MURDER AT THE RED OCTOBER

The man at the window was rich. That was clear. He was about Duvakin's height, but fuller in build, and his clothes had not come from any rag and bone shop, as Duvakin's had. He was powerful, inconceivably powerful. And now he was dreadfully quiet. And devilishly familiar.

"Well, well, Vanya . . . It's a real surprise to see you again . . . We're both surprised, I'll bet."

His host turned, with a broad smile, and enlightenment came.

"You!" Duvakin cried.

"As you see . . ."

Anger unlike any emotion he had ever felt exploded within Duvakin. Before he had time even to think about it, he had leapt up, crossed the room and landed a round-house left on his host's right ear. Eyeglasses went flying; Duvakin's awkward right slammed into the middle of a look of myopic amazement.

"You son of a bitch," Duvakin muttered through clenched teeth. His victim slid to the floor.

Murder at the
Red October

Anthony Olcott

CORONET BOOKS
Hodder and Stoughton

Copyright © 1981 by Anthony Olcott

First published in Great Britain 1982 by
Hodder and Stoughton Ltd

Coronet edition 1983
Second impression 1983

British Library C.I.P.

Olcott, Anthony
   Murder at the red october.
   1. Title
   813'.54(F)   PS3565.L28

   ISBN 0–340–33782–6

Printed and bound in Great Britain for
Hodder and Stoughton Paperbacks, a
division of Hodder and Stoughton Ltd.,
Mill Road, Dunton Green, Sevenoaks,
Kent (Editorial Office: 47 Bedford
Square, London, WC1 3DP) by
Hunt Barnard Printing Ltd, Aylesbury, Bucks.

1

"What, Mashka, what? I'm awake . . . let go of my foot, for God's sake!"

"Oh, Ivan Palych, Ivan Palych, you'd better come, there's trouble, oh, such trouble . . ."

Duvakin sat up on the decrepit day-bed, scratched the back of his head, and cast about for his shoes. He wondered vaguely about the time, but the red-tinged black without told him all he really needed to know. It was still night, and in Moscow, in December, that pinned the time down to within fifteen hours.

Dulvakin sighed, then slowly pulled one of his Belomorkanals from its cardboard pack. He stuck the cigarette in the corner of his mouth, lit it, and inhaled deeply. Exhaling, he finally looked up at Mashka, the night desk clerk on the eighth floor.

"What trouble, you goose? Trouble that you get me up in the middle of the night, that bad?"

The answer jiggled wordlessly on the badly frightened woman's several chins; she danced in part from shock, in part from her impatience at Duvakin's deliberate movements. He knew that Mashka was not normally an excitable woman, and knew too that she had an exaggerated respect, even fear, of the security staff of the hotel. Respect great enough to prevent her from idly waking even so minor a staff member as Duvakin.

"Do hurry, Ivan Palych, it's horrible, it's . . .awful! I was just lying down, for just a minute . . . it's been hard at home, you know, what with my husband sick, and the girl too . . . and well, I just couldn't, not a minute longer, and I thought well a moment won't hurt anybody . . . but then *this*! . . ."

Duvakin sighed again, then stood and grasped the sobbing Mashka by her two plump elbows, seating her on his just-vacated bed. It was always this way; no one ever seemed able to report an incident without attempting first to establish his own lack of guilt or involvement. It did not make things move easily.

"Do calm down, please, Mashka . . . now, you were napping upstairs?"

"All the rest of the girls do it!"

"I know, I know . . . what happened *after* you were napping?"

Duvakin felt a certain smugness as Mashka's tension visibly eased. By tacitly agreeing that she had been awake, he removed her negligence from the story, which now was free to tumble out.

"Well, you know, I heard an odd sound, like maybe a scream or a shout, only far away, so at first I thought maybe it was on the street . . . It was almost three, but you know how the drunks are, and what with today being Friday . . . that's how my Rodya got sick you know . . . drinking out in the cold . . ."

"Mashka, what about the sound?"

"Well, soon as I heard it, I thought I'd better sit up anyway, and then I saw someone running down the hall . . . now that is odd, I thought . . . I mean how he ran. Lots of times when we have tourists they have to run down the hall, but that's to the toilet, and they run different . . ." she giggled.

Duvakin bore this stolidly, though silently cursing the addled course of her story.

"So anyway I go to look and I notice a room is open, 852 it was, right by the corner. The outside door is open, and the inside one is closed, but through the glass I can see that the bed light is on, so I figure maybe there's a problem or they want some help, so I knock, but there's no answer so I knock harder . . ."

Here her face paled again, under the impact of her memory and the movement of her own narration.

"I knocked harder and the door swings open, and . . . lord, it was terrible . . . blood everywhere, and the room all torn up . . ."

"Blood?"

"Well, the poor dead man was lying on the floor part-ways like, so when he got his throat cut it just went everywhere . . ."

Mashka's final words faded behind Duvakin as he dog-trotted down the long corridor to the lobby. A dead man in his hotel, on his shift, and the dim-witted clerk takes two years to tell him. Finally he reached the echoing marble lobby; even at the best of times it was an uninviting expanse, and now thanks to the efforts of the night cleaners it was wet and treacherously slippery.

The doorman dozed peacefully on his stool, oblivious to Duvakin's questions. Finally, in despair Duvakin shook him by the shoulder. The stubble-chinned pensioner rolled his eyes wildly, started as fully as arthritic joints would allow, and finally stood up, his back against the wall.

"Did you let anyone out? Has anyone left just now?"

"How's that?"

God above, no! Vanya the Post! Duvakin was tempted in his frustration to slap the deaf old man, but the sight of the threadbare uniform and the greasy cap trembling in his hand was so pitiful that Duvakin, controlling himself, left him to quake in uncomprehending fear, and pushed his way through the inner door.

The bolt from the huge glass outer doors lay on the floor at his feet. Duvakin rubbed clear a space in the crimson-fogged panes and peered without hope out at the deserted street. The neon sign 'Hotel Red October' above the doors, and the distant street lamp swaying fitfully at the far corner of the street illumined tracks left in the frozen slush by crowds of passers-by. Though absent now, the crowds contrived to conceal Duvakin's quarry from him.

He drummed his fingers on the window for a few unnecessary moments, staring vacantly at the twinkle of water vapour crystallising in the air outside as he tried to gain control of his anger. He sensed the doorman behind him.

"Well now, that's that . . . best get up to the room, I suppose . . ."

"How's that, Ivan Palych, sir? . . ." The doorman had the eager posture of a dog who wished nothing more than to please.

"It's all right, Nikiforich, go back to sleep," Duvakin said, patting the old man on the shoulder.

"All night? No sir! Just dropped off, I did, sir . . ." As the old man launched into a defence for what he supposed his fault to have been, Duvakin's anger boiled up once again. Biting his lip, he pushed the doorman back into his chair, and with a sharp—too sharp, really—wave of his finger, told him to stay put. He forced a jovial wink, to try to ease the situation.

Duvakin looked at the bank of elevators, without much hope. Three were turned off for the night, while the fourth had stood unrepaired so long that it ceased to have meaning as an elevator; for all but the unwary tourist it was no more than an indentation in the wall. Since it would probably have taken less time to scale the outside of the building than to search out the woman who guarded the elevator keys, Duvakin had but one choice. Grimly he crossed the dark, echoing lobby and began to trudge up the red woollen runner of the ceremonial staircase.

Duvakin, after an endless ascent with brief rest stops, stood at long last, panting heavily, on the eighth floor. Like all the floors of the hotel it was T-shaped: in the long part of the T the rooms were given to Soviet citizens and tourists from the brother countries. The rooms in the short part of the T were reserved for foreigners from the West. While he tried to get his wind back, Duvakin looked down the corridors disappearing into rectangular gloom. Suddenly he felt uneasy. He had forgotten to ask the nationality of the dead guest. Now the layout of the floor suggested the worst. Room 852 was in the short part of the T.

To have a murder in one's hotel, on one's shift, was not in itself a catastrophe, particularly in a hotel like the Red October which was a seedy, decaying giant built during the last days of the 'cult of personality', mostly for Soviets. But it also accepted those foreigners which the Rossiya, the Intourist, and the other big tourist hotels would not or could not accept. Foreigners came in numbers large enough to warrant a tiny hard currency shop in the hotel. For the native population however, the main importance of the Red October lay in its proximity to Komsomol Square and its antheaps of railway terminals, highways, and hotels; it was a convenient warming stop for dealers in flowers, buyers of blue jeans, for all the procuring and procured. Those who mattered accepted as given that with *that* type of crowd beatings and knifings were not only to be expected, but could even be a good thing, as long of course as unpleasantries did not occur before foreign eyes.

Dead Russians were one thing, and dead foreigners quite another—foreigners were to be carted in, fleeced, and removed, happy if possible, but in any event alive.

Oh God, make him Lebanese or Italian or even Finnish—not a real foreigner! For a moment Duvakin stood still, flooded with the superstitious hope that incantations could turn the dead man into someone acceptable. Then he swore vividly and entered the open doors of room 852.

It was a double room. On either side of it stood a narrow day-bed; beside each was a dark wooden nightstand, topped with a small plastic lamp. There was a desk in the centre of the room. On it were two glasses with a half-empty bottle of vodka between them. A second bottle lay empty in the crumbs and ash littering the top of the desk, overflowing from the ashtray and saucer belonging to the buffet on the fifth floor. Both receptacles held, along with ashes and cigarette butts, the plastic wrappings from a bologna. Duvakin noted that the cigarettes were foreign.

At this point Duvakin became aware of two things simultaneously; of Mashka, stealthily watching from the doorway, where she attempted to still her panting breaths, and of his own reluctance to look at the dead man. He pulled himself together and assumed, for Mashka's benefit, a demonstratively blank and professional air. The chubby squat night

9

clerk stood pale and goggle-eyed in the cloakroom between the inner and outer doors.

A balding man lay half in and half out of the bed on the right side of the room; his shoulder touched the floor. His body was covered up to the top of his buttocks by the bedsheet, which somehow emphasised his nakedness.

The man's head was turned leftward, exposing the hideous smile of his slit throat. Mashka had not exaggerated one detail anyway—the blood. It had soaked the Oriental rug in the centre of the room and had gushed onto the rough parquet of the floor, where it mixed with the soapy orange varnish and turned a scummy brown. Only the sheets looked as Duvakin might have expected; the blood was luridly scarlet against the white linen.

"Did you touch him at all, Mashka?" Duvakin asked without turning around.

"Oh, no, Ivan Palych, no . . . dreadful, isn't it? . . . so much blood, and you wouldn't even think that a man would have so very much blood in him, would you?"

Duvakin didn't answer; still, as he sucked at his dead cigarette, he had to admit Mashka had a point. The amount of blood was impressive. He shrugged and continued in an official tone.

"Of what country is this man a citizen?" Duvakin rubbed the bald spot on the back of his head gingerly, as he often did when worried. It gave him a somewhat absurd air.

"I've forgotten . . . just a moment, I'll go to my desk down the hall, it's in the book. He just arrived this afternoon . . . speaks Russian though . . ." Her voice trailed off down the hall. Duvakin prayed that it was still too early for this to awaken guests; he had yet to get the body examined and removed.

Mashka's padding feet could be heard returning.

"American, he's an American, Ivan Palych," Mashka informed him, panting slightly.

Damn! The worst, the absolute worst! Duvakin felt doomed, locked into a ritual he would not soon escape. He angrily shoved his cigarette into the butt-filled saucer. People who let American tourists get killed do not get off lightly. He mused dully for a moment, until the sight of his own cigarette butt among those of victim and, presumably, killer, brought him back to his senses. There would be enough to explain, without including that bit of stupidity. He sighed.

"Got sealing wax up here, Mashka?"

"Of course, Ivan Palych . . ." the women said as she darted off again.

Duvakin turned out the lights and stood in the dark, waiting for the clerk to return with the wax so he could seal the room. He hated the thought of the next step he must take. Telephoning. Down the corridor he heard a toilet flush. Better call from downstairs. People were beginning to wake up.

2

Outside the night had turned an opalescent grey, very faintly streaked with pink. Little could be seen through the double windows, for they were sweating copiously, their edges etched with crystal. Duvakin, his mouth tasting of too many cigarettes and too much bad tea, sat on the creaking chair in front of his desk. He looked idly about the room, absorbed by the novelty of not sitting in his usual place at the pine table with the single drawer.

The reason for Duvakin's displacement sat behind the desk, fidgeting angrily with the telephone.

"Doesn't this damn thing work, Duvakin?"

"Usually, but you know . . ."

"What?" The man looked up sharply, all his anger and frustration at the telephone clear in his eyes, now tense and hostile.

11

"Well, morning, you know . . . had to get outside lines . . . everybody's busy . . ." Duvakin once again felt the curious inner split he had felt before. His mouth said the proper thing almost by reflex, long before his mind could collect itself. It was a reaction he disliked, but there was no doubt it had saved him from a good deal of trouble over the years.

The man across from him was youngish and dark, fit-looking but with a hint of the puffiness and clumsiness which mark the hard drinker ten or fifteen years on. His thinning hair was disguised by an oily pomade which reeked of exotic flowers. He wore a flowered tie, an olive coat with broad black stripes, and pants of some shiny purple material.

All those colours and stripes had been woven in East Germany, of fibres as unobtainable to Duvakin as they had been to his nameless forebears who had stood hat in hand while the horsemen of Genghis Khan trotted through the mud streets of their village. His own suit was a stiff, crackling sack of Russian cloth purchased in a dusty, cavernous store called by the grand name of 'Ruslan'. His own thin hair was undisguised, as was his own smell: the comfortable aroma of potato, onion and sweat.

"Well, Duvakin, it looks as though you're off the hook for this morning . . . I can't get through. We'll seal the room up again until I can get back here with a truck. No noise about this now . . . We wouldn't want this to get around." The man looked at Duvakin dispassionately. His eyes were dark, flecked with yellow.

"All right, but I don't really see how we can keep it from getting around, you know. He's not one of ours, he's American . . . He must be on a tour or have friends or something. They'll be wondering . . . We'll have to notify their Embassy, I guess . . ."

"Citizen, you are mistaken. You've done your duty, when the call went to the district authorities. That was your job. They notified us. That was *their* job. Now *we* handle this, and nobody else. And for now, I say we don't want this getting around. Understand?"

For a moment Duvakin considered taking offence at being

called 'citizen', rather than 'comrade', which would have been more proper in this instance, but he realised he was too exhausted to object.

"Of course, of course . . . so I'll just sign the protocol then, and go seal the room again." Fatigue was making his tongue feel woollen. He had been on the night shift for fourteen hours, and had not been in bed for close on twenty.

"*No protocol!*" the man boomed. "This talk has not taken place! Understand?"

Duvakin looked up, astounded. Again his mouth said the proper thing.

"Of course, of course . . . Habit, you know . . ."

These words calmed the younger man as completely as those before had angered him. He smiled, grunted, and got up from behind Duvakin's desk.

"Is that all today, so I can go home? Or should I wait around?" Even as he spoke, Duvakin cursed himself for acting so subserviently. But the presence behind this man of the gloomy building at Dzerzhinsky Place was all too clear: Lyubyanka.

"No, you can go . . . We know where to find you." The man smiled unpleasantly. "Just seal the room again, and then we're through with you. But remember—not a word, and no one should notice!"

With a loud snap, he closed his briefcase of brushed aluminium and black vinyl. Duvakin had never seen such a briefcase, except in movies, of course. CIA spies and German agents always carried them. Then the young man bustled out of the room, leaving Duvakin with a sweet odour in his nostrils and a vague, exhausted sense of having been violated.

"Vanya! What's the matter? What's up? . . . Those guys . . ." Grisha Zavalshin who came on at eight in the morning had finally been allowed to enter the room. Grisha was short and plump, with hair so blond it was almost transparent, and with what Duvakin had always considered the most cursed of all Russian complexions: a mass of pink and white in which swarm eyes the blue of a washed-out autumn sky.

"Sorry, Grisha, business. Nothing for you to worry about,

13

though. I'll be off now, and you can take over." Duvakin gave an exaggerated yawn. "I sure can use the rest." He dumped the ashtray into the filthy, open-work trash basket, and as usual all the ashes spilled on the floor. He wondered idly for the umpteenth time why anyone bothered to make trash baskets with holes in them.

"But what's going on, Vanya? Were those men from *there*?" Grisha pointed upwards, inquiring whether the two men were from *there*, from *high places*. Duvakin winked at Grisha conspiratorially.

"Can't talk about it, but it's all right . . . They came on business," he said, emphasising the last words by sketching a vague circling motion with his upright index finger.

Zavalshin stared pop-eyed at the spectral spool of tape which revolved for a second in the air. Then he relaxed, nodded knowingly. Duvakin relit his dead cigarette, muttered "So long", and left the office.

As he shut the door, with its 'Shoe Repairs' sign, he laughed. Zavalshin, simple soul that he was, would never think to read the log book, where, as required, Duvakin had given a brief description of the evening before signing out. Zavalshin was an odd little man, not given to seeking information from the written word.

Duvakin's steps echoed through the long marble corridors leading to the lobby. As he thought vaguely about the past evening, it seemed to him that it was not only Zavalshin who was odd.

Since he had entered room 852, everything had been queer, not quite normal. He had followed the correct procedure, telephoning his district militia office, where a sleepy, indifferent voice had noted his report that an American tourist had been murdered. Then he had sat down to wait. Masha had given up all pretence of work, and was sitting with him in the lobby, endlessly discussing the great event. Duvakin floated dreamily in the torrent of her words, borne along by cigarettes and strong tea. Although he had been a hotel security man for more years than he cared to count, he had no idea how long he would have to wait.

Finally, in the bleak grey hours of early morning, after Masha had finally returned home to her alcoholic husband, the two men appeared. They flashed their red cardboard passes and announced that they were from the Committee for State Security. KGB.

Although Duvakin had not expected Chekists, he was not particularly surprised. He gave them his name; they did not give him theirs. The apparent senior of the two, who was later to usurp Duvakin's desk, requested to be shown the body. Duvakin took them upstairs, and broke the seal on room 852. The two men shoved past him brusquely into the room, and set about their business with no further attention to him.

The body remained as he had left it. The warmth of the sealed room had caused the air to become heavy with the odour of stale meat. From the doorway Duvakin could glimpse the American's face; it looked piteously surprised. He had not expected to die just then, whoever he was.

The two men were engaged in incomprehensible activity: one held the two vodka glasses thoughtfully in his hands, while the other riffled efficiently, if not carefully, through the garments hanging in the birch wardrobe. The second man picked up the ashtray and the two bottles and threw them through the window. There was no crash: probably they landed in a snowbank. Duvakin was puzzled, and no less so when the first man began searching the dead man's suitcase and wallet and quickly pocketed what appeared to be an address book.

Only after this did they turn to the corpse. The blood on the sheets had turned brown now, lessening the horror of the scene. The senior agent gestured to the other, who bent down, grabbed the dead man roughly under the armpits and chucked him onto the bed.

The throat had been savagely slashed, muscles and tendons destroyed, so that the head flopped grotesquely back, whacking into the wooden headboard with a hollow thump. Another wiggle of a finger told the junior man to straighten the body. Then the finger wiggler reached into his black and olive coat and took out an American passport. He looked closely at the picture, then at the dead man's face, and back at the picture again. Then he nodded, and the Chekists left the room together.

The swiftness of their departure took Duvakin by surprise. He was only too aware of his own lack of dignity as he wavered back and forth, uncertain whether to follow the men or to stay and reseal the room. Finally he slammed the room door, locked it, and dog-trotted down the hall, reaching the agents just as they were stepping into the elevator.

Downstairs he was led into his own office, where he had to suffer through hours of brusque, unpleasant questioning. When did you hear of this? Do you know who he was? Where's the killer? Did you touch anything in the room? Why? Why not?

Duvakin's sense of event and function, already affected by fatigue, blurred over so that he found himself forgetting that he was not under suspicion for the crime.

Now, at last, it was finished. Duvakin had only to reseal the door, and his responsibility for the corpse was ended. But something gnawed at him through his exhaustion; he could not tell quite what. He stood outside the door, and smoked, tasting the cardboard filter of his cigarette. Finally he said aloud, "Well, no harm in looking one last time, I suppose." He wanted to make his own authority more convincing to himself. He sighed, unlocked the inner door and tiptoed into the room, shutting the door softly behind him.

In the gloomy light of day the room seemed shabbier and more depressing than ever. Through the windows, instead of restful darkness, could be seen the courtyard of the hotel, filled with garbage bins, yowling cats and an occasional bellowing cook in a tall white hat. Snow flakes drifted onto the slush piles, on which the ashtray and vodka bottles were not to be seen. Why had the agent tossed them out like that? Shaking his heavy head, Duvakin turned to look at the late guest.

His face was the face of a man who had lived hard. Those puffy eyes, and lined cheeks, that bulbous red nose, all of his features were familiar; they belonged to Duvakin's generation. They had been born in the Thirties, when people always said "Farewell" at parting; it seemed too optimistic to say "See you later". Duvakin himself had been better protected than most: a militiaman's son, growing up in Krasnaya Sosna, two days' train ride northeast of Moscow, the kind of place that people vanished to, not from. He remembered wraiths floating down the mud streets in the autumn mists, seeking shelter in the rotting log cabins of the backwater village.

And then the war came. The war that was to be 'quick, bloody, and on the territory of the enemy' slowly crushed the world they knew. Again Duvakin had been lucky, living well away from the front and too young to fight. But he had watched the evacuees wallowing through the freezing mud in October 1941, haggard, ghostly people. Finally he began himself to grow ghostly; meat, milk, and vegetables disappeared, and the clay content of bread grew so high it was not so much baked as fired. Time had branded his generation, Duvakin thought, as indelibly as Ivan IV branded thieves, against whose brows was pressed a spiked 'T' of red-hot iron.

Another thought crossed his mind. He laughed, somewhat ashamed of his maudlin reflections. The corpse might be about his age, but he was *American*! In 1940 he was probably playing baseball or something, not starving to death in a rural village.

The fog in Duvakin's brain lifted a bit: his instinctive suspicion rose. Several times that day he had found himself thinking of the corpse as Russian. Why? Duvakin saw nothing in the face that was particularly compelling; high cheekbones, blue eyes, now obscured by the milkiness of death. Maybe Slavic, maybe Jewish, maybe some sort of mix. Slavic faces were not as distinctive as Russians liked to think, and heaven knows enough Slavs had gone to America. The corpse had the tan of a man who had worn sleeveless undershirts all his life, just as Duvakin had, but that was hardly conclusive evidence. Jewellery? Nothing special, a wedding band, but on his left hand, not on his right, as a Russian would wear it. The tattoos on his forearms and the thumb joint of his right hand . . .

Duvakin slapped himself in the forehead. "Damn! I *am* tired . . ." It was the tattoos. On the right arm was a miniature of two skeletons dancing some sort of jazz dance, while the left arm bore a crude snake and dagger. The folds of his thumb joint held the faint rays of something like a sun rising. Or setting. The tattoos were lopsided and crude, the colour of a bad bruise. Tattoos of ash and urine. Duvakin had seen other foreigners with tattoos, with their rainbow colours, fine shapes, elaborate workmanship. *These* were tattoos as Russian as those he saw on every subway, every bus, and every beach.

"Poverty's a terrible thing, eh?" Duvakin whispered to the corpse in a bantering way. "Couldn't even afford a decent tattoo, had to do it yourself . . ."

Well, finish up and then off home. Duvakin reached into his pocket for the glob of wax and the thread to seal the door. Humming to himself, he began to place the thread on top of the wax. He was almost through; he would soon be in bed. The spool bobbled a second on the wax as Duvakin juggled with it, and then dropped onto the floor.

It was nowhere to be seen. Duvakin stared earnestly at the floor, cursing. That was the only spool he had; he did not want to return to the first floor to get another. He got onto his knees and peered under the bed. It was too dark to see anything. Hopelessly he thrust his arm under and groped about . . . Clunk.

Something larger than a spool of thread was under there. He lay flat on his stomach and reached as far as he could. Even as his hand closed around the object, he knew it was a matryoshka, one of those gay stacking dolls that tourists loved to take home with them.

"Well, at least you had time to buy a few souvenirs . . . Who for, I wonder?"

Duvakin looked at the doll, with its painted smile and rosy cheeks. He shook it, listening to its rattle with satisfaction. Six dolls inside there, at least. He looked at the dead man with a sense of guilt; he had thought of Lenochka, Tatyana's daughter. He was going to see them tomorrow. He could forsee the pleasure this doll would give Lena. It quickly outweighed his sense of duty. What conceivable good would the toy do the dead man now? He pocketed the doll.

Then he sealed the room and walked down the hall to the elevators.

3

"When does three come?"

Duvakin slowly tore himself away from the window and turned towards the kitchen door. Tanya's five-year-old Lena stood on the sill, shaking a cheap toy clock in a futile attempt to discover the time.

He walked across the crackling tiles of the kitchen and bent gingerly over the little girl.

"This is three . . . see? Soon. Is three when mamá comes home?" Duvakin was uncertain of his tone. He was not in the habit of speaking with children.

Lena had very large brown eyes, brownish skin, and lashes almost velvet in texture. She answered seriously, "No, that's when Mighty Mouse goes on . . . Mighty Mouse!" she squealed in anticipatory joy and ran into the large front room, where the television was.

Duvakin shrugged; the name meant nothing to him. Some children's show. He straightened and returned to the kitchen window.

The view was staggering, the more so since even the idea of a view was so uncommon. Tanya lived in Matveevo, one of the newest of Moscow's 'micro-regions'—this grand name was given to planned neighbourhoods which, at the stroke of

19

the designer's pen, devoured the villages that had surrounded old Moscow. Where log cabins and old orchards had stood, there suddenly sprouted fourteen-storey buildings, asphalt streets, co-operative apartments, and the forlorn wilting trees of new parks. These micro-regions usually stood for years in the middle of mud lots or dust bowls, unserviced by shops, transport or telephone. In extreme instances of bureaucratic absent-mindedness they sometimes lacked even water and electricity.

Duvakin's dislike of this urban frontier living was dissipated by the magnificence of Matveevo's setting. From Tanya's eleventh floor apartment one looked out in two directions. In the room where Lena now sat enthralled before the television set, the window faced the lights of Solntsevo twinkling against the streaked vastness of the evening sky; while from the kitchen one had a view of the Ramenka River valley with the Lenin Hills beyond, where the gilt spire of Moscow University vaulted into the sky.

Today this view looked like a painting. The sky was clear for the first time in months; all day the world had glittered under the false warmth of the winter sun. It had been cold and grew colder now as the early December dusk drew on. Duvakin could make out the thick hoar frost on the university spire. Puffs of steam wafted over the hockey rink at the foot of Tanya's building, where the neighbourhood boys were banging one another expertly onto the boards. Farther off, little knots of skiers could be seen trudging slowly up and down the valley.

Duvakin pulled a straight chair close to the window and sat down, his elbows resting on the sill. He lit a cigarette and mused happily in the red-gold light of the setting sun. It was the perfect way to enjoy winter.

A key rattled in the lock after a time, and Lena ran from her room yelling "Mama! Mama! Mighty Mouse! Mama!"

Duvakin stood up, feeling somewhat awkward. For the first time he was greeting Tanya at the door, rather than vice-versa.

"Tphoo! It's freezing! . . . Hello, my darling . . ." Tanya came in and bent immediately to kiss Lena, simultaneously holding out a cardboard box for Duvakin to take.

"A torte? . . . You shouldn't . . ." Duvakin took the box and stopped talking, realising that now he was unable to help Tanya remove her coat. A slow blush of confusion rose past his collar.

Tanya laughed as she shucked her coat and hung it on a hook by the door.

"So you got in all right? Good. Come on, put the cake down! No, not there . . . In the kitchen!" She took his arm and manoeuvered him down the short hallway and into the kitchen.

"Sorry I had to run out like that, Vanya, but there wasn't a thing in the house . . . and then the queues! They keep promising to open the other store, but . . ." Smiling, she made a wave of dismissal. "Sit . . . You want tea of course?"

Duvakin felt too off-balance to trust his voice, so he simply nodded, smiled, and sat. After a moment's thought, he stated the obvious.

"Lena let me in."

Tanya smiled at him over her shoulder, while she rummaged about in the cupboard for the kettle. She began to hum softly to herself.

As usual, Duvakin fought briefly against confusion before allowing himself to drop into a pleasant embarrassment, disarmed by her energetic presence. Tanya Kaplan was fated, it seemed, to keep Duvakin off balance. It appeared she knew this, and enjoyed it.

She was about a dozen years younger than he, still in full bloom. Almost as tall as Duvakin, she was so slender that she appeared to be taller; if account was taken of her stack of uncontrollably curly hair she *was* taller. Duvakin remembered how difficult he had found it, when he first met her, to reconcile her last name with her blue eyes and the auburn-shaded honey of her hair.

No doubt he had betrayed his surprise, because she had said, "My husband's name." "Husband?" Duvakin had asked, too quickly. "Former . . ." She had smiled, and he had smiled back.

They had met at a dull drunken birthday party thrown for himself by Duvakin's childhood friend Volodya Ishakin in a vain attempt to soften his entrance into his second half-century. Duvakin had gone only because he thought he should: he detested large parties and he had fallen out of the habit of heavy drinking, but Ishakin was his friend and benefactor, so he had gone. In fact Ishakin's benefaction had been the single act of obtaining for Duvakin his present post at the Red October and his room near Novoslobodskoe Metro. After that Duvakin had apparently vanished from Ishakin's mind.

Which was Volodya all over, of course. He and Duvakin had in their childhood in Krasnaya Sosna been united more by circumstance than friendship; Duvakin's father was chief of the militia, Volodya's the director of a food trust, and so both sons fell into the chasm between the merely mortal and the immortals of Stalin's regime. Elevated above the common herd, yet not considered good enough to play with the children of the town's real officials, the two boys had turned to one another out of necessity, and so had remained friends until after the war, when Ishakin had been drafted.

He reappeared in 1962, driving a shiny Pobeda over the ruts and mudholes of the main street of Krasnaya Sosna. Duvakin was by then a militiaman, and his polite inquiry into the nature of the driver's business led to a reunion, the warmth of which quickly turned forced. Ishakin had become a somebody, director of a hotel in Moscow, in possession of an apartment on Gorky Street, owner of a car. Like most Muscovites, he became nostalgic for his village in the summer, and so he came to pass his holidays there. His voluntary rustication consisted largely of drinking bottles of Granny Tulyachka's homebrew (illegal, but as much a part of the village as the goats in its central square). On one oppressive, lightning-flecked evening, this had led to Ishakin offering Duvakin the job of security officer in his Moscow hotel. Equally in his cups, Duvakin accepted, and the following

November he received an official order transferring Lieutenant of the People's Control Duvakin, I.P., to duty at the Hotel Red October. Where he had remained ever since, unnoticed and without further benefactions.

Ishakin's party had been much as Duvakin had expected it would be: fairy-tale quantities and varieties of food and drink; numerous, greedy and sycophantic guests in a huge apartment with expensive furniture. Duvakin, acutely conscious of his frayed cuffs and clumsy plastic shoes, had drifted off to the sidelines.

Tanya had taken refuge there. Her hubsand had only recently left her; she was as moody as Duvakin, and they had fallen into conversation. When the evening ended Duvakin said untruthfully that he lived in her direction; they shared a taxi. She invited him to tea the following afternoon. Since then they had spent one or two afternoons a week together.

Now Duvakin sat in what had come to be his usual place at the kitchen table. His back against the wall, his elbow on the table, he comfortably smoked his cigarette. The setting sun shone on cake and teacups; Tanya rattled dishes in the cupboard. In the next room the television made muffled noises, punctuated by squeals and chortles from Lenochka. Duvakin felt utterly at peace.

"It's nice here, Tanya," he said.

"It is, isn't it? Glorious day today, but cold. Everywhere you go people say, 'a real Russian frost' . . ." She laughed, tilting back her head, and then sat down with him and began to pour the tea. Lemon slices floated on limpid steaming pools; there were slices of creamy torte on china plates. He was solidly and stupidly in love with Tanya; her every movement and gesture seemed to him to be a miracle. He felt constrained to be courteous and gentle with her even to the point of immobility.

"So, Vanya . . . What news on the organs? Taped any good conversations lately?" She smiled, but her words held a barb.

"You never let up, do you?" Duvakin avoided her eyes and concentrated on the indentation in her right cheek.

She laughed and patted his hand. "Sorry," she said. "It's a stupid joke."

"It really bothers you that much?" he asked.

"What? The hotel militiaman business?"

"Well, the whole thing . . . How I work . . ."

"I don't know, Vanya. It just seems . . . Well, I've never known anyone from the KGB before." It was impossible to tell whether she were being naive or not.

But today, after he had had his own visitors from the KGB she hit him on the raw.

"Damn it! You know I'm not a Chekist! I'm in the militia!"

It was too loud, too heated. The tea sloshed in the cups, from the impact of his fist on the table. He did not realise he had done that. Tanya looked startled.

"Mama?" Lena appeared in the open kitchen doorway. She looked upset. Duvakin realised that loud male voices were unusual in this apartment; his anger subsided.

Tanya went to Lena.

"It's all right, little sun. Uncle Vanya was just telling a joke. How's Mighty Mouse?"

These were the magic words. Lena whooped, "Mighty Mouse!" and rushed back into the large room that served Tanya as sitting room, dining room, bedroom and playroom. Tanya closed the glass kitchen door and returned to the table.

"I'm sorry, Tanya," Duvakin muttered miserably, tracing his tobacco-stained finger on the oilcloth.

After a moment, Tanya reached across the table to pat his hand again.

"No, it's my fault, Vanya. I didn't . . . Well, I just didn't know that it was so . . . important . . ."

Duvakin looked up; he was surprised by the entreaty in her face.

The swiftness of the change in her attitude and the sincerity of her concern combined with his own guilt over his outburst to tempt him to a confessional mood. He was not fond of unburdening himself. His adult life had been passed without close friendships, and he had always felt demeaning the drunken honesty of strangers sharing a litre or two.

"Oh, it's not important, I suppose," he said uncertainly.

"It is, though. You got so upset. And I don't want you angry with me . . ." She spoke the last words softly, in an intimate tone.

He felt his reserve crumbling. This was the first time Tanya had spoken to him in that tone of voice. This seemed to be a natural advance in their relationship. He took a deep breath and tried to express his thoughts.

"It's the way people always say it . . . Like it was something filthy. My father hated it, as long as I can remember, and I suppose . . . Well, it rubbed off . . ."

"Your father . . ."

"He was commandant of the station in our village . . . Also the only militiaman. In fact, so was his father, and his father before that . . ."

"Not militia, surely!"

"No, no, not then. Police then, before the Revolution. But it was the same thing . . . And people said Third Section, then OGPU, KGB . . . and we weren't."

Duvakin had been happy to move to Moscow so that he could escape the oppressive weight of his family's tradition of service to the public order. In Krasnaya Sosna the name Duvakin was synonymous with militiaman; even as a toddler Duvakin had been treated as a future gendarme. Moscow gave him anonymity. Too much, he realised. Tanya's interest and concern made him aware of how lonely he was.

"I hadn't realised that there is . . . Well, much difference. I mean, I know that there are divisions and so on, but . . ."

"But, a Judas is a Judas?"

Duvakin was impressed by her even through his annoyance. Where a flirtatious woman would have protested, Tanya merely looked at him gravely, bit her lower lip, and nodded.

"Have you ever seen an old drunk out in the street? In a November sleet storm, let's say . . . Or two lads who get the wind up their tails and start poking each other with bread knives? *Somebody* has to take care of them!" He did not add that for more generations than he knew one of those some-bodies had been a Duvakin.

"But the hotel? That's different, isn't it? Foreigners, hard currency stores, surveillance, spies . . . all that kind of thing?"

"Foreigners mean things to steal, honey for flies. Students so anxious to speak Russian they don't notice their new friends are drug pushers. Lost passports. Fights . . ." He trailed off as the events of the day before returned to him. His sense of wellbeing dissolved in the memory of the dead American and the two slimy creatures from the KGB. And the doll. He had completely forgotten that he had brought the matryoshka doll for Lena. Now he felt awkward. Doubly awkward. The context was not one which would encourage the giving of presents and the source of this present could not be told. He felt tired and disgusted, his pleasure gone. He waved his arm angrily. "Ahh, the devil take it! I can't explain it! . . . What's it to you anyway? I can leave if it upsets you so damn much!" He slipped deliberately into the familiar, anxious to be as coarse as possible.

Tanya tightened her grip on his hand.

"Please don't . . . It's not worth it . . ."

She answered him in the familiar, but she was as gentle as he had been crude; his anger melted away. He smiled, and was answered after a brief pause by her smile.

"More torte, Vanya?" she asked. Her voice was still husky and forced, but it was clear that a crisis had passed.

Duvakin looked at his plate. He had stubbed out his cigarette in the chocolate cream. He blushed in confusion.

"Please . . . I suppose I can't have more, though . . . I haven't had any, yet . . ."

Tanya laughed. She took his plate to the sink, and brought him a fresh one. She began to cut the torte; Duvakin half-listened while she told him how she had come upon the cake, about the queues, the mystery of the cake's name—Goose Foot—and much more. He was entranced by her graceful movements.

Lena appeared in the short hallway and, bored, began to slide the glass front of the bookcase back and forth, back and forth. Duvakin watched this incomprehensible game for a while before he remembered the doll.

26

"The programme's over, I see. I forgot to tell you . . . Well, I brought a little present for Lena." Cautiously he resumed the use of formal speech.

"Oh, do show me!" Tanya spoke still in the familiar. He looked at her with silent thanks, and then rose and opened the glass kitchen door to cross clumsily to the coat rack in the hall. His left foot was asleep.

"Uncle Vanya! Uncle Vanya!" Lena chanted. Duvakin thought she might be better off outdoors, where the crisp air could help her dissipate her energies. He was aware that mothers lived in constant fear of chills and sniffles. Perhaps the doll would serve as a substitute for a brisk walk; Lena was beginning to get on his nerves.

"Uncle Vanya has a present for you, Lenochka," Tanya said.

"Really?"

"Really!" Duvakin answered forcefully. He did not feel comfortable with this small person, but he tried to act a jovial role. He fumbled in the greasy pocket of his overcoat through gloves, handkerchiefs and innumerable wads of used bus tickets.

The doll emerged bright and shining.

"Here, little one . . . For you."

Lena took it from him suspiciously, and shook it. It rattled.

"It's broken!" she whined. "Mama, its arms and legs fell off and *listen*!" She held it up and shook it again.

Duvakin was as puzzled as he was disappointed. Could it really be true that Lena had never seen a matryoshka before?

"Good Lord, Vanya, a matryoshka! Wherever did you find it?" Tanya squatted down beside her daughter and took the doll. "I haven't seen one in absolute ages." She spoke softly to Lena. "It's not broken, my love . . . Look, see what happens . . ."

Tanya twisted off the top half of the doll, very slowly, to draw the interest of the fretting child. A smaller doll was revealed, nestling within the bottom half. Tanya's eyes glowed; she pulled the doll from her mother's hands.

"And it still rattles, Mama!"

"It does, doesn't it? Better take it into your room and find out why."

Lena disappeared into the small room that was hers. Tanya straightened up and watched her daugther shut the door. She turned to Duvakin.

"Don't worry, Vanya . . . She loves it. She just hadn't seen one before."

"Odd though," Duvakin said, when they were comfortably back at the table, and fresh tea had been poured. "Odd that she hasn't seen those before. I always thought they were as Russian as . . . well, black bread . . ." Lamely he finished the cliché.

Tanya shook her head.

"No. It's years now that they're almost impossible to find. I remember, what? . . . two years ago? Anyway, Sasha and I looked all over for one for Lena's New Year's present—and never got it. And usually Sasha was good at that sort of thing . . ."

"Sasha?"

"My husband. Former . . ." Tanya and Duvakin concluded the sentence together, laughing.

This was the first time since their meeting that Tanya had spoken of her husband.

Duvakin looked for a cigarette with exaggerated calm. He wanted desperately to know more about her marriage, and at the same time was terrified of what he might find out. His hand shook as he got the stale tobacco glowing. Finally he asked in a tight voice. "What was he? I mean, how . . .?"

"A man. A normal man. And as far as how, how what? How did we fall out? How did he make a living? What how?" Though her tone was bantering, Tanya's face suggested that it would cost her to speak of the past, and that she was hesitant.

"Not my business, of course . . ." Duvakin brushed a fallen ash from the tablecloth onto his trousers. He brushed it from there into his cupped palm and held it there.

Tanya fetched an ashtray to which she tenderly guided his

hand, cupping hers around his. After a pause, she rose and began to pace the kitchen.

"It's not a nice story, mostly because it's not unusual. I generally don't see much point in going through it, but . . . Well, I suppose I want you to know . . ."

Duvakin wondered why. He sat, following Tanya's restless pacing with his eyes. As she walked, she hugged herself with her long thin arms, and spoke softly, almost to herself.

"The usual thing, really. Marriage at the institute, out in the provinces. Kaluga, to be exact. Sasha couldn't get into any of the universities of course, because of the Jew quotas, but he's bright . . . Clever, too. So he did well in the engineering line, and got an assignment to a foundry there. Some kind of top-secret work. We did very well, with my salary at the press . . ."

"Press?"

"Oh, I worked for a publishing house there . . . Technical things, local histories, bad poetry . . . The usual provincial stuff . . ."

Tanya fell silent, her eyes unfocused. It was difficult to tell where her memories carried her; Duvakin dared not interrupt her a second time.

Finally she began to speak again.

"Anyway, Sasha was ambitious and Kaluga wasn't enough. He was forbidden to discuss his work, so I really don't know what he did, of course . . . Mostly there were a lot of trips. Moscow, Leningrad, the Baltics, the East . . . But mostly Moscow. Finally he announced one day that we were being transferred to Moscow."

Again she stopped speaking, and Duvakin found himself recalling his own move to the capital—the bustle, the excitement of new wealth, the myriad streets, the complexities of the metro. It was intoxicating, while the novelty held.

"He was still travelling though, and pretty soon he started going abroad. Always alone, of course. Neither one of us has any family to speak of, so I had to be his anchor . . ."

"Anchor?" Duvakin frowned.

"Oh, you know . . . His guarantee, what he leaves behind

so he won't forget to come home." Tanya smiled thinly. "Anyway, that's when I had Lena. I was bored and lonely . . . and then he began to be sent to the West, and finally he was two and a half months at some place in Italy. . . What? Two years ago? . . . and when he came back he decided he needed someone younger and prettier to go with his lovely Italian clothes . . ." She stopped, her words slowly becoming a soft sigh.

For a time both were silent. The radiator gurgled and spat. The sun was just at the edge of the world; Tanya's hair and skin were honey shot with copper; ruby tears trembled at the edge of her large blue eyes. For a brief moment her beauty seemed to Duvakin unworldly, a miracle; she inhaled deeply, smiled, and the world returned to normal. When she began again to speak her voice was business-like and detached.

"But he did the right thing. He was very kind. He spoke to his boss . . . oh Lord, what was his name? Krakmalov? Kabakov? Some sort of big wheel, with an unpleasant name . . . I remember—Korshunov. Anyway, Sasha spoke with him and then Korshunov spoke with that Ishakin, and between them they got me fixed up in this apartment. I don't know how they did it, but I've got permanent registration here in Moscow and they juggled the living space allotments around so that I could get all these rooms . . . And the job at the book-store is enough to eat on . . ."

Duvakin was unable to think of an intelligent response. He was bewildered that anyone could consider Tanya to be old or ugly. He shook his head. And Volodya, the son of a bitch! He *had* done well, if he was able to rig living space and registrations. Rigging Duvakin's was one thing: he was one of Volodya's colleagues, and certainly he had no more space than the law allowed. But to fix up Tanya in these three huge rooms . . . That was something.

"I guess that explains why you were at Volodya's birthday party . . ."

"Volodya? . . . Oh, you mean Ishakin. I'm not sure why I was invited, but I did feel obligated . . . It worked out nicely, didn't it?" She smiled.

Duvakin felt a thrill of pleasant alarm, a new sensation for him. He had not experienced a relationship like this before. To remain stable for months—friendly, polite, somewhat distant—and then suddenly lurch forward into warm intimacy . . . A new sensation, and one that threw him even further off-balance and frightened him a little.

"It did, it did . . ." he said, gruffly. "The tea and all . . . It's pleasant . . ." He ended with a wave of his hand.

In the silence that followed, Duvakin brooded over his own powerlessness and insignificance. Not for him the fixing of permits, the ability to travel abroad, to wear nice clothes. He was certainly aware of how he must appear to anyone: failed, aged, poor, impotent. Looking at Tanya who was all limbs and lines, he realised the true folly of dotage: to think that so marvellous a creature would find in him anything more than a sympathetic ear. She had known people and places he could never know. Uncle Vanya he must be for Tanya, and Uncle Vanya he would remain.

He drained his teacup, savouring the lemon scent of its deep blue interior. Then he wiped his mouth and stood up.

"Well, best be off, I suppose. Work tonight . . ."

Tanya put her hand on his elbow.

"Please . . . It's early. Not even on five yet." She looked up at him.

Duvakin had not led a celibate life, but he knew little about love. He did not know how to decipher the silence between them, and it troubled him. As when a foreigner in the hotel spoke to him in some unknown tongue, Duvakin longed to understand and could not.

They both stood, immersed in the tensions and balances of their relationship. It took a moment for an alien sound to impress itself upon them. Lena was vomiting.

Tanya wheeled and dashed to the hall. She flung open the door to the toilet, where she scooped up the little girl and cradled her in her arms. Duvakin stood at a diffident distance.

"Lena, my darling . . . What's the matter?" The child was limp; her head rolled alarmingly on her mother's arm. Duvakin could see that her eyes would not stay open.

31

"Mama . . ." she said drowsily, indistinctly. "I'm sleepy . . . The candy made me sick . . ."

"Candy? What candy?" Tanya looked first at Lena, then at Duvakin, who was as puzzled as she. "In the doll?"

"Mmmm . . ." Lena's voice trickled off into silence.

Duvakin strode into the little girl's tiny room, which held only a pine cupboard and a day-bed.

Pieces of the doll were scattered about the red tartan cover of the bed; all tops and bottoms of various sizes. The pieces of four dolls. And a plastic bag, about the size of the three inner dolls. Duvakin riffled quickly through the toys and pillows on the day-bed, knowing even as he looked for them that the missing dolls were not there.

A doll from a dead man's room, he thought bitterly.

The bag was filled with a white colloidal powder. As he picked it up a whoosh of the stuff escaped. Even as he was convulsed in sneezes, Duvakin was reasonably certain of what he held.

A plastic bag filled with heroin.

4

When he shut the door of the phone booth behind him, Duvakin had an uncomfortable sensation: the roof of the booth was as low and its sides as close as a sarcophagus. There was actually no real advantage in closing the door: not only was there no one else in sight on the street, but four of the booth's nine glass panes were missing. He fiddled with the door, knowing that he was stalling.

His endless nights at the Red October had taught him that the routine of night security guard had a limited number of variants. Small items—fights, drunks, petty thefts—were his to deal with. Everything else was supposed to have the same response: call the militia and wait.

Saturday morning he had discovered a dead body and had done the right thing. He had called and waited, and the two KGB men had appeared. Thus the KGB seemed to have jurisdiction over this case. The heroin had come from the dead man's room. Thus he undoubtedly had to notify the KGB about it.

But he had been bumping his head for hours against the question. *How* to notify the KGB.

It was an odd thing, like contacting God. Everywhere all about, but damned hard to put your finger on. A two-year-old child knew the building at Number One Dzerzhinsky, the yellow building with its set of forbidding thirty-foot high parade doors. People avoided coming close to these doors even when the sidewalk was crowded. But how to break through the magic circle? He didn't know the names of the two gaudy boys that had searched the American's room. He didn't know which division had sent them. Hell, he didn't even know if they *had* divisions.

All he had, in fact, was a telephone number that had been given to him eight years before, when he had first come to Moscow, 'to be used only in the most extraordinary circumstances.' He had heard these words so often that he had gathered the impression that the phone number was not to be used at all. For eight years he had had that number tucked into the recesss of his wallet. It was now barely legible.

And what if the number had been changed? What if the phone should be out of order?

He sighed, and finally began to dial. To remain standing in the gloomy slush of the booth was to court death by freezing. And he could hardly wander around Moscow with what looked to be a hundred or so grams of heroin in his pocket. He spun the flimsy plastic dial, taking care to hold the icy receiver a good two inches from his ear. The seventh digit. Then some random noises. Clicks. Hissing, distant voices, another click. Then silence. Swearing, he decided that the call must have cancelled itself. Just as he was about to hang up, the phone rang. He was startled. Never had he encountered a phone line so free of interference. It must be a separate system entirely. The phone continued to ring. He slipped two kopecks into the slot. Someone had answered.

"Yes?" A man's voice, neutral, almost curt.

"Is this the—could you tell me where I've reached?" Duvakin found himself speaking in the squeaky voice of a schoolboy. He cleared his throat.

"Wrong number, friend . . ." The voice was trailing off, hanging up.

"Wait! Is this the KGB?" Duvakin shouted desperately into the phone. He looked around nervously. No one had heard. The street was dark and deserted. The phone connection remained intact, anyway.

"KGB? It's possible . . . Who wants to know?" The voice was now completely neutral; not curt.

"Lieutenant of the People's Control Duvakin Ivan Pavlovich. Assigned to the security staff of the Hotel Red October." Duvakin hoped he sounded business-like; he suspected he sounded subservient.

"We don't deal directly with the People's Control, Duvakin, as you know . . . Why are you calling this number? Where did you get hold of it?"

"It was issued to me eight years ago, for use in extraordinary circumstances . . ."

"Well?"

Duvakin explained as briefly as he could, taking care to skip over the actual discovery of the doll and the way in which the contents were revealed. This made his story rather disjointed, but he counted heavily on his effective ending.

Not without reason.

"Heroin? What makes you think so?" Hostility disappeared from the unknown voice, replaced by controlled interest.

Duvakin ran quickly through his qualifications for thinking so: a brief seminar, some newspaper articles about the decline of the West, a few internal bulletins circulated to the security staff of hotels where foreigners stayed.

"Who was this American, this stiff?"

"I don't know, I wasn't told . . . I mean, I know his name . . . Miller, Andrew Miller. But that's all they told me."

"Miller, Miller . . ." There was the sound of paper rustling. "No Miller here. Hang on a second, will you . . ." This was not a request. Duvakin clung to the silent phone.

He could not guess how long he stood there waiting. He shifted from freezing foot to freezing foot, and blew on his fingers to warm them. The wind was rising, obscuring the distant lights of the buildings with snow devils. Far overhead stars twinkled coldly. He began to worry seriously about frostbite.

At long last the phone came back to life.

"Duvakin? It appears that this matter will require some consideration, and some help from you. Be at Number 7 Dzerzhinsky tomorrow by ten. Understand?"

"Ten in the morning?" Duvakin knew the question was idiotic, but he could not help it. "I work all night. First thing in the morning?"

"Yes, without fail. And ask for Colonel Polkovnikov. Be so good as not to forget."

The phone went dead.

The desire to restore circulation to his numbed feet was only partly the cause of Duvakin's savage stomping as he headed down the slope towards Matveevo's train station; the larger part was disgust, anger at his own acquiescence. His own cursed rabbitry meant he was now going to have to work all night, then go meet that damned colonel after no sleep. It was only as he slithered down the steep hill to the tracks that he began to realise that the man on the phone had not given him any choice.

The day's anxieties slipped away in the crush of the train and the subway. It was a special time, just two weeks to the New Year celebration, and all of Moscow was in motion, desperately hunting out special tidbits. Despite the crush, most people seemed in a good mood, enjoying the holiday atmosphere. Gypsy girls with billowing bright coloured skirts hawked home-made cosmetics by Kiev station, their gold

35

jewellery bright against the filth of their faces. Farther down the platform, beneath the harsh violet lamps, an enormously fat woman was selling piroshki, enveloping herself in clouds of steam each time she opened her box to serve a customer. In the metro the crowd laughed good-naturedly when a drunk was refused admission, on the reasonable grounds that he was carrying loose eggs in a net bag, through which the eggs dropped one by one. When Duvakin got off at the library stop, where the Arbat, Kirov, and Fili lines crossed, he was stunned by the crowds. As he descended the stairs he saw an undulating carpet of grey fur hats, through which bobbed tightly wrapped fir trees. It was a pleasant sight, the more so since this year Duvakin would have someone to spend the holidays with.

By the time he reached the hotel he was humming to himself.

"You on again tonight, Nikiforich? We see a lot of each other, don't we?" Duvakin patted the doorman on his creaky shoulder. The old man looked up with rheumy, eternally startled eyes. The loose skin on his neck wobbled.

"Yes, sir, it does . . . Colder though when I was a lad."

Duvakin laughed. One does not come without cause by the nickname Vanya the Post. He clapped the old man on the shoulder again, and went down the hall, diffidently flattening himself against the wall as the richly dressed foreign tourists passed him on their way from the restaurant to the hard currency shop.

He paused near the cavernous restaurant, inhaling with pleasure its warm smells; then ducked down his dark, tiny hall to the door marked 'Shoe Repair'. He barged in, exuberantly chucking his coat in the direction of the clothes tree.

"Damn it, Duvakin! You've knocked over my ink!"

"I'm sorry, Dima . . . Careless of me." Duvakin looked without interest at the pool of ink that was soaking into the new *Evening Moscow*. He daintily wadded up the mess and threw it into the waste basket.

"That better?" he asked airily.

"Damn it, no . . . I still had two to go on the crossword . . . And there was a bit in there I hadn't read about bananas for the holiday . . ."

Dima had joined the regular rotation only a few months before; Duvakin did not know him well. Nevertheless he disliked him already, partly because Dima, like every new man in the last eight years, had managed immediately to land a day shift, and partly because Dima was not a likeable sort. Duvakin knew he was old-fashioned, but he did not admire these breezy young men with their stylish clothes and their crossword puzzles, who switched instantly from the formal to the familiar and who took as an insult one's failure to respond in kind. Somewhere Dima had a wife and children who developed grippe whenever it looked as though their husband and father might have to work an extra shift. Duvakin looked at his colleague, his lips pursed.

Then he sighed, shook himself slightly and relaxed. It was silly to allow Dima to spoil his good mood. He began to hum again.

"You're happy tonight," Dima said suspiciously. "You . . . you didn't . . ."

"What?"

"You didn't *find* anything, did you?" Dima's bovine face looked at Duvakin insinuatingly.

Duvakin stopped humming. What was the man driving at?

"Find anything? Like what . . . You lose something?"

Dima's eyes appeared to glitter shrewdly.

"Find, you fool . . . *Find!*" It was only when Dima began to wink theatrically at Duvakin that he realised what was up. He felt an enormous, irrational relief. Dima had in mind shopping, not purloined evidence.

"You mean because I'm humming? It's not what you think. Just had a good day, that's all." Even as he said it, Duvakin realised that the phrase was wrong.

"Don't tell me then. But I think it's pretty low," Dima said huffily.

"No, I don't go in for that, you know that . . ." Duvakin realised that it was futile to protest. "Oh hell . . . Go up to the

37

Yaroslav station, there's a bunch of Armenians selling tangerines there . . ."

"Thanks, friend!" Dima was already at the door.

"Whoa! Is there anything I should know about? Anything come up?" Duvakin grabbed Dima by the sleeve of his overcoat. Suede. How the devil had Dima come up with a suede coat?

"No, just the usual . . . Let go, Duvakin!" Duvakin released the suede, and Dima thought for a moment. "Nothing worth mentioning . . . That tattooed devil Sasha showed up again, sniffing around a bunch of tourists, but I clobbered him a good one on the ear. Then that fucking number two elevator stopped between six and seven again— no foreigners on it this time though. Oh—a big group of Americans are coming in tonight, late . . . Russian winter festival and all that. They'll be up on eight . . ."

"That guy was removed all right, then?"

"What guy? Somebody up there that shouldn't be?"

Duvakin looked intently at Dima. There was no slyness behind this question. Evidently he really did not know about the body in 852.

Duvakin shrugged. He sure wasn't about to be the one to inform him.

"Nothing. Just a little matter from Friday night . . . It's all taken care of."

Normally Dima would have been suspicious about being excluded; now he had his mind on tangerines.

"Okay then—I'm off," he said, and rushed out.

Duvakin chuckled to himself, and settled back with a cigarette. Thank God it was Sunday. He could sleep maybe, get a little rest before that interview tomorrow with the Colonel. He had not had much experience with mysteries in his career, and he was glad of it. In Krasnaya Sosna the work had been simplicity itself. Deaths were caused by exposure or old age—except once, when one drunken Kaban brother plunked his kindling axe into another drunken Kaban brother. There had been no mystery there: the killer had passed out on top of his victim. Beyond that the only sleuthing he had ever had to do was to find out who was pilfering supplies from the local kolkhoz construction.

The country. In some ways he wished he had never left it. Thoughts of Tanya, however, gradually overcame memories of sunny fields and damp woods. When Lena got well . . . But he could not sit there dreaming all night. Reality began to press in on him. Cursing, as he did at the beginning of virtually every shift, he opened the desk to take out the log book and sign in.

But Dima must have moved it. That was odd. He turned out the drawer, and then opened another drawer and rummaged through that. He was not certain of the function of the log book, but for eight years he had opened and closed each shift by signing it; that was now as automatic a gesture as lighting a cigarette. And in eight years the book had never been moved from the top drawer of the desk.

Damn it. Only a new man like Dima, with his head stuffed full of crosswords and bananas, would think of moving it. Duvakin got up stiffly and went to the wooden wardrobe on the far wall. The cabinet was so rarely used that last January someone had stupidly pasted the year's list of social obligations right over the crack, and there it had stayed all year, undamaged. Until recently, it seemed. Now the red and gold document dangled loosely; a large chunk was torn from Lenin's brow. A fragment of paper remained on the frame, held by a lump of flour paste.

It was a miracle that Dima hadn't put the book somewhere even harder to find, or rolled it up into cigarette papers . . .

He opened the door and, sure enough, the big vinyl ledger lay among forgotten papers on the top shelf. Duvakin took it down, noticing that Dima had contrived to misplace the metal ruler that served to mark the current place. The man had his head in a shopping basket.

Duvakin flipped through the pages, looking for his place. There was December, there was last week, his own hand, Grisha's, someone named Pavel whom he did not know, then Dima. He skimmed mechanically through Dima's entry, contemptuously noting spelling errors, and then signed his name and the time he had come on duty.

After a moment he remembered that Saturday morning he had written his entry on a left hand page. But the entry was now on the right hand page.

It was one of those things; a feeling that something didn't jibe. He turned the pages slowly back to his Friday night entry.

Lieutenant of the People's Control Duvakin, Ivan Pavlovich, reports that his post was assumed at 20:00, 17 December.
On quitting my post I have the following to report:
   A) Transgressions of the public order, two fights induced by drink;
   B) Crimes against state property, none;
   C) Crimes against private property, the disappearance and presumed theft of a galosh (left) from room 512A.

And so on.
Right down to 'I quit my post at 8.00, 18 December, I.P. Duvakin'
Period.

Duvakin stared at the rough green paper. His handwriting, his name, the right date. But not the entry he had written thirty-six hours before, reporting the discovery of one dead American male. That record had apparently vanished.

For a brief moment he wondered if he had gone mad. Then he thought of something. He remembered that stupid left galosh. He flipped back through the book, looking for December of the previous year.

He found it. December 7, a year ago. The two fights, the lost galosh and, of course, no dead man.

He flipped back to the recent entry and compared them. Except for the changes in date, they were identical. But that made no sense at all. Leaving aside the mechanical question of how there could be two identical reports like that, what

40

was going on? It would be nonsense to think that someone had taken the log book and doctored it to make a dead American disappear.

It would only make any kind of sense if that log book held the only record of the death in the world. Then a murder would become a non-murder.

But it was not the only report. All right, there might be hundreds of reports like that in the local militia office; it might pass unnoticed. And maybe Intourist could misplace a foreign visitor and not get excited. Maybe there was no one in America who would care enough to come looking for the man.

But the KGB was in on this too, that was the stupid thing. Duvakin thought of the arrogant little beast who had commandeered his desk the day before. It was hardly likely that *he* would pull his hooks out of a thing like this. So what on earth was the point? Yet there it was. A fact.

The wisest thing—much as he hated it—was probably to call the secret number again. There was heroin. There was the altered log book . . . He was out of his depth.

"Never rains but what it pours," Duvakin said aloud. He knew that he was trying to trivialise the thing; he had begun to feel anxious. He dialled the number. At least his office was warm, unlike the draughty phone booth.

The phone circuits opened. The stillness on the line was eerie, unlike any phone lines he had ever used. It rang.

"Yes?"

"Colonel Polkovnikov please," Duvakin said. He tried to sound confident.

"Wrong number, chum," the voice said. The line remained open.

Duvakin, confused, stammered out the history of his earlier call, trying to keep the unknown listener on the line.

Finally the man said non-committally, "That so? Hang on a second, I'll go check."

Duvakin sat, listening to the silence, glad he was indoors.

"Duvakin?" This was a new voice. "Polkovnikov can't come to the phone now. He said you should talk to me."

Duvakin was somewhat emboldened by the interest in this new voice. He gave a report which he felt was professional, uninflected and objective.

"Hmmm. That's hard to swallow. Are you sure?"

Duvakin was offended.

"Yes, I'm sure . . . What d'you take me for?"

There was a muffled sound. The other man appeared to be talking to someone with his palm over the mouthpiece. Then his voice returned.

"Listen, Duvakin. This sounds important. Hang on to that book . . . I'll be coming over as fast as I can. Understand?"

The line went dead.

Duvakin felt almost cocky as he replaced the receiver.

Gradually, he relaxed, even growing drowsy. Yawning exaggeratedly, trying to clear his head, he looked at the clock.

Since he had no idea where the KGB man might be coming from, he could not know how long he had to wait for him. Certainly at the least a half hour. Maybe an hour. Getting anywhere in Moscow took an hour, and if he was coming from way out beyond Marina Roshcha . . .

Probably there was time to get a cup of coffee. He picked up his briefcase. The woman at the fifth floor buffet generally had a few oranges or other rare goodies tucked away for her special friends. He was going to need something to re-establish himself in Tanya's good graces after what had happened to Lena. A kilo of nice oranges would turn the trick.

As he walked down the long, empty corridors he kept seeing Tanya's face as it had looked in the ambulance. Frightened, grateful to Duvakin. Frightened of Duvakin. Hell, what a mess, and he hadn't been able to explain anything to her. He had used what little pull he had and managed to get Lena into the clinic normally reserved for foreign tourists. At least he had done that.

The clanking elevator deposited him on the fifth floor. The night duty woman was asleep at her desk. He should have awakened her. But why? Nothing was going on. The only sounds were random clanking noises, snatches of radio music, some laughter. Normal hotel noises. As he walked to the buffet he found himself hoping desperately that there would be oranges. He had to regain his position with Tanya and Lenochka.

The buffet was crowded; the one group that was there drinking fortified wine was unpleasantly raucous. The windows were opaque with fog, the coffee machine steamed merrily, spewing wet grounds; a few sausages bobbed in greasy water. The tables were sticky with cheap cognac and spilled mustard.

Duvakin spotted a dried orange peel curled among crushed egg shells at a corner table. A hopeful sign.

"Hello, Ivanovna. How's it going?"

"Hello, Duvakin . . . You haven't been up to see us in a while. You look thin . . . Like some sausages?" She indicated the big vat behind her.

He laughed. "No, thanks. Just a cup of coffee, if you will. Double sugar." After a moment he held up his briefcase and silently mouthed the word, Oranges?

Ivanovna peered owlishly through her round steel glasses, and nodded. She gestured with her finger to Duvakin to put the briefcase behind the counter, which he quickly did. She kicked it out of sight.

"Cold, isn't it?" Duvakin asked uncomfortably. He never knew how to hold a conversation during operations of this sort.

"Minus forty tonight, they say."

"Imagine that . . . That's cold, all right . . ."

"Cold indeed . . . Well, here's your coffee, comrade . . . And the other . . ." She mouthed what Duvakin took to mean 'later'.

He nodded and went into the other room with his coffee.

The raucous group were just finishing the last of the cognac they had managed to wheedle out of Ivanovna. The law prohibited the selling of strong drink after seven in the evening, but Duvakin knew that the clock generally had a way of stopping in hotel buffets. Besides the wine they were now about to order was perfectly legal, and only slightly less

43

potent than the Dagestani cognac they had just finished. Duvakin's stomach flip-flopped at the thought of it. He found a stand-up table in a quiet corner, and gulped his coffee quickly.

He spat out the grounds and glanced back into the kitchen. Ivanovna was too busy to allow him to catch her eye. She was trying to decipher the accent of an Arab who wanted to buy something. To Duvakin it sounded as though all the man's 'b's' should have been 'p's'.

Oh well. Later. The oranges would wait.

He returned to the lobby, where the staff sat and dozed in clumsy uncomfortable furniture, waiting for the Americans who would arrive later.

Sunday night. Even the bar was empty.

Great, thought Duvakin. Once he had talked with the KGB man, he could look forward to a long evening of doing nothing. He couldn't really sleep, but he could doze, and maybe it would not seem so long until tomorrow.

He rounded the final corner and entered the pitch-black corridor that led to the shoe repair office.

He dug into his pocket for the key, and when he inserted it in the lock, something huge and heavy crashed into the back of his neck. He crumpled to the floor, unconscious.

5

Something cold and wet struck him across the face. Duvakin struggled up, discovering to his regret that he was still alive. Movement shot pains from his shoulders through his neck to explode in his head. He collapsed again and gradually the room became clearly visible.

He lay on the office day-bed, beneath the bright ceiling

light. Something moved near his feet; slowly he looked in that direction.

A short stocky man was sitting on the desk chair, which he had pulled next to the day-bed. His legs were crossed, and his pale blue eyes watched Duvakin with calm, detached interest. In his hands he idly twisted a wet hotel towel—the instrument no doubt which had effected Duvakin's return to the world.

Duvakin rolled onto his side, his back to the stranger. He had no desire to ask questions, although he supposed he ought to ask some. It was quite clear what had happened, although for what reasons he could not imagine. The office had been ripped apart: desk drawers turned out, the contents of the cupboard dumped onto the floor, where his overcoat lay, still attached to the capsized coat tree. A couple of empty vodka bottles stood on the desk; gradually Duvakin realised that he himself reeked of vodka.

"Looks bad, doesn't it? Drunkenness on duty, destruction of state property, hooliganism, maybe even a few tricks with currencies, because the merely mortal haven't been able to buy that vodka for five or six years now, and here you are just a few doors down from the hard currency shop . . ."

Duvakin rolled over again to look at his visitor who, smiling pleasantly, reached into his suit pocket and brought out a pack of cigarettes. He offered them to Duvakin, who hesitated.

"Foreign?"

"German. Not our Germans."

Duvakin took one, allowing the stranger to light it for him. He drew deeply on the cigarette, pain throbbing through the back of his neck. "Not bad . . . What time is it?"

"Little after ten," the man said.

"So. I come on duty at eight, drink myself into the blind staggers, waltz around like an elephant in a china shop, pass out, and then wake up two hours later stone sober with nothing more than a headache . . ." Duvakin's voice trailed off. He touched the back of his neck gingerly to see whether his last words were true.

The man laughed. "Me, I'd say a performance like that

45

should get you title of Master of Sport, or maybe Hero of Labour . . ." He paused. "Pity you didn't really do it."

"I didn't do it?"

"It was a good job, it really was. When I arrived the scene looked perfect. Just a couple of things they overlooked. The door was unlocked, which didn't seem likely for a man bent on liquid refreshment without benefit of collective aid, and on duty too . . ." He smiled. It was clear that he was enjoying himself. "Another thing—I don't see how anyone could manage to fall against both a cupboard and a desk and knock all the papers out of each of them. And at the same time neatly slit the lining of his own overcoat."

"Did I break anything? Is there any blood?" The visitor obligingly held up a pocket mirror. Duvakin was horrified to see that his old familiar face was caked in dried blood. He touched his noise. It did not feel broken.

"You're damned lucky, Duvakin. It takes a good solid whack to make your nose bleed like that. Maybe your friend hit you a bit harder than he intended; he wouldn't have gone to all this trouble for a dead man, would he?"

"Give me another cigarette, will you . . . And you can put that towel away," Duvakin said. He sat up and put his feet on the floor. "Perhaps you'd be so good as to tell me how you enter into all of this?"

"You made a phone call about eight o'clock?"

"KGB?"

"No, why should I be KGB? CID, criminal investigation."

"CID?" Duvakin felt curiously cheated, as well as sheepish about the timidity with which he had spoken on the phone. There was nothing particularly awe-inspiring about CID.

"And what would you call a mother-naked dead man, a bag of heroin, and a hotel security man laid out like an Easter piglet? Political?"

It was a relief, at least. This man seemed ready to take the weight from his shoulders, a weight which had grown far too large in the last two days. He began to feel more confident, and professional, since his responsibility for the dead man in room 852 would last at the most for another two hours or so.

46

Duvakin attempted to ignore the sensation that his brains were spread on the floor for passers-by to stomp on, and decided to give a good account of himself before he was rid of that damned dead American once and for all.

"Have you identification, comrade?" he asked officiously.

The stranger sighed, placed his cigarette in the corner of his mouth and reached into the breast pocket of his coat. He pulled out a red cardboard rectangle which opened like a book. Printed on the right hand page were the words, 'Criminal Investigation Division' with a photograph of the man's face underneath, obscured by a scrawled name. The left hand page said that the bearer was Bezimenov, Mikhail Sergeevich.

"Sufficient, comrade Duvakin?"

"Yes, thank you, comrade Bezimenov. Should we get down to it, so that your people can finish the business?"

Bezimenov's face congealed slightly; it became cold and distant. He did not appear to care for Duvakin's new air of professional courtesy.

"I'm afraid that is my line you've taken there, Duvakin. We've got a few more things that we'd like to hear from you, but there's an awful lot more that you've got to hear from us. Understand?"

Only too well, Duvakin thought. He was still involved in this mystery. He tried to bluff his way out, however, despite his aching head.

"Damn it, you're CID! My job is just to guard this hotel and report to the proper place if anything comes up. I did my job, now it's your turn! What could you have to say to me?"

Bezimenov spoke mildly, but his words were harsh. "Remember that *we* tell you what your job is, Duvakin. And it is possible that I was mistaken about all of this . . ." He indicated the chaotic room with a sweep of the arm. "Do you know the penalties for this sort of behaviour?"

Only too well, Duvakin thought, staring at Bezimenov. He was fascinated despite his anxiety. Something really big must be afoot if the CID were going to push him that hard, that early. Slowly he nodded.

"All right," he said. "You win. I'll listen."

"Sorry, Duvakin. But this is an old problem you've wandered into, and we're a little short-fused about it."

"Old? But I only found that American Friday, or Saturday morning really, and reported it right away. And the heroin . . . that was today. If it really is heroin," he added. It might be in his interest to appear as ignorant as possible.

Bezimenov got up and put on his coat.

"Let's go get some coffee, comrade Duvakin, and we'll have a chat." As he spoke he made a circular motion with his finger at the ceiling. Duvakin's confusion deepened, but he got up and began to assemble the rags of his overcoat. Why would a CID man suspect a hidden tape recorder?

"Here?" he asked, hoping Bezimenov would understand the question.

He laughed. "Duvakin old boy, remember the fairy tale about Ivan the Fool, how he grabs hold of a rope and discovers it a bull's tail? My friend, you are in the same situation as Ivan, although you don't seem to know it yet. You can't let go, so you'd better hang on!" He laughed again, and took Duvakin's arm.

They followed the trail of corridors to the lobby, and went through the double glass doors. As they walked Bezimenov kept up a friendly chatter which would suggest to any on-looker that they were just two old pals, ducking out for a quick one.

The air outside was freezing cold; Duvakin winced as he inhaled it. The sky was clear. He could feel the mucous in his nose gelling as he breathed. He spat experimentally, shaking his head when he heard the slight crackle of ice hitting the pavement. He pulled his ravaged coat about him. In vain.

"Sorry, Duvakin . . . It's going to get colder too, but not like in the Far East, of course . . ."

"Look, Bezimenov, what is this? I can't leave that office for long . . ." And besides, he added silently, I'm freezing.

"Wait until I explain a bit more, and then you'll see. It seems best out here, not to take a chance on extra ears . . ."

"But that's the security office, for God's sake!"

"In which you got pole-axed. Shut up and listen!"

They walked slowly down the block and around the corner: two friends taking a leisurely stroll through deserted streets on a freezing evening.

To Duvakin Bezimenov's story seemed incredible, like some spy book about America. But there appeared to be no question that he held an enormous bull by the tail.

Andrew Miller was apparently not a stranger to those whom Bezimenov called 'us'; he had travelled in the Soviet Union a dozen or more times in recent years, always on different tourist routes. His fluent Russian he explained to his Intourist guides by saying his parents were refugees, escapees from the days of the Black Hundreds, and that his name was really Melnik, translated by his father into Miller, when he arrived in America. Now that he was a grown man of means, he said he had conceived a desire to visit Russia out of a love for his 'native land and language'. Not an unusual story. It was one that brought Intourist a nice pile of foreign currency every year.

Miller's game had been blown early on, and entirely by chance, Bezimenov said. Duvakin was struck by this admission: he had never heard a superior officer suggest that anything ever happened except through his own native brilliance. But chance it was; Miller had happened to eat at the same table with his female Intourist guide on the first day of his first tour. He was tired from his flight, but happy and talkative, obviously delighted to be speaking Russian. The girl enjoyed chatting with him; English she found an effort. When his soup arrived Miller ate it Russian-style, with the spoon held like a scoop in his right hand, and his black bread held in his left hand as a pusher. The Intourist guide found this endearing; Westerners she thought ate in a prissy manner. In fact most Americans did not care a lot for cabbage soup; she was fascinated to see that Miller not only ate his with appetite, but wiped his bowl dry afterward with his black bread.

Not only that, but, conversation suspended, he licked his spoon dry and shoved it with a quick movement into the top of his boot. She was gathering herself together to warn him of the consequences of theft when a shudder seemed to pass through him. He took the spoon out and put it back on the table.

Nothing else untoward happened that day or at any time on the trip, but the guide was a trained professional. She reported the incident to her superiors, along with her suspicions of Miller.

After some little search, these suspicions were confirmed. The guide had never seen an American lick his spoon. Americans were much more prone to disgustingly wasteful gestures, like putting out their cigarettes in the soup. But she had read about behaviour like Miller's, in a story set years ago, during the unmasking of the cult. The story was set in a prison camp.

Over a period of weeks investigation and supposition brought together a coherent story, which was finally deposited at what Bezimenov called 'the appropriate place'.

The fact was that Miller was no Miller, nor had he ever been a Melnik. He was a Gorazhanin, an American-born soldier of Russian parentage. After the war he had been stationed in occupied Vienna, where he was picked up one night in the wrong sector on real or concocted charges of black-marketeering, and whisked away into the interior wastes of the Soviet Union. On the way he had stopped off at Steplag, Peschanlag, and so on—the file had all the names, as well as a list of the jobs he had worked in the camps. The file carried no details about the actual man. By 1956 Gorazhanin had spent ten years among the lost souls, and his sentenace was to last for another fifteen. The times were such, however, that he was granted 'clemency'. He was released, taken to a train station and put quietly on a train bound for Vienna. He had two thousand American dollars in his pocket, and a skilfully forged American passport.

He disappeared from the Russian sphere and was not seen until his reincarnation as Andrew Miller, in a group of American tourists.

Bezimenov confessed that this reappearance puzzled 'us',

since it was doubtful that anyone would feel nostalgia for such a life. However since Miller left the country with his group, the incident was considered closed; nothing was done except for the issuing of a warning to the visa people about the need for vigilance.

"In short," Bezimenov concluded, "we decided he had simply acted on a whim. To be noted. But nothing to worry about."

And then Miller's name and picture turned up among the visa applications of another tourist group.

The first reaction was to reject the application, but then someone a little wiser and a little higher up decided that Gorazhanin-Miller was either a lunatic or someone who could be most interesting; in any case it might be profitable to allow him in and keep him on a long, sure leash.

And so matters had remained. Gorazhanin showed up about once every six months, sometimes with groups, sometimes alone. He was always friendly and outgoing, not inquisitive, not bold.

He managed to remain enigmatic—sometimes he lost his tail, sometimes he ducked out to make a phone call from a random booth, and sometimes he chatted briefly with apparent strangers. It was hard to decide: he might have lost his tail by accident; the phone calls always appeared to be afterthoughts and were always short; the chance encounters involved people whom the security organs knew always tried to befriend foreigners. A couple of times these friendly types had been pulled in for questioning; but these sessions did not prove to be worth the effort. All of Miller's conversations seemed to have been acceptably innocent—just the usual touches of anti-sovietism, some banter about the black market, and so on.

"The problem was that while nothing quite hung together, it wouldn't fall apart either." Bezimenov rubbed his ears, apparently to keep his blood circulating. He dug a pack out of his coat and offered a cigarette to the shivering Duvakin. "We could have picked him up for currency violations or we could just have denied him entrance visas. But it was never worth it. If we tried to jail him the FBI would jump down our people's throats in New York, and if we expelled him or refused him, then we would never find out what was going on."

"And what was going on?"

"That, my friend, is where you enter the picture. We had just about had it with this clown. Four years we were following him, listening to him, shaking him down every time he went through customs, searching his room when he was out . . . And nothing. We found nothing. Then this afternoon we got your report. Murdered, slit throat . . . the doll . . . Things started to come together a bit. We've been doing a hell of a lot of work in the last few hours, I can tell you that."

"And?" Hurry, hurry, Duvakin begged silently, hopping from one foot to another. Bezimenov had unfortunately become so absorbed in his own story that he had stopped moving.

"And? Well, we don't have the whole thing yet, but we are looking for patterns, trying to fit what we already have. The big mistake we made in the first place was to look for something political . . . espionage . . . it never fit the facts. When you made your report, we ran it all through again and some things turned up. Of the people that Miller ran into, at least one was always queer, homosexual. But not just free-lance . . . Each of them was under the protection of thieves, they all had connections. And remember that Miller was ten years in the camps . . . with the thieves."

"So he was hooked in with them, eh? What, currency? Smuggling?" Duvakin was very cold. He did not see how he connected in any way with all of this. He wanted to ask why, if they knew so damn much, he had to stand outside like this and freeze. Instead he asked, "And the heroin? Was Miller on drugs?"

Bezimenov looked at Duvakin with mild incredulity.

"No . . . And if you will allow me to add one more interesting coincidence, we can be done." He smiled a thin smile. Duvakin knew that he had better damn well listen.

"That fact—that coincidence—the only consistent point

of reference in all of Miller's trips is that he always passed through the Red October."

"But . . . You know as well as I do that tourists never choose their hotels, that they're placed in them!"

"I didn't say he stayed here, I said he passed through. Sometimes he stayed. Sometimes he dropped in to change money. Sometimes he came to the bar. But he always bought something in the tourist shop . . ."

"So?"

"So . . . It's the only constant in all of these damn trips. That's what's 'so'. Which means that this hotel is somehow connected to what's going on. It can't be that he came here *each* time by chance. Oh, every tip looks good on the surface, but think . . . What's here? Komsomol Square? He's going to come all the way from the centre to look at four train stations and an elevated train? Shopping? When everything worthwhile is down at the Rossia or out at Novodevichy? To drink? Hungarian scotch and Yugoslav gin? No, little friend, it was something else, and it brought Miller not only to this hotel, but all the way from America . . ."

Duvakin involuntarily followed Bezimenov's gaze. The hotel hunched gloomily the entire length of the block, a dark fortress with a few yellow lights which twinkled in the frozen air. "What in the hotel? Why?"

"That, Duvakin," Bezimenov said slowly, "is what you are going to find out."

"Me?" Duvakin whirled to face Bezimenov. "Me? I'm in god-damned security! I'm no CID man! What can I find out? Why don't you people do it . . .?"

"There's a number of ways that I can answer that. I could say that he was your dead man, on your shift. Or I might point out that since whatever it is is in your hotel, you are the only one who could conduct an investigation without tipping our hand, without seeming out of place. You could be said to have an interest in all this, since that rap you took was no real love pat. Or, I could just say that we asked you to do it . . . which means," his voice became flatter, "you will do it. Understand?"

Duvakin could feel still the pain at the base of his skull, the taste of iron which follows a hard blow to the head. He *was* involved, that was true enough. Which meant two choices. Let go of the bull's tail and be trampled by Bezimenov and his friends. Or hang on to the tail and ride that like a tick. And follow the bull wherever it might go.

He sighed, "You win . . . What am I to do?"

Bezimenov laughed. "You have an appointment down town tomorrow morning, don't you?"

"I thought . . . Well, doesn't this talk . . .?"

"Take its place? No, it doesn't. I'm just an errand boy tonight; Polkovnikov wants to see you himself. Besides, I've got a month in Pitsunda coming. I start Saturday."

Whoever Polkovnikov might be, he rated being called 'himself'. And Pitsunda? God, what would Duvakin give for even five minutes at the Black Sea?

"All right, comrade Bezimenov, I'll try . . . but remember, I work tonight. All night."

"My friend, you won't try, you'll *do*. Goodnight and goodbye, comrade Duvakin. I hope your head improves." Bezimenov quickly shook Duvakin's hand, and disappeared down the street.

Duvakin watched him go for a moment, then turned and dog-trotted back to the hotel on clumsy wooden legs. Once inside he suffered agonies as his fingers and toes began to warm up. It was in December that he most felt the need for warm clothes, and the hopelessness of getting them. No money, and the whole of winter before him. He sat at his desk in the 'shoe repair' room, and looked through the window at the foggy red glow of the hotel sign. He felt trapped. In winter, in this hotel, in this mess.

One hell of a mess. He looked at his coat again: the lining was a mass of fluttery ribbons. Then he glanced at his watch and sighed. Still hours of work ahead of him. He had to see Polkovnikov at ten; he ought to sleep, but he knew he could not. Despite his misgivings, he felt some excitement at the thought of doing real work, of perhaps finally moving up in the world. At the same time he thought that Bezimenov's metaphor was inadequate. It was not a case of having a bull by the tail, but of riding a tiger. Working with *them* . . . You reached your goal, but the trick was arriving astride the tiger and not inside it.

He got up and stretched his aching body, and then began to pace the floor. The back of his head was swollen and fiery to the touch, his office was torn apart, and his clothing was in shreds. This was not a game; it was deadly serious.

But there was no *sense* in it. Someome had bashed him hard, and tried to discredit him. They had tried to get him fired, or even sent to jail. But what was the reason? Jealousy? A desire to replace him on the night shift in a rundown hotel, for one hundred and eighty-seven rubles a month? Maybe they wanted his room, which used to be the dining room of a working-class apartment and which was now part of a home for nine families. Could anyone be that desperate?

And why would anyone want to take this room apart? The ceiling light illumined the tattered day-bed, the desk, the wardrobe, two hard chairs, a framed certificate of socialist merit, and over it all a penetrating smell of vodka. That was all there was. What else could it have held?

It would seem that he had been knocked unconscious so that someone could search this room. But why go to the trouble? And why pour vodka all over him? If they wanted to search the room they could have lured him away by a deceptive phone call or some kind of disturbance in the hotel or even outside it.

Brooding, he picked up his overcoat for the umpteenth time and suddenly realised that it was *he*, not the office, who had been the object of the search. Otherwise why rip out the lining of his coat? Why knock him out? And if he was the object, it could be for only one reason . . . that damned doll. He laughed shortly. All day that doll had been on his mind, for one reason or another.

It would have been hard to find a hiding place safer than the locked buffet on the fifth floor, beneath the oranges

55

that Galina Ivanovna had presumably stuffed into his briefcase.

He laughed again and began painfully to clear up the mess left by the disappointed searchers.

6

Duvakin squeezed out of the Number Nine trolley just behind Children's World and headed up the gentle slope that leads toward Dzerzhinsky. He picked his way gingerly across the enormous parking lot at the upper end of Kuznetsky Most, to avoid being run over by the strapping lads who were dashing about in their Volgas. The KGB parking lot was filled with more cars than you ever saw parked in Moscow, all either black or a bilious green. The KGB seemed a very open secret; all the car licences had the same prefix, MOS, and all the drivers were hefty and overfed.

As he crossed the street, making for the blue and white mansion further up Dzerzhinsky, his heart beat more rapidly than he liked. He tried to pretend to himself that it was the walk uphill.

At Number Seven he grasped the wooden handle of the huge parade door and, taking a deep breath, was able to pull the door open.

He wasn't sure what he had expected to find inside. He faced a dark hall into which stared tall blank doors. From somewhere came the slow tapping of a one-finger typist. When his eyes had adjusted somewhat to the gloom he saw a staircase on his right with a sign high up on the wall: 'Reception'. Upstairs. He trudged slowly up, trembling. It was cold in there.

On the second floor were more enormous doors, three

times higher than Duvakin, their glass covered by yellow curtains. Again he had to take a deep breath and pull hard. Why did doors always have to be so massive and so heavy?

There was a large waiting room containing several pinewood armchairs covered with a burlap kind of fabric, most uncomfortable looking. Clumsy side tables held yellowing copies of *Pravda*, *Izvestiya*, *Soviet Sport* and *Bulgarian Woman*. On the far wall was a large map of the Soviet Union; some cities were marked with flashing lights. The other walls held plaster replicas of the seals of the republics.

The room was already filled with people; Duvakin could not perceive them as distinct individuals. They were like actors in a play. The setting seemed to demand a pudgy, balding man by the window, smoking nervously as he stared into the street; an old woman with a wrinkled, tanned face and weepy eyes, her head covered with a white kerchief and her feet thrust into ragged felt boots; a neat middle-aged woman sitting quietly by herself. And another blank door at the far end of the room.

And no receptionist. It was almost ten o'clock. They had emphasised that he be on time. He had grabbed a few minutes of sleep, slipped away from Zavalshin to get a glass of lukewarm cocoa and a dried-out sandwich, retrieved his briefcase from the buffet and caught the trolley. Riding public transport in Moscow in the morning was a hell of elbows, shoulders and briefcases. Duvakin had to take two trolleys and a bus to reach his destination. Moscow was so damned big. The trolleys were packed, the melting snow sloshed up and down the aisles as they stopped and started. During the trip the sky turned from black to dove grey.

Now he stood and waited, his tired, aching head refusing to function any further.

At long last the far door opened and two women walked out, chatting brightly. At the same moment a voice from a hidden loudspeaker said, "Next!" The pudgy man at the window automatically stubbed out his cigarette on the floor, looked around nervously and bent down and picked it up again. There was no ashtray; he put the butt in his pocket, and walked quickly to the far door.

Duvakin followed him, trying to act as though he knew what he was doing. He walked into a small boxy room holding two desks, four straight chairs, a cupboard and another door.

The man at the right hand desk looked up, silent and rather stern.

"Good morning, comrade," Duvakin said, with cheerful assertion. "I'm Duvakin. Lieutenant Duvakin."

"So?"

"I was told to come here. By ten."

"And you're here, aren't you?" The man returned to his work, his interest apparently exhausted. At the other desk the pudgy man was being lectured by a sour-faced woman with hennaed hair and gold teeth. He tried occasionally without success to interject a remark.

"To see Colonel Polkovnikov," Duvakin said softly.

Duvakin's man looked up again, this time with somewhat more attention. The questioning light in his eyes quickly subsided; had Duvakin been someone to fear, he would not still have been standing there like that. The clerk pointed at the floor with an exquisitely sharp pencil.

"Wrong floor. Downstairs. Room 28."

Duvakin, sighing, turned back toward the door.

"Just a second, citizen. I'll call and tell them to expect you."

He rapidly dialed four digits with the pencil, then swore and hung up. He redialed, and his face assumed a respectful expression. This Polkovnikov must be somebody, all right. The telephone conversation was too soft for Duvakin to hear. The clerk put the phone down and said, "Go on down. They're waiting."

Duvakin retraced his steps, turning down the corridor at the foot of the stairs. He followed this corridor, turned again, followed another corridor, and made another turn.

The door to room 28 was a solid padded barrier of maroon leather and brass studs. He knocked, but even he could hear nothing because of the padding. For some moments he stood, screwing up his courage and then, with a physical effort, pulled the huge door open.

This office resembled his own. No waiting room, just a desk and a wardrobe with a coat-rack at the door. Two chairs. And a man behind the desk. Good Lord, where do they get them? Again blond, around thirty, in decent physical shape, beefy, with eyes a little puffy from drink. Indistinguishable from a hundred of his colleagues.

"Yes?"

The tone was neutral, indifferent. This tone was beginning to irritate Duvakin.

"I'm Duvakin. Colonel Polkovnikov wanted to see me."

"Oh, yes, Duvakin. Have a seat. He'll be in directly. Cigarette?"

Duvakin carefully fished one out and lit it at the man's lighter.

"West German?" he asked, inhaling.

"Sure are . . . You like them?"

"Mmmm . . ." Duvakin was not sure about the proper response to this question. He sat down on one of the straight chairs. The other man also sat, not quite watching him, but not looking away either. Duvakin could hear his own wrist-watch ticking.

Finally there was the sound of a door opening somewhere to the right, and someone bustling about. The man behind the desk looked in the direction of the sounds. After a bit came the sound of another door. Doors, Duvakin thought.

"Duvakin? How do you do, comrade? I'm Colonel Polkovnikov."

A trim man with a large nose stepped, it appeared, from the wall. As he straightened up to greet Duvakin, he appeared to be two metres tall. Duvakin, staring upward, grimly shook hands with this giant.

Polkovnikov guided him around the desk and past the wardrobe, where there was a door hidden from view by the cupboard. Duvakin stood in the middle of a large, opulent room. The Colonel shut the door behind them. Red Georgian carpet on the floor, a dark wood desk with a felt top, a chair covered in leather, dark panelling on the walls . . . The room was not only richly appointed; it showed no signs of wear. Duvakin knew now that Polkovnikov was a very large cheese indeed.

"Sit down, sit down, comrade. Cigarette?" Polkovnikov strode to the desk and snatched up a cigarette box of Karelian birch. Duvakin mutely held up the cigarette he was still smoking, and shook his head. He decided to plunge in.

"You asked to see me, comrade Colonel?"

Polkovnikov looked at him attentively for a few agonising seconds. The glittering blue eyes took his measure.

"Duvakin, we've got a problem, and we need your help."

Polkovnikov spoke as though he were asking a favour. Bezimenov had demanded co-operation as a duty.

Polkovnikov sat in his large leather chair, silently swivelling in it, and glancing about the room. He began to play with the desk, moving knobs, opening and closing drawers. It was a very clean desk indeed. Duvakin's mind was beginning to wander when the Colonel suddenly sat forward and began to speak softly. His tone was so conspiratorial that Duvakin involuntarily drew closer to him.

"Duvakin, we know you're a smart fellow, we've had a look at your file . . . And you've had some time and reason to think about all of this . . . What strikes you as odd?"

Duvakin sat frozen. The mention of his file had pithed him like a frog, for it had raised a threat of unknown and unknowable proportions. To suspect one has a file is one thing; to be told not only that it definitely exists but that authorities are examining it, is another thing entirely. And what was *not* odd about dead tourists, dolls filled with heroin, militiamen attacked by night . . .?

"I'm not sure what you mean, comrade Colonel."

"Bezimenov spoke with you?"

"Yes . . ."

"About Miller?"

"Yes . . ."

"So. What do you make of it all?"

Duvakin did not like all this; he was not used to being questioned by his superiors. He paused, hoping that Polkovnikov's questions were rhetorical, and that he would begin to speak himself. But as the silence dragged on, he realised he had to offer something: a guess, a few conclusions. Miller was carrying heroin, he said, maybe for a gang . . . Maybe they had an argument . . . Maybe he had met the gang in prison . . .

"Duvakin, you've just told me how to make a bicycle . . . And I already know how to make a bicycle. So. Nothing seems odd to you, hm?" Polkovnikov got up and began to pace seriously. Duvakin felt hopelessly lost. The Colonel sat down again and leaned forward, once more speaking almost in a whisper.

"Duvakin, when you called us about that doll, we started doing a little digging, a little checking, some thinking, and there were a few odds and ends that stuck out. All right, you say Miller was carrying heroin and selling it in the West, maybe for a gang. He met his gang maybe in camp. Now they had a fight and he gets bumped off. Think for a minute. Miller gets out of the camps in 1956 and then shows up *twenty years later*? To run heroin? Why? We think there have to be only two possible explanations. First, let's say Miller comes back on his own and contacts somebody, and arranges the whole thing. That's possible, but it's got problems. One, who does he know to contact after twenty years? How does he know where to get hold of them, whether he can still trust them . . . A lot of water goes under the bridge in twenty years . . ."

Duvakin thought of his own face, twenty years before. Pink cheeks . . . and a full head of hair. He sighed. It was one hell of a lot of water.

Polkovnikov continued in his conspiratorial tone.

"And that's not all. Say he can do all this—get in contact, set the thing up, even arrange for payment, though that's not easy. But even so, where is he going to get the heroin from? No gang is going to sit around with sacks full of it, waiting for some damn Auntie Mashka to walk in and ask for a couple of grams. And Miller's on a tight schedule, because he's with a tourist group. But let's say that they even get around this one, that maybe he doesn't bring anything in or out the first couple of times, that they just set it up. You know what it takes to make heroin, Duvakin?"

"No, comrade Colonel . . ." Lord, he thought. Imagine answering that question affirmatively.

"The flowers are easy enough to grow, Georgia or Kazakhstan or somewhere like that . . . Keep the locals looking the other way, get a bit of time free from work, watering . . . The devil knows that any one of those blackass Turkmen can figure out how to do that. It gets rougher, though . . . You need laboratories, chemists, equipment. Now, mind, I'm not saying that this stuff can't be found, but it all takes grease to run quiet and smooth. Lots of grease. Not just money, Duvakin . . . Influence, risks, letting people in on the enterprise. Duvakin, this isn't a pastime for drunken pickpockets! We're talking chemists, people with education!" Polkovnikov spat the word. "And Duvakin . . . No protector is going to stick his neck out for some guy he hasn't seen in twenty years and can't touch as soon as he's across the border. Miller trots off to America with his ass full of money, and what's this gangleader here got? Two handfuls of smoke! Or worse . . ."

Duvakin suddenly realised where Polkovnikov was headed, and he froze. As the realisation grew and strengthened he felt both satisfaction at the way awkward bits now slipped into a pattern, and horror at the pattern that they made.

"Or the second explanation . . .?"

"Or, my little friend, the second explanation . . ." Polkovnikov once again halted, to scrutinise Duvakin's face. Duvakin, squirming inwardly at the intensity of the Colonel's ice-blue eyes, managed to preserve a calm façade. "The second explanation . . . Let's turn the thing around, assume that we already have our flowers, our chemists, and our heroin. And our gangleader who is smart enough to know that there is no real point in the whole exercise if he can't get that powder out to the West. So you need a Westerner—let's say for the sake of argument, a Russian with an American passport. Somehow word gets to him, in he comes, takes the stuff out, brings things back into the country. Not much difference between the two versions, you think? Think what it takes to make it work . . . One, how to contact Miller? Two, why Miller anyway, and how do we know that he's going to come? Three, how can we insure that he'll do what we want? I mean, sell the stuff and bring us back the profit . . . and there's the problem too of how to bring the profits back, in what form."

Polkovnikov fell quiet, apparently ruminating. Duvakin was virtually certain now that he knew what Polkovnikov was leading up to. Better that Polkovnikov should cross his own t's.

Finally Polkovnikov spoke, but in a tired, quiet voice.

"I've thought about this so many times since they got me the information, and it always seems to lead to the same place. Someone who knows Miller and can control him, can contact him . . . and without attracting our attention. I thought at first that it wouldn't be that hard—after all, we don't let that many people out. A gypsy and his god-damned dancing bear, a basketball player, maybe . . . One or two fairies from the ballet. But how does the contact take place? The bear pees on the hotel carpet, the gypsy telephones while our man watches them mop it up?"

"Our man?"

"Not yours and mine . . . Ours . . . The nanny. But they get watched too closely, it wouldn't work. Any basketball player that doesn't take his five dollars and head for the first blue-jeans store in New York we watch *real* close. So we don't have anybody that can contact Miller *and* guarantee him *and* keep him on the level . . ."

Polkovnikov leaned even farther forward, speaking with more force. His words reached Duvakin as puffs of air mixed with saliva.

"Duvakin, anybody who could do all of those things is somebody who can come and go as he likes. And that, Duvakin, means we are after somebody *big* . . ."

"We? You and me? Big what?"

"Big," Polkovnikov said, pointing upward. "High up . . ."

Mother of God, Duvakin thought. He kneaded his wrist bones with his finger tips, sensing their awful fragility. Why me? "And where do I fit into all of this?" His question was soft; he did not want to hear the answer.

"In the middle, little friend, right in the god-damned middle! Duvakin, four years we've watched Miller, watched him closely, and until yesterday afternoon we didn't have the faintest idea what the hell he was up to. Not that we know that much now . . . We've traced back as much as we can, but those idiots we have out pounding pavement, half of them can't tell the difference between hard-boiled eggs and their own balls . . . And so what we really have is a lot of guesses, conjecture, suppositions. Duvakin, we can point you in the right direction, but you're the one who's got to run it down."

Duvakin suddenly felt the accumulated weight of his fatigue. He looked at his watch. Twenty-five hours since he had last been in bed. And he'd not had much more to eat than those slices of Tanya's torte.

"I'll do it, comrade Colonel," because I have no choice, he added inwardly. "But please . . . I'm worn out . . . I haven't slept . . ."

Polkovnikov looked at Duvakin with amusement. After a moment he rang a concealed bell; the young man from the outer room hurried in.

"Sir!"

"Tea . . . Sasha, isn't it?"

"Yes, sir! Two, sir?"

"Yes . . . Plain for you, Duvakin?"

"Yes . . . Well, lemon?" Duvakin asked, then fished for a cigarette. He discovered he had none, and sighed.

"You heard the man, Sasha. And bring him some cigarettes too. A carton, maybe."

A carton? Duvakin sat dumbly. While they waited for Sasha to return, Polkovnikov chatted amiably about the weather, the time of year, the pleasures he looked forward to at his dacha during the holidays.

Sasha returned with a tray holding two steaming glasses of tea and several rectangles of sugar wrapped in paper. And a carton of foreign cigarettes. Polkovnikov smiled and winked. Take, enjoy, his expression said. This is only the beginning. We take care of our own. Duvakin smiled weakly. Avoiding the Colonel's benevolent eye, he fumbled with the unfamiliar cigarette wrappings. He succeeded in extracting a cigarette. Inhaling deeply, he composed himself in his chair and forced himself to look Polkovnikov in the eye.

"You feel better now, more alert?" the Colonel said, smiling. Suddenly his smiled disappeared. His face was hard as flint; so was his voice. "Because I go through all of this *once*. And you get it. Understand?"

Duvakin nodded.

"About all we know about Miller is that he was damned good. He never saw the same people twice, never repeated himself. Except to go to your hotel. So. Our track goes through your hotel. That gives us a place to start. Now whoever this person is that we're after, he knows that hotel very well. He knows, for example, where a phone call about a dead American would go, and he knows what to do about it."

"What do you mean?"

"I mean, little friend, that we never received any call from you about Miller. Your first phone call to us was about the heroin. After that call we checked around; whoever it was had the whole thing covered. The tracks were covered. The log book, for instance . . . How do you think that got done?"

The log book. That had happened so long ago that Duvakin had almost forgotten it.

"I don't know, comrade Colonel. I . . . Really . . ."

"Ever hear of Xeroxcopying, Duvakin?"

"Yes, sure . . ." It wasn't a lie; he *had* heard of it. He didn't know what it was, though.

"It's an American toy. We got it—oh, nine, ten years ago. It makes copies, like photos, on almost any kind of paper. You take your December 7 page, fudge up the numbers a little, copy it on this machine, and then stick the original back in December 7 and take your December 17 page out," put the new one in place and presto! Your dead American is a lost galosh. All you need is someone who can take a security ledger from a hotel, take it to a photocopy machine, use it no questions asked, and return it without being noticed. Do you know where there's a machine like that, Duvakin?"

Duvakin made a noncommittal sound.

"No? Well, that puts you in a *big* majority . . . there's maybe three hundred of these machines total—and not one that doesn't have at least three rings of security around it. You want to guess what sort of person can get through those rings, Duvakin?"

"No . . . I mean . . . You said he was big . . ."

"We're trying to check those machines out, the few that someone might realistically have been able to use, but it's pretty damn touchy, I don't mind telling you." Polkovnikov grimaced and looked at Duvakin, almost as if he expected sympathy. "Damn tough, we don't want to flush our bird too soon. So. We need you."

Duvakin wanted now only to speed things along. He was almost indifferent to anything but the thought of his own bed. He smiled to himself as he remembered that his sheets had just come back from the laundry, stiff shiny sheets, crackling with starch, smelling of fresh linen. "Yes, comrade Colonel," he said. "What is it that you wish me to do?"

Polkovnikov stared at him hard enough to make him forget his sheets.

"You like those cigarettes?"

Duvakin held the cigarette at arm's length and squinted at it, as though to render an objective judgment.

"These? Sure. They're pretty good. They burn damn fast though . . ."

"Duvakin, there's maybe a million people within two kilometres of here who would do almost anything to get their hands on a carton of those cigarettes. Do you know what a carton like that costs on the black market? Fifteen, maybe twenty rubles—if you can find them at all. That's more than you make in a day, Duvakin."

He was not surprised that his salary was public knowledge.

"So, Duvakin, why does the trail lead through your hotel? What is the only starting point we have in this whole business?"

Polkovnikov was forever urging him to speak, to come up with conclusions. He could not think, he could hardly move, he was not sure that he could summon the energy to go on living. For the first time he noticed that the room had no windows. There were curtains, but no windows. Duvakin flipped open the unfamiliar cardboard box and pulled out another cigarette. He put the pack on the edge of the desk and reached for the lighter, missed it and knocked the packet off the desk. He bent down to grope for it and suddenly sat bolt upright.

"The doll. The heroin was in the souvenir doll. Of course, the Beriozka shop . . ." Duvakin, looking directly into Polkovnikov's cold blue eyes, was once again intrigued by the mystery.

"That's right, Duvakin," the Colonel said, as if he were encouraging a slow-witted child. "That means we ought to start in the Beriozka, doesn't it?"

"That's only for tourists, though . . . They'll only sell to foreigners with Western money . . ."

"That's partly right, Duvakin. Legally, they only sell to foreigners. But . . . Well, let me put it this way. What foreigner in his right mind is going to pay forty or fifty rubles worth of hard currency to acquire a short-wave radio that is the size of a suitcase, and made in Latvia to boot?"

"You mean a Leningrad? But they cost about a hundred sixty . . ." Duvakin stopped abruptly as he grasped the point. Less than a month before Volodya had appeared in the office, delighted at having found a Leningrad for one ten. "Black market, you mean."

"Oh, not always. We make it pretty damned hard for people to get their hands on Western money and we watch the stores very closely. We make sure that everyone who shops in them is foreign. But people try pretty hard too, and there's a lot of money in it. So that's what we want you to do, Duvakin. That's where we're going to start this thing off."

"You mean move up the tail and try to find the bull," Duvakin murmured.

"How's that?"

"Nothing. I'm—Well, I'm tired. But wait a second. I can't do it. I don't have any foreign money."

Polkovnikov fished in a drawer and threw a packet on the desk.

"And what do you call this?"

A rough roll of bills of various sizes and colours, worn and dirty, tied with a string. Like something hoarded up, hidden away, illegally gotten and treasured. "Pick them up, have a look at them," Polkovnikov said. "They're real. We don't know how careful our bird is; they look like something a security man in a cheap hotel might gather over the years."

"And you want me to try to buy something. In the Beriozka at the Red October." Duvakin picked up the roll and hefted it. How much money was it? "But they all know me there, and besides . . ." What the hell, he thought. "Our shop is just a little one. All it's got are some dolls and some crummy balalaikas and a lot of vodka . . ."

Polkovnikov laughed, rattling the spoons in the glasses of tea. "Couldn't resist a peek, huh? Oh I know, I know . . . Line of duty and all that, eh? Well, you can satisfy your curiosity now, to your heart's content."

"I can buy anything I want?"

"No, Duvakin. You can start there. But, as you say, they know you in the Red October, and you'd have to be pretty damn dumb to buy from your own hotel. Unless of course you were working with one of the salesgirls . . . which," Polkovnikov said casually, but with delicate emphasis, "we know you aren't."

"So?"

"So, Duvakin, you're buying there for a reason . . . Remember, they know you have the doll, and they haven't been able to get it back. You haven't been to your room yet, have you?"

Duvakin looked at Polkovnikov despairingly. Not that too, please, not that . . .

"Yes, I'm afraid so, Ivan Palych, I'm afraid so. We sent a man over there yesterday . . . Seems he was the second man to come 'look at your radiator' yesterday. None of the other people admit to being around the apartment, of course, so no one remembers a thing."

"What was . . . did they . . ." Duvakin could not find the words. His misery was total, and he was not consoled even by Polkovnikov's first use of his name and patronymic.

"The place was pretty thoroughly torn up, but nothing was destroyed. See what I'm getting at, Duvakin? They know you have the doll, and they can't get it back, they don't know where it is or what you've done with it. Or why. But so far, to them you look pretty damn clever, and they will probably be willing to listen to a proposition about getting it back . . . if you go about it right. In general, though, you probably know that they won't be overly particular about how alive you are after they have the doll . . ."

"So," Duvakin concluded for him, "I can play things pretty much as I want to."

"That's right," Polkovnikov said and began to rise; the talk was at the end.

"Wait a minute, comrade Colonel." Duvakin stood up first and leaned over the desk. "I know what *I'm* supposed to do, but where do 'we' come into all of this? How do I get in touch with you again? Are you going to be behind me?"

"Duvakin, you're a pretty slender reed, but you're all that we have to hang onto. The only reason that we've even got you into this is that we can't seem to get into it any other way. If one of our boys was to start coming around now that they are missing that little toy of yours, and with one dead American to their credit already . . . Bang, the shop closes down and that is that. We need someone whose angle they don't know, who they can't yet figure . . . This one is yours, Duvakin. You know our number—there's always someone there." Polkovnikov stood up and straightened his uniform. Duvakin had to lean back to look him in the face.

"But, Colonel, what if I have to get through to you fast? I mean, they've been a little . . . slow . . ."

"What do you want, Duvakin? A password, like in some spy novel?" Polkovnikov looked at him so benignly that Duvakin suddenly thought he might pat him on the head.

"Well, no . . . But you know . . ."

"Just call and ask for me. Tell them your name, of course . . ." Polkovnikov pressed a button at the edge of the desk and the door to a concealed closet swung open. He went over to it and pulled out an enormous overcoat and a thick woollen scarf, which he began to put on.

The man with the indistinct face looked in from next door.

"Sasha, take Duvakin here and show him out. Take good care of him. He's one of us now." Polkovnikov winked at Duvakin, who was too dazed to respond. "And Duvakin! Let me wish you good luck. You can be of great service to the Motherland, comrade!"

This was Polkovnikov's first mention of the Motherland, and something about it sounded false. Forced. Perhaps this late-blooming patriotism was for Sasha's benefit. Or was Polkovnikov sincere?

"Thank you, comrade Colonel. I'll do my best." Duvakin felt like a bit player in a movie about the Great War.

"And take care, Duvakin." Polkovnikov's voice softened. He sounded almost embarrassed. Then at once he spoke more loudly, professionally. "And Sasha, make sure he signs for the equipment, of course."

"Of course, sir," Sasha said. The Colonel's back disappeared through another concealed door.

They walked back to the outer office. "Sign for what equipment?" Duvakin asked. He was acutely aware of Sasha's gentle but insistent hand at his elbow.

"Sit, please, comrade," Sasha said. He dug through papers in his desk drawer.

Duvakin began to repeat his question, when Sasha took something from the drawer and set it on the desk before him.

"It's nothing, really, just a formality, for internal accounting. That is a lot of money you've got there." He began to write as he spoke. "Sixteen pounds sterling, eighty-nine dollars American, fourteen dollars Canadian, one hundred twenty francs . . ." He finished counting and writing in silence. "A nice bundle, my friend." He extended the inventory and a pen to Duvakin, who signed it quickly and rose, buttoning his overcoat as best he could, torn as it was.

"Just a second, comrade, That's not all."

Duvakin stared at him, puzzled. Sasha smiled and pointed with the end of his pen at the battered vinyl briefcase.

"The doll."

"The doll? But that wasn't issued to me."

"And you aren't going to keep it either."

Duvakin agreed sheepishly; he would not know what to do with it anyway. He took it out. Sasha opened the doll and quickly examined its contents. Then he wrote out another form and handed it to Duvakin along with the doll. "Approx one hundred grams heroin."

"Before I sign, just out of curiosity, how much is that worth about?"

"Thinking of setting yourself up in business, are you? . . . I'm not positive, I would guess about five or six thousand. It depends . . ."

"Five thousand rubles! I don't make that in two years!"

"Not rubles, Duvakin. Dollars." Sasha leaned back in his chair; he was enjoying himself. "On the black market that's worth somewhere between fifteen and twenty thousand rubles."

Twenty thousand rubles. Duvakin slowly put the doll back into his briefcase. That was every kopek he had earned since he had come to Moscow, and then some.

He rose to leave. "That it?"

"Yes, you can go, Duvakin." Sasha's attention was already absorbed by his papers.

Duvakin stood for a few long and foolish moments. Finally he said, "Do I get a copy of the receipts?"

Sasha looked up. His stare was reminiscent of Polkovnikov's.

"No," he said.

Oh, well. Duvakin looked at his watch; he had been awake for close to thirty hours now. His head ached and his tongue felt as though it were coated with tar.

On the way out he got lost once; he was corrected by a savage old woman who sat at a desk in the corridor, checking passes. She looked up from her magazine and told him to get out of there. He retraced his steps, walking past countless doors, from which came the sounds of typing, voices, more typing . . . until finally he found the doors which led to the street.

Planting his legs, he gave a solid heave; the enormous doors yielded slowly and unwillingly. He stepped over the slush grate and out onto the street. The sun must have appeared; he felt blinded.

When his eyes adjusted to the light he walked back down the hill toward the KBG parking lots. As he was crossing Dzerzhinsky for the Kuznetsky Most side, he looked left, down the hill toward the centre of town. The sun was at a high point, writhing in the clouds just above the brick yard and yellow stucco of the Kremlin. The north tower and its ruby star were outlined against the sky. Closer by Felix Dzerzhinsky stood on his pedestal, a gloomy figure, looming above the square. Crows flapped black and melancholy across the faintly visible sun.

The trip from Dzerzhinsky to Tanya's apartment was worse than a nightmare for Duvakin; in a nightmare at least he would have been asleep. There was an endless procession of jolting subway cars, shoving crowds, transfers between lines, escalators . . . He had the ill luck to doze off on the Ring Line and miss the Kiev Station stop, which meant that he had to ride all the way around to Gorky Park and back. The Matveevo train was packed with sportsmen and shoppers: skis, ski poles, skates and bundles continually jabbed, poked and crushed the luckless traveller. It seemed an age before Duvakin found himself before Tanya's door.

He stood, savouring the warm cabbage-scented air of the hall. Finally he rang. And knocked on the door. Silence. He rang again, then called, "Tanya! It's Vanya!"

Again a long, long silence. Duvakin felt defeated. He could not bear the thought of leaving, nor of facing the scene that would result if he did what he wanted desperately to do, and fell asleep right there in the hall. A drunk, they would say, and have him hauled away.

"Tanya, please . . . It's Vanya."

Slow steps sounded on the parquet; the flimsy peephole opened in the door. The lock rattled. The door slowly opened. Tanya stood with her hand on the knob, her eyes averted.

"May I come in?" Duvakin asked, puzzled.

She nodded. He stepped inside and she closed the door softly behind him.

"You have a key, Vanya," she said. Her voice was tense.

After a moment a sheepish grin spread across his tired face. Of course. She had given him the key when they put Lenochka in the ambulance.

"How is she?" he asked. He still wore his overcoat.

"They say she'll be all right. They're only going to keep her for a few days or so. Thank you for getting her admitted there. Everyone is so kind . . ."

She still sounded tense and preoccupied.

"That's good news then."

An awkward silence followed. They stood in the entrance alcove. Duvakin stifled a sigh. The natural ill ease of the poisoner before the mother of his victim. Duvakin thought grimly. Finally he could stand it no longer.

"Could I sit down for a minute, Tanya? I'm pretty tired. I'll go in a moment, I promise you. But . . . I can't face the train right now . . . No sleep, you see . . ."

She looked up and met his eyes for the first time. Her expression changed from coldness to warm sympathy. Lord, Duvakin thought, I must look awful.

Then without warning Tanya began to weep silently. Transparent tears coursed down her cheeks.

Awkwardly Duvakin put his arm around her. She stiffened slightly, and then allowed herself to be drawn into his friendly embrace, where she sobbed quietly for a while. Finally she stepped back, wiping the tears away with a swift gesture of her palm. Her smile was forced and fleeting. She took him into the kitchen. He gave her his coat and sank down on his accustomed seat.

"There's tea yet, Vanya. Let me warm it up for you." She smiled, this time more genuinely.

The first flakes of another snow storm were just filtering through the icy fog. Duvakin could see nothing through the window. Tanya bustled about the kitchen, asking when he had last eaten, what he would like to eat, and so forth. He relaxed, a pleasant drowsiness spreading through his body. Quickly the meal was placed before him; an enticing steam rose from meat patties.

He ate silently. He had not realised how hungry he was. He was intensely grateful for the warm fatty meat, the sharp mustard. Finally he said, "Are you angry with me, Tanya?"

She shook her head gently. "No, Vanya, not now. I'm even grateful . . . for the hospital and so on . . ."

"Why didn't you answer the door? I mean, if it's all right to ask . . ."

She paused a moment. "Oh, I don't know . . . It was silly, stupid even. I . . . Well, I realised that I didn't know you all that well after all . . . And you did have the key, and then the doll'. . ." She looked down at her hands, which were nervously drumming on the table. "Well, I might as well tell you. I was mad at first because I thought it had to be you that stole them."

"Stole what?"

"My books."

"What books?"

Tanya burst out laughing, throwing her head back slightly. Duvakin was distracted by the beauty of her throat.

"I'm sorry, Vanya . . . Forgive me, do. I'm just so tense, and the whole thing is so confused. Of course you don't know what books!" She stood up, apparently more to work off tension than to get the tea, with which she returned. "Everything has been so strange . . ."

The story came out by degrees. She had returned from the

74

hospital late Sunday evening, assured that Lena was in no danger and was sleeping comfortably. She had let herself in, had a quick meal and then prepared for bed. Something about the apartment bothered her, but she couldn't place what it could be. She assumed it was simply nerves, after the fright over Lena. It was when she was folding down her couch to make up her bed that she noticed two books were missing from the bookshelf on the wall. Her library was small; she knew every book in it.

She looked all over the apartment, considering that she might have set them down somewhere, or that Lena might have moved them somewhere, unlikely as that was. But they were nowhere to be found.

"So I figured at first that you had taken them, Vanya. Forgive me. I'm ashamed now, but you had the key . . ." She took his hand. "I'm sorry . . . As soon as I saw you at the door I knew I was being an idiot."

The hairs on Duvakin's neck had risen in alarm, but he tried to keep his questions calm.

"That's awful, Tanya . . . You're sure they couldn't be lying around somewhere, or maybe you lent them to a neighbour? Or to some visitor?"

"No, I was reading one of them just a week or so ago, the Bunin. But I really know because I could tell that the apartment had been entered while I was gone. That was why I felt odd all evening."

"What do you mean?" Duvakin pushed away his unfinished dinner and reached for a cigarette. He had pulled the pack partway from his pocket before he remembered he had only those damn foreign cigarettes. Awkward to remind Tanya of his access to special goods, now that one of them had put her daughter in the hospital. He fished out a single cigarette and lit it.

"After I noticed the books were missing, I looked all over, as I said, and I kept finding things that weren't where they should have been. You know, like a souvenir on the wrong shelf, or Lena's doll in a place she couldn't reach, the dishes moved . . . Little things. That's why I felt odd. Nothing big enough to stick right out. Just slightly off. But it was obvious when I really started looking."

Duvakin inhaled deeply and let the smoke drift out through his nostrils. A search, he thought, which means they have been here too. Any hesitation he had felt about helping Polkovnikov to catch these people disintegrated into a firm resolve.

If they knew that he had been with Tanya between Saturday morning, when the doll had fallen into his possession, and Sunday, when Tanya was at the hospital, then they were good. And they wanted that doll badly, as the dull ache in his neck still reminded him. He took another drag on the cigarette and looked at Tanya. She was thinking, her head bent, her fingers toying with a button on her blouse. She looked so brittle, frail . . . Thank God, thought Duvakin, thank God she wasn't here when they came. Or had they known that too? That she was gone.

"I wouldn't worry, Tanya . . . Probably just some workman that the housing people sent over to look at the radiators. They give them keys, you know . . . And they're the most incredible thieves. One of the people in my apartment came out of the bath to discover that both left shoes were missing from his only two pairs. He raised the devil over it, until he got them back . . ."

"How did they manage that?" Tanya asked, intrigued.

"Masterpiece of criminal investigation. They went looking for one-legged repairmen . . ."

Tanya smiled and slapped him gently, a playful punishment for his frivolity. Then she said, "I suppose you're right, but it is a shame. Whoever it was, he knew his books. Those two were real finds, completely irreplaceable now. I wonder if he took them to read or to sell?"

"Sell? How much could a couple of old books be worth?"

"Vanya! Where have you been in the last ten years? You really don't know?" Tanya was both astonished and charmed by his simplicity. Duvakin shrugged helplessly.

"Vanya, legally you could get ten, fifteen rubles, and oh, four, five times that on the black market . . ."

The black market again. Duvakin was beginning to regret that he had stayed so much away from all the haggling and dealing. Two lousy books and it would take him ten days of work to buy them. Or if he worked very hard for ten years and didn't eat, he could afford to buy a hundred grams of white powder. Maybe they would throw in the doll for free, he thought bitterly.

"Vanya, are you feeling all right? You look pretty tired."

"Oh, I'm all right . . . I just haven't had much sleep lately."

Tanya stood and took him firmly by the arm. She virtually dragged him to his feet, and guided him into the next room. She stood him against the wall and indicated with a stern shake of her index finger that he was not to move.

"What are you doing?" he asked feebly.

"Making up the bed for you. Now hush . . . I'll only be a second."

"But there's no need, really . . ."

"Hush!" she continued to work.

Duvakin watched her flat, elegant hands gliding smoothly over the sheets and thought sadly of his own apartment, where the searchers had not bothered to be careful as they had here. He tried to rouse himself to an adamant refusal to stay in Tanya's apartment and could not. The crackling linen sheets, the warm room, Tanya's sure movements, her obvious concern for him . . . He felt himself sliding gratefully into acceptance even as his mouth formed his objections.

"Now get into bed and get some sleep, Vanya . . ." Tanya said, slipping out the door, the curtains pulled. Duvakin sat heavily on the edge of the bed in the darkened room and began peeling damp shoes from stiff socks. Well, I'm in her bed now. He smiled as drowsiness folded over him.

7

Duvakin stood in the hallway trying to look nonchalant, and silently cursed both Polkovnikov and himself. What had escaped their attention was that he could not drop into the dollar store casually, for the obvious reason that it was never open during his working hours. He had already raised eyebrows and invited inquiry simply by showing up at the hotel when it was neither night nor pay day. A stern look and brisk nods of greeting had carried him to the door of the shop. There he foundered. He stood by the huge porcelain urn and smoked a cigarette, trying to look as though he were simply finishing his butt before going—legitimately—into the store.

The problem was that he knew so damned little about what he was going to do. The black market. People always spoke of it as though it were an entity, a place. The question, "Where did you get it?" might be answered, "Cheremushkin market" if the object of inquiry was a kilo of tomatoes or a loofah sponge; "the black market" if it were a suede skirt, a mohair scarf or a pair of Japanese tyres. Duvakin's only experience with this amorphous market had come during his years of buying homebrew from Auntie Tulyachka back in Krasnaya Sosna, where she was established as an institution by the regional Party committee. Beyond that he knew about the black market only from movies and books, except for a few exchanges of money and goods that he had observed at train stations.

Not that he could turn back now. With a sigh, he crushed out the last few millimetres of his American cigarette against the urn. Squaring his shoulders, he gave the briefcase a solid heft, took a deep breath, and pushed open the frosted glass door.

As he had expected, there were no customers in the shop. The tourists were now being carted about Moscow in their Ikarus buses, so the salesgirls sat idle, nodding vaguely to music on Radio Moscow, and looking out the window.

Along two walls stood high metal racks filled with hundreds of bottles of vodka. There was a rack of cigarette cartons, and a rack of boxes of chocolate, some of them dusty and faded. On a large rack in the centre were art books, wooden carvings and balalaikas. The girls sat behind a glass counter which held the more valuable items: watches, silver and enamel cognac cups, buttery lumps of amber, black and gold lacquered boxes. It was odd. There were items there that Duvakin had not seen in twenty years or more, and still he did not find the room impressive. Perhaps it was the sight of all that vodka. Alcohol in large quantities always depressed him. There was a deadly monotony about the state spirit stores, with their mountainous stacks of bottles in wire baskets.

Duvakin had moved part way around the room before one of the girls looked up from a novel she was reading.

"You! Citizen! What are you doing here? This is for foreigners!"

Duvakin noted her lapel pin. A Young Communist. As were her two sisters behind the counter, who were so accustomed to this sort of scene that they did not pay any attention to it. He decided to affect a mysterious bearing.

"Not citizen, girl. Lieutenant." He looked at her sternly. Momentarily she checked herself. He fumbled in his pocket for another cigarette, bringing out the red and white pack.

The sternness of his rebuff had only slowed her down. She was gathering herself for a new assault when she saw the pack, foreign cigarettes, available only to the few.

"What is it you want, comrade?" she asked, in a guarded, neutral tone.

"Just looking around."

Wrong answer, he realised at once. She frowned.

"On business," he added quickly.

"What business? By what right? You get out this instant or I'll call my superior!"

Duvakin, cursing himself for a fool, forced a stern and exasperated look upon his face. Coming close to the counter, he leaned over and whispered, "Internal security . . . Delicate matter. We're checking . . ."

She looked at him through painted eyes, and then grunted and looked away. The security thing seemed to have a surprisingly minimal effect on her. Normally it overcame most opposition instantly. These girls must be used to security people, working as they did in the midst of foreign goods, and foreigner's goods.

At least she was quiet. He returned to his slow examination of the shelves. The girl hissed at him, "Cultured people do not smoke in shops!" Hastily he stubbed out his cigarette.

He circled the centre rack carefully, examining everything on the shelves. He was stalling, hoping that a clue of some sort would present itself to him. Books, slides, tin samovars, chocolates, and finally, on the second circuit of the shelves, the nesting dolls.

They stood, with cheerful empty grins, in tight ranks of purple, red and yellow, in several sizes and varieties: some were inlaid with straw, some just painted, and one type was not a woman, but a man, a fierce antique warrior. Duvakin did not know what to do next. Surely Miller had not simply strolled in here, grabbed a doll at random and strolled out with twenty thousand rubles worth of heroin. There had to be a system, some method of signalling.

He picked up a doll that seemed to be the same size as the one he had found under the bed, and turned it over in his hands. He rattled it, rotated it, and shook it again. Nothing. Just the idiot smile every time it faced him.

He propped his briefcase on the bottom shelf and opened it quietly. Deep within the bag lay the doll. Surreptitiously he fished it out and compared it with the others on the shelves. They were all about the same size. Their colours varied, but the painted expressions were roughly the same. They seemed to rattle the same way.

He remembered the long hours he had spent in his childhood winters poring over copies of *Kolkhoz Lads* and *Friendly*

Pals. In those magazines he had liked especially the stories about Arctic explorers and brave soldiers, and the puzzle pages, with one exception: the puzzle in which one had to find the hidden differences between two apparently identical objects. Duvakin tried to solve these puzzles only when there was absolutely nothing left in the magazine to occupy him, and no reason to go outside except to pee in the snowdrifts.

The puzzle was even more annoying now. He tried concentrating harder, but then he began to think about himself thinking, which made him feel even more helpless and angry. He dropped the doll back into the depths of his bag, where it lay repentantly on its face; its back with its braid tied by a bright painted ribbon faced Duvakin. He angrily replaced the shop doll on its rack, conceding defeat.

But he had noticed something. Absence is more varied and sly than presence. It took a moment for it to register.

The braid.

Quickly he checked the rest of the dolls on the rack. No braids anywhere. He glanced into his briefcase again. Now that he had noticed it, the yellow hair and red butterfly bow seemed to stand out like a beacon.

It seemed the first step was taken. What next? The shelves held crude souvenirs of a Russia that had not existed for sixty years, if indeed it had ever existed, and the odds and ends of an incomprehensible West. He sighed.

"May I be of some help, comrade?"

Standing by the door was a strong upright woman of middle age, her hair a high bleached blonde tangle. She wore a dark blue suit with a lapel pin that said 'Beriozka'.

"Perhaps. You are . ." Duvakin tried to approximate Polkovnikov's brusque tone.

"Liudmila Grigorievna, the administrator of this shop." A wave of her plump white hand indicated the sullen painted girl. "Valentina phoned me. May I see your documents please?"

This Liudmila Grigorievna seemed promising. Her voice and her smile were pleasant. Duvakin was accustomed to the iron self-confidence which lay beneath such voices and such smiles. The smile did not extend to her eyes. She was an authority.

"Of course," he said, staring hard at her. "But is this the wisest place? It is, shall we say, a *particular* affair . . ."

"Ah yes . . . Please, comrade. Follow me."

Duvakin cast a triumphant glance at Valentina as he departed in Liudmila Grigorievna's wake. Zealous Valentina only looked bored.

He knew their destination, even though he himself had never been there. Down the corridor, through gigantic curtained parade doors, and down a flight of stairs to the series of offices labelled 'Laundry', 'Locksmith' and 'Vice-electrician'. It was in those rooms that the Beriozka's administration functioned.

Liudmila Grigorievna opened the door to the vice-electrician's office. It was similar to Duvakin's, but it had no window or any visible means of ventilation. On the desk were an enormous, well-used abacus and a brand new machine of some sort, with a keyboard of numbers. There were several cabinets and wardrobes, and a great deal of paper.

Liudmila Grigorievna took her seat with a stately air. She leaned forward the proper degree to indicate co-operation without servility, but with perhaps a touch of condescension.

"I'm listening, comrade. How may we be of service to you?"

This was a moment that he had been dreading. He was reaching the limits of his ability to anticipate events. For the first time in his life he wished he knew more about illegal operations.

"May I offer you a cigarette, comrade directress?" He asked, stalling.

"Foreign, aren't they." A statement, not a question.

"Yes, care for one?"

"No, I do not. Thank you."

As he struck the match he noticed her eyes following the pale yellow flame.

"Don't mind if I smoke, do you?"

"No. If you must . . ."

"Might as well come to the point then," Duvakin said, desperately. He had flung himself into this conversation and he did not know how to continue it. His only hope lay in deliberate vagueness.

"I have been told elsewhere"—a wave of the hand and a shrug of the shoulder—"that perhaps you could be of some assistance on a problem."

"I've already indicated our willingness . . . Perhaps if you could show me your documents and indicate the nature of the problem . . ."

His heart thumping irregularly, he reached into his inner pocket and brought out his cardboard identification folder.

"This is of course not all of it, because the problem is one of—well, supply . . ."

He watched her closely, hoping that she would betray some response to his transparent hint. Damn it, he was going to need some help if he were going to become a black marketeer.

Her face was wary, distant. "You have other documents?"

A hint? If so, of what? Duvakin cursed to himself.

"There *are* certain others, yes. But of . . . a more delicate nature, so to speak . . ."

"I see. And ought I to see them do you suppose?"

Was she playing with him? Did she know what he was getting at? Or was she in fact innocent and puzzled? He decided on a test.

"My . . . umm . . . colleague in this affair, comrade Gorazhanin, ought perhaps . . ." he trailed off. There was no reaction to his planting of Miller's real name. Of course that meant nothing. It had been a stupid test. Now he had to continue putting cards on the table until one worked.

"You are, I know, a person in a position of great responsibility, comrade directress, and I'm sure the Motherland appreciates and trusts you . . ." As he spoke Duvakin rummaged in his black satchel for the roll of foreign currency. He brought it out, still blethering. "You will understand of course that the problem in question and this response in the direction of a solution originates at a high—the very highest—level . . ."

Casually, while he spoke, he transferred the roll of money to the outer pocket of his jacket. Slowly. In full view of the comrade directress.

Her eyes took in the roll, the size of an eight-kilo sledge hammer, and never flickered. God above, Duvakin thought, either the woman is excellent or a total idiot. His possession of that money should have been called into question by her immediately. Instead she looked at him expressionlessly. She was waiting.

"As you can see the nature of this problem is such that we require some assistance in its solution. And . . . well, of course, you no doubt are aware of the many ways in which official gratitude can be expressed. Materially, and of course more . . ."

At least with Auntie Tulyachka and her bootleg vodka all one had to do was enter her hut, say "Two bottles", and pay the money. Here he had to blether at this woman-shaped piece of furniture and try to figure out what might be going through whatever comrade directress used for brains. The situation was awkward. She did not know him, and she had reason to be cautious. He had heard that the government did in fact use provocateurs who behaved just as he was doing. People found guilty of black marketeering on a sufficiently large scale could be shot. He had to go on prattling and hope for the best.

"The part which you are asked to play in this exercise is, as you might surmise, quite small—yet most vital. A part that requires little effort on your part, but which could reap large . . . shall we say benefits . . .?" The woman was still an unblinking blank, but she had not stopped him. He decided to switch from the carrot to the stick.

"The part however is a serious one, a most vital one, and I think it is only fair to add that certain quarters would be most unhappy—even, we might say, displeased—by a refusal to co-operate in so negligible a way in a communal effort, a comradely effort to erase a problem so serious, so grave, so . . ." Adjectives tumbled to his tongue in varieties of increasing stupidity. He stopped to stub out his cigarette.

The blonde blank shifted position slightly, adjusting herself in her chair more comfortably. Her eyes never left his face, nor did her expression alter. He was beginning to feel that he was beating his head against a very hard wall. And that made sense, really. The directress of even so decrepit a hard currency store as the one in the Red October could be expected to be someone unusually trustworthy, a Party type.

Duvakin was defeated. He might just as well go back to Polkovnikov and admit it. He wasn't the type to go chasing murderers and dope traffickers. He was the type who got slugged from behind. Period.

He stood up slowly. The angry buzzing of the fluorescent lights reinforced the silence in the room. Feeling like a helpless failure, as he prepared to leave he babbled in mock anger.

"I am most sorry then, comrade, that you have chosen to take this attitude. I can only imagine what would be the consequences if all our citizens were to take this attitude. Not to mention of course that this problem affects not us primarily, not the people of our generation, but rather the youth, the youth of our country who will be building the future . . ." He returned the useless wad of money to his satchel. Swept along by his own voice, not really thinking, he took out the doll and began to gesticulate with it. "And truly, comrade, is this so large a thing to ask, when it would bring such joy to some small heart . . .?"

"May I see that, comrade?"

Duvakin stopped short, with his mouth open. Liudmila Grigorievna looked up at him with a slight smile, and extended her hand. Slowly he rolled the doll into her outstretched pink palm and sat down. Idiot's luck, it would seem. At least she had said something.

She turned the little purple and yellow doll about in her hands, examining it. Duvakin said tentatively, "It's got a braid."

She looked up, now frankly appraising him. Wondering.

"So this is the sort of problem which interests you," she said softly. "Interesting. But not small, comrade uh . . ."

"Duvakin."

"Comrade Duvakin . . . You are I think connected with this hotel?"

"High security, eight years . . ." Duvakin did not know why he added the last bit of information, but it apparently meant something to Liudmila Grigorievna.

"Eight years? And on the night staff the entire while? Mmm-hmmm . . ." A pause. "I believe perhaps I will take one of your cigarettes now . . . You have a name besides Duvakin?"

"Of course . . ." He fumbled clumsily with the intricate red and white pack. The sudden thaw in her manner had thrown him off balance. "Ivan Pavlovich. Oh, don't worry, it's not the last one. I've got more . . ."

She laughed as he clumsily crushed the pack's last cigarettes in the cardboard top. He rummaged furiously in his satchel and finally produced another pack. But when he looked up a pack with a camel on its side lay on the desk, and Liudmila Grigorievna was already smoking. And watching him, with a broad, almost flirtatious smile on her bright red lips. Her teeth were solid gold, top and bottom. She licked a fleck of tobacco from her lip, and plucked it from her tongue with long scarlet nails.

"Eight years on the night shift, mmm? You have a family, Vanya?"

"Not really . . . Mother died during Khrushchev . . . Not because of him I mean . . . But you know. During."

"No wife? Kids, Vanya?"

"No, I've never . . . I mean, not that I don't want . . ."

"Girl friend?"

Duvakin felt like an idiot, sitting there while a woman about ten years his junior asked him such questions, which he was stupid enough to answer. And by what right did she call him Vanya? And why did it make him so nervous?

"I'm not sure that I see what business . . ." He felt the blush creeping across his bald spot.

"I'm just curious, Vanya, just curious."

"About what?"

"Oh, about why a man like you might be interested

in . . . helping solve that problem which interests you," she said, still smiling. "What are you thinking of?"

Duvakin was at a loss for an answer. Almost unconsciously he put his hand into the outer pocket where the money had been. The gesture was meaningless, but in this new world of hints and suggestions it seemed to convey something. The woman nodded understandingly.

"A common problem, most common, comrade." She appeared to be musing. Finally she leaned forward and crushed out her cigarette. "Well, perhaps I can be of some assistance after all."

Duvakin felt conflicting emotions of relief and fear. Much as he would have hated to tuck his tail between his legs and return empty-handed to Polkovnikov, still Polkovnikov was a known quantity, more or less. What might happen now, here, was not known. Luidmila Grigorievna dialled a number on the telephone and assumed the waiting expression of one who concentrates all her attention on one ear. The call apparently went through.

"Hello. Hello. Liudmila Grigorievna. Hello!"

She swore like a trooper, slammed down the receiver and repeated the process.

"Hello? Liudmila Grigorievna. No, that was me, I just phoned. No, I know . . . But I thought you might be interested . . . If you'll wait a second I'll tell you. Quiet a moment! A doll with braids has turned up . . ."

That apparently had some effect. Liudmila Grigorievna fell silent and listened, nodding occasionally. Once she turned to Duvakin and gave a friendly comic shrug. At last the unheard tirade appeared to draw to a close.

"All right, of course. Yes, yes, I understand. Certainly."

She was muttering to herself as she hung up. She turned to Duvakin, rearranging the blonde curls which had suffered during her conversation.

"It appears that my superiors have some interest in your problem, comrade."

"That's good news. Now perhaps . . ." But there was no stopping her.

"However . . . the problem cannot be properly handled in this office, as I'm certain you will understand." The circular motion of her finger, meaning 'extra ears'.

"I'm afraid that I do not quite understand, comrade directress."

"My superior asks that you deal directly with his office." She smiled a brilliant golden smile. "He would greatly appreciate having you meet him this evening."

"Evening?"

"This evening," she continued smoothly, "in front of the Maly Theatre, if you will. He suggests seven o'clock."

"Seven? But I have to—well, work . . ."

In fact it was not a large problem; all he had to do was call in sick and someone else would be press-ganged into the night shift. But it would be the first time he had deliberately played hookey. The prospect was oddly thrilling.

"Seven. And he asks that you bring the . . . your . . . the necessary documents and . . . ummm . . . samples."

"Seven? The Maly? But how will I find him?"

"You won't. He'll find you."

"How will he know who . . ." Duvakin paused. He did not really want to know how they would recognise him.

"Just be at the Ostrovsky statue at seven, comrade." She smiled a last toothy golden grin and waved him out the door. He nodded and smiled weakly in reply.

For better or for worse he had taken the first step.

As he trudged back up the stairs to the ground floor, Duvakin thought of the look of surprise frozen on Andrew Miller's face, of Lena vomiting, of Tanya's burgled apartment . . . Years of ceaseless repetition had left him deaf to government pronouncements about socialist morality and the spiritual loftiness of the New Man. Doubtless every government blethered in the same way, and probably most citizens did not bother to listen; they were too caught up in the problems of everyday life. Duvakin certainly was. In his life he had seen many people, and he knew them not to be terribly different one from another. In the army, his village, the hotel, they were just people, without elevated morals or philosophy. Volodya and his incessant bargain hunting, the gypsies and their eye-shadow, Tanya with her books. Hell, even him, with his oranges. Everyone had an angle, or was looking for one. But all of that was natural, it was life, the way things were done. It didn't cause anyone any harm.

In a way it was even fun, a series of small triumphs—buying daffodils in a February sleet storm, scalping two unwanted theatre tickets for the young swain seeking a warm place to spend a few hours with his girl, finding a pair of leather shoes the right size. The worst thing about the black market was obviously that it tended to pull almost all useful or valuable objects into its vortex. Even so, it was something one could live with.

What the devil, one *had* to live with it. But not murder, not burglary, not drugs, he thought, as he walked through the gloomy lobby and out the double doors. The cold immediately penetrated his tattered overcoat. He laughed grimly. A briefcase loaded with untold wealth and he was wearing an overcoat not even fit to cradle the head of a drunk in the gutter. He stepped into the freezing slush and joined the crowds jostling their way to the metro stop. The dark browns, blues and blacks of the crowd blended imperceptibly into the ochre of the buildings and the grey of the air.

Suddenly his eyes watered with affection and anger. Not much of a world, but it was his world, his only world. And there could be no place in it for people like those on whose trail he was now set. And if fate was such that he, Duvakin, had been chosen to do something about them, so be it.

8

Holding his briefcase under his arm, Duvakin jogged rapidly in place, drawing a few curious stares but little else. He forced himself not to look at his watch; he had already looked at it a hundred times in the last fifteen minutes. His contact could not possibly come from Karl Marx Prospekt; traffic rules would make it impossible to stop or turn. Petrovka was more promising. Huge Chaikas which always bore a Someone came into view with almost every change of the traffic lights. Each time Duvakin's heart beat faster. He could not say why he was so certain that his contact would appear in a Chaika, but he was. The Chaikas always turned right, though, just past TSUM department store and halted before the brilliantly lighted columns of the Bolshoy. There must be a big concert tonight.

The wind was rising; across the street the enormous crush around the tram and bus stops was beginning to thin out. Duvakin realised with alarm that he had lost the feeling in his right hand. He dusted the snow from Ostrovsky's feet, put his briefcase down there, and began furiously to shake his arm. Finally feeling returned, with pins and needles. Growing angry at his contact's tardiness, Duvakin huddled against the statue to protect what little body heat he had left, while he fished in his breast pocket for a cigarette.

"So you're looking for dolls, eh?"

Duvakin started, dropping the glove he held under his arm.

"Beg pardon?" The man who had tapped him on the shoulder was short and bulky in a heavy sheepskin coat. He wore a hat made of some exotic fur—wolf perhaps. The face buried in this luxurious winter clothing had dull, small eyes, a battered nose with prominent red veins, and black teeth which had been replaced here and there by steel.

"Dolls."

"Well, yes, perhaps . . ." Duvakin was not sure what to say. He looked expectantly over the man's shoulder for the Chaika which must be waiting at the curb.

"Follow me then." The man walked briskly away.

There was no car. Duvakin stood surprised while the stumpy man faded quickly up the street. And if he did not hurry he would lose the contact completely in the crowded dusk. He scooped up his glove and his briefcase and scrambled after his indifferent guide. The man did not look back once, and his pace was so rapid that it was only as they crossed the deserted park behind TSUM that Duvakin managed to catch up with him.

As they waited at the light to cross over into Neglinnaya Street, the man made it clear that he was there only to lead the way, and that any attempt at conversation would be fruitless. All in all it was just as well there was no Chaika: it might be safer to be out on the street with this sullen companion. Although a long mysterious evening lay ahead. Duvakin's throat was dry. He swallowed rather painfully.

A few street lights poked dimly through the bare branches of the boulevard park. The sign of the restaurant Uzbekistan gleamed in blue neon, bathing in its light the knot of people who stood outside, waiting for tables. Duvakin's guide pushed indifferently through the shivering crowd. Duvakin hung back, embarrassed to follow, yet appalled to think that he might have to stand outside, perhaps for hours. Protests arose from the gelid line while the stumpy man knocked loudly on the glass doors of the restaurant. The ancient doorman could be seen rising unwillingly from his chair, sauntering to the door, ready to repeat for the thousandth time that there were no tables. However when he saw Stumpy he became attentive; the door opened to admit him. Stumpy entered the restaurant lobby and turned to look back for Duvakin, who had just begun to wade frantically through the crowd. The stumpy man nodded at the doorman and the door remained opened wide enough for Duvakin and his briefcase to slide in sideways. A flurry of plaintive protests and proffered bribes floated about the doorman as he bolted the door again.

They checked their coats in the crowded cloakroom. Duvakin, as unobtrusively as possible, checked his briefcase as well. The attendant handed them their claim checks. Duvakin trusted to the fierce protectiveness of the Russian cloakroom attendant for the safety of his satchel.

They stepped up the short flight of stairs of the lobby. The

Uzbekistan was perhaps Moscow's best restaurant. Duvakin had never expected to enter it. An evening here might easily cost him a week's wages. Only the most highly placed people could penetrate this place, precisely because it was the Uzbekistan, home away from home for the countless Uzbeks, Tadzhiks, Turkmen and other Central Asians who seeped into Moscow. It was at the Uzbekistan that they gathered, instantly transforming the tables into facsimiles of their native Chaikans as they sat, feasted and chattered in their incomprehensible tongues.

Duvakin was as overpowered by the rich smell, and the cacophony of shouts, bits of song, and breaking glass overlaid with the constant hum of voices, as he was by the deep blue arabesque painted on the ceiling, or the Persian murals on the walls.

Most Russians disliked these almond-eyed, olive-skinned people: the men wearing black skull caps and the women in bright scarves and brilliantly coloured smocks. Their stubborn adherence to their native dress and even to their chaotic religions, combined with their incomprehensible refusal to learn the Russian language, brought contempt and anger on their heads. They responded to this by becoming even more clannish while they were in Moscow, often spending entire days gathered at the richly loaded tables of the Uzbekistan, yielding space only through exhaustion or fear.

Normally Duvakin paid no attention to Asians, but now he remembered rumours and stories that he had heard all his life: they caused a shivering down his spine and a queasy feeling in his stomach. Polkovnikov's plot seemed to be working, which was good, but if the answer they sought lay in Central Asia . . . Duvakin felt that he may already have greatly inconvenienced this particular group of Uzbeks. He sighed deeply, trying to aerate his mind, and calm his nerves.

Stumpy walked up to the administrator who sat at the door, and spoke with her briefly. She listened, scowling, very similar in appearance to the Red October's Liudmila Grigorievna, and then pointed a crimson-tipped finger to the left. Stumpy signalled to Duvakin with a nod of the head.

They went down a corridor, past a bar, and down another corridor, facing which were a series of closed doors bearing name plaques: Bukhara, Khiva, Registan . . . The corridor was unimposing, but Duvakin knew that behind these doors were private rooms, the most exclusive part of the restaurant, where its true opulence could be found. At the last room, the Shakh-i-Zinda, Stumpy knocked. Duvakin tried to decide whether that thumping contained any signal. After a brief pause the door was opened by a dark-skinned man with an aquiline nose.

Duvakin followed his leader through the door. He could not stop grinning nervously. The room was crowded with men, and with a long narrow table that ran down the middle. Crumbs, crusts, empty bottles and cigarette butts were thickly strewn among sumptuous plates of salad, fruit and fish. The air was heavy and sweet. Someone had spilled champagne.

What appeared to be scores of men sat and even squatted, hiding the walls almost entirely. It seemed that every black eye was on Duvakin, as he squeezed into the room. The silence was eerie, but Duvakin recognised it: it was the silence of insiders watching an outsider, a newcomer; the silence of underlings awaiting the pleasure of their overlord before announcing their own reactions.

The overlord was obviously a large man sitting at the table's centre, to whom the beak-nosed man said, "He's here".

And in fact, Duvakin thought, here I am. He stood near one end of the table: the crush of Asians parted to let him through, and then closed behind him. An unnerving sensation. He fought off a moment of irrational panic: after all, his old familiar Russia lay not two metres away, through the window and across the courtyard. It only seemed as though he had been transported to the tents of the Golden Horde.

"Welcome, friend Ivan Palych. Sit, drink, eat maybe, eh?"

The host had spoken. The silence had been so profound that Duvakin was startled to hear it broken. For a moment he did not understand the words, although the man's Russian, heavily accented though it was, was very clean.

"Sit, sit . . . What the matter is, don't feel like drinking, maybe?" The dazzling gold smile did little to warm the rest of his face.

Duvakin, temporarily deprived of the power of speech, looked vaguely for a seat. The big man twitched his head. A vacant seat appeared immediately to his left. As Duvakin slid awkwardly into it, the host leaned over and filled his glass with vodka. Export vodka. For foreigners.

"Good thing you come, Vanya, damn good thing! We been hope you come. Here, drink with Ishan!" He held up his own glass, vodka dancing tremulously along the rim.

"Ishan?" Duvakin had finally found his voice.

"Ishan? Me! Come, you don't want drink with Ishan?" Duvakin recognised the threatening undertone which he had come to know well since Friday night. He hurriedly raised his glass with forced enthusiasm.

"No, of course not. Or yes, I mean . . . Come, let's drink to our new friendship!" He extended his glass to click against Ishan's. But Ishan's glass remained on the table.

"For friendship? No, everybody always drinks for that, but is it serious? No, you just go outside, look . . . What you see? Fightings, people hitting each other on heads, knives . . ."

He smiled and drew a thumb the size of a bottle neck across the folds of his throat.

"No, my friend, another toast . . . How about 'May all our wishes be fulfilled' . . . or 'To the success of our enterprise!' or perhaps . . ." Here Ishan looked around at his minions, who still watched the scene in silence. "Or maybe the best toast of all, eh? 'May this not be our last drink together!' Eh?"

Ishan raised his glass suddenly and smashed it against Duvakin's, splashing vodka over his guest's arm and shoulder. The room erupted into noise as the two men drank together, and festivities returned to normal.

Ishan put a heavy arm around Duvakin's neck, shooting skyrockets through his still-tender skull.

"So, Vanya, what brings you our way, eh?"

Duvakin, wincing, leaned forward into Ishan's fiery breath.

"You talked with Liudmila Gri—"

"Listen to me, friend Vanya. That Liudmila, she's a nice bit all right, but you took chance. Start at wrong end, so to say . . . And with a woman, that's no good!" He made an obscene gesture and laughed heartily at his own joke. Duvakin smiled.

"Well, then, Ishan, I suppose you know why I'm here. Dolls, you might say . . ." Duvakin felt his replies were most effective when they were meaningless.

"Dolls . . . Matryoshki . . . A subject near to my own heart. But why you interested? You want collect them, eh?" This was the question Duvakin had been dreading.

"Well, is there a place where we can talk? I mean, to ruin so gracious a banquet with talk of business . . ." Duvakin felt he was rising to the occasion with Oriental politeness.

Ishan put down the fork he had raised part way to his mouth.

"Talk," he said.

"My reasons, is it? Well, first I should say that it is *our* reasons . . I mean I represent . . . or could represent, somebody else—others. If our contact prospers, there might be further . . . work." Duvakin was not quite sure why he had pluralised himself. Although he did in fact represent others, this was the last piece of information he wished Ishan to acquire.

"That is understood, friend Vanya. But what is your interest, that's what I would like to know." Ishan's lupine eyes seemed to hang on Duvakin's words.

"Our interest? Mutual . . . satisfaction, I suppose you might say." Duvakin reached for a yellow and white slab of smoked white fish. He was not too agitated to remember that he had not eaten white fish for years.

"That too I know, friend Vanya. But we are to talk of what? Deliveries from you or to you, so to speak?"

Duvakin ate slowly, eyes on his plate, trying to collect his wits. He had grown to hate these conversations, loaded with free-floating pronouns, hinting at Lord knows what.

Nervously abandoning his food, he dug out his cigarettes and lit one, and then quickly offered the red and white box to his host. This gesture of belated generosity seemed to have been a good one; Ishan's manner grew less overbearing and more friendly.

Duvakin drew in a lungful of smoke and exhaled slowly. "Our interest at this point is . . . preliminary," he said. "Investigative. Maybe that would be the better word." He was telling as much of the truth as he could. Ishan's broad Tartar face showed very little, but he seemed to accept this answer.

"I see," he said, toying with a spoon. "I see. Big outfit?"

Duvakin took another deep drag on his cigarette. The other guests were laughing and drinking and yammering away in their own language. Here and there among the black skullcaps were a few shaggy karakuls, above sharp-beaked, savage-looking faces. No one seemed to be paying any attention to Ishan and himself, but he had a strong suspicion that Ishan would have only to wiggle his finger for the Russian visitor to be filleted like the white fish. In the meantime the background chatter provided excellent protection against chance 'ears'.

"Big outfit? Yes and no. Depends on what you mean by big. There's a lot of . . . responsibility that they have . . . that we have . . . We could work well together, you know."

Ishan looked at him appraisingly. His gaze held steady for a disconcerting length of time. Then unexpectedly he leapt up, smiling his golden smile.

"My friends!" he cried to the room at large. "Let us drink again!" The men in the room reacted instantly, as Duvakin had thought they would. They toasted first both Duvakin and Ishan, and then one another. Ishan continued to address them.

"My friends, I drink to the health of my friend Vanya! May he always be well! May his sons have only sons! May his wife always be beautiful, strong and silent! And may his friends become my friends, and the friends of my friends! Vanya!"

"Vanya!" The room chorused, and clinked and gulped.

There was a moment's silence as the vodka took away their breath. At that things became even more chaotic than before. Everyone looked expectantly at Duvakin, who could feel the vodka working its way up his neck and into his head. Rashly he offered his glass to one of Ishan's underlings to be filled. Then he got to his feet.

"Ishan!" he said, holding his glass high. He did not know whether he were sober and simply feigning euphoria out of politeness or if he was so drunk that he thought he was sober. In either case, he choose to ignore that part of his mind that was desperately warning him to be suspicious of Ishan's sudden improvement as a speaker of Russian.

"Ishan! I thank you. I am honoured to be called your friend! I drink to your health, that our association may be long and profitable!" Again the room drank, clinking and laughing. Duvakin congratulated himself; it seemed he was hitting all the right notes. Eloquent, but not more eloquent than the host. Polite and warm, but still he had said nothing. Ishan beamed.

Duvakin's head was swimming when he sat down again. He was going to have to work to keep his wits. He lit another cigarette.

"Vanya, Vanya . . ." Ishan said. He leaned forward awkwardly. He intended apparently to whisper to Duvakin, but he failed to come anywhere near his ear. Duvakin felt his unease about his own sobriety disappear in the face of Ishan's obvious inebriation. The poor fellow clearly had a long head start. Duvakin slipped a supporting arm under Ishan's shoulder and helped the man find his ear.

"Vanya, you 'n me frien . . . be friend, we are, you know . . . friends the most important thing."

"Ishan, Ishan . . . We have to talk, Ishan . . . Wake up . . ." Duvakin suddenly realised that he could be in bad trouble indeed if his new-found friend were to pass out. He tried to shake him gently, but it was not easy. Ishan looked large and flabby, but Duvakin's fingers reported solid muscle beneath the fat. "You shouldn't drink so much, Ishan," he scolded frantically.

A voice on Duvakin's left suddenly addressed Ishan in an incomprehensible tongue. Duvakin turned to see an impassive olive face looking at Ishan over his shoulder. He turned back to find himself staring into Ishan's serious and dead sober eyes.

"My friend Mukhtar there says that you are clean, that you have no electronics and no papers . . . Other than these, of course."

Ishan held up Duvakin's wad of foreign money. Duvakin's hand moved instinctively to his jacket pocket; he cursed himself for an idiot. Never had his pocket been picked so neatly. Muckhtar could probably have taken his black cotton underwear as well, if he had wanted it. Duvakin tried to put the best possible face on it.

"There was some doubt?"

Ishan ignored Duvakin's question, studying him as though he were a small boy, or a lamb being sized up at market.

"Friend Vanya, could it be that you are truly what you claim to be?"

He decided to brazen it out, a decision he would not have made two glasses of vodka earlier. "Trust, Ishan, is the basis of all good things. And without it . . ." He made a splitting gesture. Plucking his money from Ishan's fingers, he stood up. As he had feared, his attempts to edge his way to the door were fruitless; the crowd that had parted to let him through did not now yield a millimetre. Ishan watched him silently for a moment.

"Sit, Vanya, sit . . ." His hand was on Duvakin's arm, a friendly insistent pressure. "Don't be angry, there's no point in it. We have a lot of things to discuss, we do . . . So sit, have a bite to eat . . ."

Slowly Duvakin sank back into his seat, reminding himself that he represented vast organs of state power. He failed to feel comforted.

"All right, Vanya, so let's say that you are what you say you are, that you represent somebody, somebody who likes favours and who can do favours for us." Ishan paused, while the babble of voices rose up around their conversation, protecting it. "Let's suppose that you are just that . . . What is our deal to be? Why are you here?"

Duvakin had tried to prepare for this question, of course. The trouble was that he knew so little about the black market. His limited contacts with it had taught him that the market's speciality was whatever was hard to find: water-melons in winter, leather miniskirts, Japanese spark plugs. Tanya's books, maybe. All those things cost a lot of money when they were bought 'on the left'—but not twenty thousand rubles, not wads of incomprehensible currencies, like the one he had snatched back from Ishan. What in hell could that amount of money be used for?

"Ishan, let's be honest." He was tired of his own constant confusion. He plunged in, determined to be done with ambiguity, at least. "Our discovery of your . . . property and your . . . former colleague . . . That was the first time we were aware of your . . . enterprise. So we are naturally interested, but cautious . . . This is something in the nature of a shopping trip."

"You mean an expedition to see what there might be, eh?" Ishan fished a cigarette out of a silver case. "Vanya, I'll be honest with you too. We don't know you, my friends and I. We like working with comrades. Our comrades. That way things stay comfortable . . . so to say." The Uzbek's large satiny hands cupped an invisible globe. "And another thing. You don't know what we deal in. Maybe you don't need it, maybe it's not what you want. This isn't GUM, you know!" Ishan exploded in appreciation of his own wit. His laughter was echoed by his followers, although they could not possibly have heard the joke.

"Well," Duvakin said, "if you don't want to deal, you don't want to deal." He lit a cigarette, and mechanically shook the box. It was nearly empty, and it was the last pack. Astoundingly, the carton had melted away in a couple of days. He found himself dreading having to go back to his Russian brand.

"Vanya, to be honest . . . Why the hell should we deal with you? Life is going along just fine now. We are happy, you can see that." He flung his arms wide, encompassing the room.

"But Ishan, think for a moment. Maybe we're the ones who don't have to deal with you, understand? I seem to remember that we have something of yours. Twenty thousand rubles worth . . ."

Ishan's face suffused with sudden rage. "Thirty-two! But you couldn't get more than eight hundred for it! Might as well sprinkle it on borscht like dill, for all the good it will do you."

"Perhaps . . . But right now I can think of a way I could get two thousand easily." Duvakin sipped his wine delicately. He was finding this role rather comfortable.

Ishan unexpectedly smiled his gilded smile, no longer angry. "That's right, that's right . . . A reward for finding lost property, eh? A pretty good reward." His hand dipped into his pocket and emerged holding a pile of crisp notes, deep purple in colour. Fifties. Duvakin watched Ishan's fingers rapidly peel off forty bills. Almost an entire year's salary for Ivan Duvakin, Lieutenant of the People's Control. He was ashamed even to think of it, but there it was. More than he would ever have all at one time. All he had to do was hand over the doll, take the money and then inform Polkovnikov about the Shakh-i-Zinda Room at the Uzbekistan and friend Ishan. Omitting to mention, of course, that pile of money the colour of a bad bruise.

"Dollars," he heard himself saying. "Or four more stacks of that stuff."

"Two thousand dollars!" Ishan's eyes opened wide. In surprise. Or perhaps respect? Duvakin felt he had made a lucky guess. It was about right, a quarter of what the doll was worth, or a third if you counted in rubles. That was significant to Ishan, it appeared. Probably he was thinking that if Duvakin and his 'group' could ask for that kind of money, they would know how to turn over foreign money. And they would know what the ruble was really worth, as opposed to its 'official' value. Ishan frowned.

"So, Vanya. Two thousand dollars or ten thousand rubles,

eh? And you can use it?" He looked at Duvakin's shabby suit; his cracked plastic shoes were safely hidden under the table. "That might change things . . ."

"That is our offer, take it or leave it." Duvakin was pleased with himself. He had said the right thing and he had fought off his surge of greed at the sight of those purple bills.

Ishan turned and began to speak rapidly and incomprehensibly to a countryman on his right. Duvakin lit his last cigarette with regret. The company appeared to be tiring. They were growing more subdued. The alcohol and close air must be having an effect.

Ishan turned back. "It's a lot of money, Vanya. And then you would be getting a bonus besides."

"Such as?"

"Well, you have me—your friend Ishan!" He beamed and threw his thick arm around Duvakin's neck. He withdrew it to pour himself a glass of wine from a tall bottle covered with tassels. "Think for a moment," he said. "I give my little present to you, you give yours to me, we say thank you very much and that's that. No more friends! Maybe better to be friends for long time, eh?"

"Meaning?" The noise in the room had died away and Ishan had slipped into his comic Russian routine. Why?

"Meaning, friend Vanya, that life is long and has curious things in it. Places to go, women to meet, things to see! Who knows where life takes us, eh?"

"So what are you suggesting, friend Ishan?"

"A second meeting, tomorrow maybe. A little drink, a little fun, eh?" Ishan winked and flicked his middle finger against his throat, in the time-honoured gesture for imbibing. "Because, my friend, you know I could not possibly have your present here, because I did not know you were coming, eh?" He gave a broad wink and a hard dig in the ribs that brought Duvakin to the edge of tears. "And then too . . . you don't have my present with you either."

He had actually forgotten his checked briefcase. As long as he had his aluminium claim tag, he was safe. No cloakroom attendant ever gave up a checked item without a tag. That damned doll, perhaps all that was keeping him alive at this moment, was out in the cloakroom buried under the remnant of his oranges. If they had the doll . . . how Duvakin would then be disposed of was a problem he preferred not to contemplate. They had not shown inviting courtesy to Miller.

"And so?"

"And so we must meet again tomorrow some time."

"Here?"

"No, no. It's no good to mix too much business with too much pleasure, you know. No, we meet . . ." He appeared to grow thoughtful, to stare off into space. He stared so long that Duvakin followed his gaze.

The room was not totally Asiatic, after all. A few Russians were scattered about. Three, maybe five. Ishan was looking directly into the eyes of one of these Russians.

The man noticed Duvakin's stare. Their eyes met. The man rose and bowed in mock solemnity.

"Well, Vanya," Ishan said. "I can't think of a good place. It's winter outside. Cold, you know . . . So maybe we pick you up in a car, show you around a little, eh? Maybe you like to meet some more of my friends. Talk some business, eh?"

Somehow Duvakin began to feel that he might not be master of this situation. It was beginning to look as though he had spent the entire evening talking to a man who was not what he appeared to be. The last thing he wished to do was climb into a car with any of this jolly band and depart for places unknown.

But what could he say?

"All right. When?"

"Let's say . . . Three, tomorrow afternoon. And the place . . . Hey, Petka, got any good ideas?" Ishan casually addressed the Russian who sat across from them.

"Lomonosov Prospekt, up by the new circus, on Lenin Hills. Look for a maroon Volga." It was not a suggestion, from the Russian. It was an order. In a nice way, of course.

Then Ishan's arm fell across Duvakin's neck like a club, almost driving his face into his wine glass.

"So, that's a good idea! Friend Vanya, that is when we will

talk business, tomorrow at three, you be there! And for now, let us have some fun, my friends!"

The door leaped open magically and more liquor appeared. Lead seals flew from fresh bottles of vodka; here and there bottles of champagne exploded. Waiters squeezed in and out, bearing huge platters of delicacies. The volume of noise increased. Duvakin, groping for a cigarette, discovered that someone had put a new pack of some foreign cigarettes next to his plate. He lit up and coughed, taken aback by their strength.

Ishan laughed and slapped him on the back, again almost knocking his head to the table. Ishan was now the living embodiment of a host: offering people food, pouring out vodka, joking and cajoling. Vodka splashed freely about.

Duvakin would have liked to leave but he knew they were just entering the serious phase of the banquet, when toasts and drinks would come in rapid succession. The custom of drinking only to toasts had in Duvakin's experience led always to toasts of increasing silliness, since each toast had to be replied to. "To Lomonosov!" Ishan might say, and Duvakin would have to answer "To Ulugh-Bek!" If Ishan toasted Moscow, Duvakin would have to answer with Tashkent, and so on, each toast followed by a glass of vodka.

Ishan rose to his feet and began to speak, a sort of preoration to his toast. His Russian lapsed again into caricature, a puzzling phenomenon.

"My friends! And you all my good friends! Tonight I even make a new friend! Life is good thing, eh? New friends, new surprises! Friendship is good thing, I like it . . . Friends live good, help each other, do things together . . . So me, I drink to friendship! With all of you . . ." Here he indicated the room with a sweeping gesture of both arms, unfortunately spilling his vodka as he did so. The rhythm of his speech was not interrupted; Mukhtar quickly refilled his glass. "I drink in friendship with nice Vanya here . . ." He dramatically indicated Duvakin, spilling vodka on his suit. "And I drink to friendship of peoples everywhere! To great friendship of Uzbek and Soviet peoples!"

Soviet peoples? There were Russians and there were Uzbeks—250 million people—and not one would call himself a Soviet! Duvakin automatically tossed off his vodka and took an egg basket filled with red caviar. As he swallowed the drink the absurdity of the toast hit him and he burst out laughing.

9

"More tea, Vanya?"

Duvakin huddled into a blanket, croaked an affirmation, and with an effort shoved his cup forward. Tanya uncurled herself gracefully from the stool and walked to the aluminium pot which bubbled and steamed on the yellow-blue gas flame.

Duvakin might have felt worse in his lifetime, but he could not at the moment remember when. He looked out the window at the indifferent grey sky. Afternoon again. Almost one. He groaned.

"Here you go . . . Poor baby." Tanya's eyes were filled with amused concern. A hangover is inevitably funny to the person who does not have one. "Do you remember coming here at all last night?"

Duvakin thought back. All he could remember was the dreadful panic he felt when he opened his eyes and realised that he was lying in an unfamilar room. He had assumed the worst and cried out. Which, thank the Lord, brought Tanya running.

"No, I didn't know where I was when I woke up—or came to. What time did I get here? Late?"

"No, no. It was early, around ten or so. I was just sitting reading when the driver came up to get me. She said you had given this address and then passed out in her cab. She found my key in your pocket, and then she helped me get you up here. She was nice, but Lord, she was business-like when she threw you into the elavator! She told me she had a lot of practice doing that with her husband . . ." Tanya fished a cigarette out of Duvakin's pocket. It was bent and still damp with vodka or something, but she managed to light it.

"It's pretty embarrassing," Duvakin said. "And the worst part is, I don't remember any of it. I don't know what happened . . . I usually don't drink so much . . ." He felt the tea slowly working its way through the cracks of his ravaged body. As it did so he felt a tinge of inebriation. Which explained something.

"Spirit alcohol! That's what it was!" he exclaimed forcefully, and immediately regretted it. Catherine wheels exploded in his head.

"Spirit alcohol? But Vanya, that's so strong . . . Why . . .?"

"We were drinking in a restaurant . . ." The effort to answer and to think at the same time was beyond his present powers. He fell silent and lit another of the soggy cigarettes. So . . . They had slipped him spirit alcohol instead of vodka, sometime during the interminable toasting. Almost pure alcohol, enough to fell a tree. Certainly it had levelled him. Presumably then he had passed out, and was dragged from the restaurant and chucked into a cab. But why? They could not have wanted to see if drink would loosen his tongue. Spirit made you so drunk you made no sense. He was getting normally drunk anyway. Could it have been misplaced hospitality? Spirit was fairly rare, a standard black market item. Like the cigarettes he had been given. Maybe it was a demonstration of their wares? Then another idea occurred to him.

"Tanya, did I have my briefcase with me last night?"

"Sure. There it is, over there. Shall I get it?"

"If you would . . ."

He was unquestionably feeling somewhat better. The sight of Tanya crossing the room improved his spirits wonderfully.

"Ahh," she said. "You're feeling better. But what's the joke?"

"Nothing, nothing . . . Thanks." He burrowed into the black vinyl case. Oranges, papers, sections of old newspapers, the glove whose partner he had lost long ago, old bus tickets . . .

"Well, that explains it," he muttered. He felt defeated, scared.

"Explains what? Something missing?"

"That damned doll."

"The one you gave Lenochka?" Tanya was calm but wary.

Duvakin huddled deeper into the blanket around his shoulders. His coat hung over the back of a chair near him. He reached for it awkwardly; the chair tipped over. Tanya caught it as it fell and righted it. She handed Duvakin his jacket. He noted her distant, puzzled expression. After searching his jacket, he finally accepted the fact that the doll was gone.

"And the money too . . ." he sighed, already feeling some of the relief that occurs when one knows that the worst has happened. Hope was gone, but anxiety went with it.

"What money? The doll . . . What's happened, Vanya?" Tanya's face was grave. She placed one delicate hand on his arm.

He was duty-bound not to speak of his work, and particularly not of this operation. At the same time, the affair was poised to crush him like a juggernaut. He had lost contraband worth around thirty thousand rubles, and foreign money in Lord knows what amount. He had signed a receipt.

Loss of equipment was the most serious failure of all. Perhaps if he had come back to the Colonel with the whole thing solved, with Ishan and his friends in a shopping bag, then he might be forgiven the loss. But now what did he have? He could tell Polkovnikov about the menu and decor of the Uzbekistan, he could describe Stumpy, Mukhtar and Ishan, as well as the Russian, Petka, who seemed to be giving orders. And whose full name he did not know. In other words, he could tell them very little.

In short, he was as good as wearing stripes already.

He felt like weeping.

"Vanya, Vanya, darling, what's the matter? Lord, you look awful! Please, you can tell me, I'll help you. Vanya, my love . . ." She was kneading his arm in her anxiety.

He looked at her sharply. "Love . . .?"

Her face flushed. "That was forward of me, wasn't it? Well, it's said. Yes, my love. I don't want anyone to hurt you. Please tell me. what's the matter." Calm and maternal, she took his hand and stroked it.

Duvakin felt on overwhelming need to unburden himself and be consoled. The weight of what he had been carrying since Friday night was now too much for him. Almost uncontrollably he told her the story.

He tried to skirt the questionable bits, such as the origin of the doll. Tanya listened quietly. Her blue eyes were unfathomable, but her hand remained on his arm.

"And that's where it sits right now. I can't go back, and I'm terrified of going forward . . ." The problem, once explained, was more tangible, and less awesome. However a solution was as far away as before. He smiled weakly.

"Vanya, poor, poor Vanya . . ." She stared at him, her underlip caught in her teeth. "Vanya, I'm frightened for you."

"There's no need," he said mechanically, patting her arm. But that was idiotic. If ever there was a time when there was a need to be frightened for him, this was undoubtedly it.

They sat without moving or speaking. Duvakin could hear the distant noises of other apartments; even the curious 'tick-bong, tick-bong' of his wrist-watch. Tanya stroked his hand gently, in tune with her own thoughts.

At length she stood up and said, "Look, my darling, why don't you go wash up and I'll make you some eggs or something. Then you can get ready to go. It shouldn't take too long to get over to the circus from here. We can get you a cab . . ."

Her business-like tone surprised him. She looked grimly determined.

"Why? Where am I going?"

She was already setting the table. "You don't want to be late for your meeting . . ."

"I'm going?" It was absurd, but her brisk air of certainty gave him hope.

Her voice came in snatches as she moved about. "Yes, you must . . . There's no other way . . . You must . . ."

She put down plates and looked directly into Duvakin's eyes with great concentration.

"It's the only way out, the only way you—we—have left is to go forward. You have to know more, you have to get information. They have the doll, yes, but you don't need the doll. It's information you're after."

"How is it you know all of this?" He was sufficiently buoyed by her energy to rise up and move toward the bathroom. At the same time he was taken aback by her strength of will. She was not the fragile, vulnerable creature he had thought her to be.

"Vanya," she said, tensely, "there's a good bit you don't know about me . . . about Sasha . . ."

"He was a Chekist?"

"No, no . . . Oh, it was a long time ago . . . Go wash up and get ready! I'll put the eggs on, then I'll write down everything you told me, and you can sign it, all right? Now get moving." She pushed him into the bathroom cubicle and shut the plywood door firmly behind him.

As he washed he thought that perhaps she was right. All might not yet be over. Ishan and company had what they wanted, but he had taken from them something that they would not be able to steal back. Information. And of course Ishan did not know how much he really did know. Maybe they would not show up in the maroon Volga this afternoon. Maybe now that they had the doll the whole thing would fall through. But he had to show up, in case they did. It was the only way he could escape the consequences of having lost the doll and the money.

He scraped at his face with Tanya's dull razor. In the mirror he looked wrinkled and haggard. His bloodshot eyes were puffy. Polkovnikov behind, Ishan and the maroon Volga

108

ahead . . . His arms and shoulders were white and stringy, almost the colour and texture of his undershirt.

"Hurry up, Vanya. It's getting late . . ."

He emerged. At least he was dressed and cleaned up. It was better to be doing something.

"Sit, eat. After all, you might be drinking again." Her smile was not genuine. She was making an obvious effort.

Duvakin himself put forth some effort. "A wonder, Tanya, you're a real wonder!" He sat down to a plate filled with scrambled eggs, fried baloney and a half tomato. "Where on earth did you find a tomato?"

He was surprised at his hearty appetite. He had not realised how exhausted he was, how depleted his resources.

"More? Some more tea?" She had finished washing the frying pan, and put on the teapot. She got a cigarette from the pack in her pocket, and rummaged around in the cupboard for matches.

Here she was, Duvakin thought, Lord knows how much younger than he, and pretty and well-off. And she was calling him 'love'. Why? He stretched hugely, feeling his muscles uncoiling under protest. It was curious . . . He was in the worst predicament of his life. And yet he felt happy. He even felt lucky. He looked out the window at the swirling grey of the sky. Occasional snowflakes floated there, appearing neither to rise nor fall. He did have some information, after all. True, it wasn't much. In fact, that and five kopeks could buy him a ride on the metro.

He took a sip of hot tea, and lit a cigarette.

"Ah, Tanya, that's more like it. I haven't felt this well since all of this began . . . Lord, could it have been only last Friday night? I feel like I've been miserable forever, worrying about that damned doll."

"I'm glad you feel better," she said. "You should, things are marvellous. All that's wrong is that you owe the State untold sums of money, and you have a date with a gorilla from Uzbekistan. Come on, keep your mind on things. We have to make an official report."

She disappeared into the front room.

"But why the report?" Duvakin called after her, alarmed by her coldness. "What for, in case I die?"

She came back with paper and ballpoint pen, and sat down at the table.

"That's not so amusing, Vanya," she said quietly. Her lip trembled.

Clumsily he stroked her arm. "I'm sorry . . . It was only a joke . . ."

"It's all right. I'm just worried for you. For us . . . for Lenochka . . ." She drew a deep breath. "Listen, we write up this report. We leave out the doll and the money. We set a time . . . If I haven't heard from you by whenever we decide . . . Midnight? . . . I get hold of Polkovnikov . . ."

"And they search for me. In the largest city in the world . . ." Duvakin tried to keep his tone light. It was hopeless.

"You have maybe a better idea?" Her voice was like ice. She stared at her trembling hand, holding the pen. After a silence she looked at him. "I'm sorry, Vanya. That was mean. But we have nothing else, nothing you can hold over them to protect yourself . . ."

She began to write in a round clear hand. The pen leaked.

"Give me names, addreses. You have no photographs . . . Oh, well . . ."

Photographs, addresses, names. 29 Neglinnaya. The address of the Uzbekistan. Ishan. Petka. Liudmila Grigorievna, of course. He sighed.

He went out into the hallway to get his coat, such as it was. Tanya's front room with its glossy pine table and its day-bed covered with a greenish cloth looked huge and empty. Three rooms were too much for two people. For a woman alone. He imagined himself living in this apartment, padding to the kitchen in slippers, sitting in the blue chair by the radiator. It would be so nice. He would not accept the possibility—perhaps probability?—that he might not see another day, let alone a future life in this apartment.

"Vanya, come sign this!"

"I'm coming . . ." He looked at the front room once more, trying to engrave upon his memory the blue armchair, the bookshelf, the pictures on the wall. Then he returned to the kitchen. He felt as though he were going to sign his own epitaph.

10

He stood on the far side of vast Vernadsky Prospekt. Of its four corners, the circus side was the least used, and was now almost deserted. The sun was at the horizon and the wind was rising. The few people on the streets were huddling in the open-sided bus shelters or trotting into the metro station. Duvakin pulled his ragged raincoat tighter, while he waited for the sign opposite him to flash its green cut-out of a walking man.

Then he crossed quickly. Even so at the opposite side his heels were nipped by traffic turning left. Past the corner, beneath the dome of the new circus, was the huge complex where in the summer reflecting pools and fountains shimmered. Now it was an open wasteland. The wind gathered up slashing ice crystals. He turned his face away and stamped his feet.

"Hey, Vanya! Friend Vanya!"

It was Ishan. Waiting there for a moment he had thought they would bother no further with him.

He trudged through the squeaky snow, toward the maroon Volga. His stomach fluttered and his legs trembled. If only he could keep it from showing.

"You're right on time, Vanya, right on time! Worse than a German, you are!" Ishan displayed his golden teeth.

He got out of the back seat and stood invitingly by the open door of the car. In the daylight his face looked puffy and dissolute, the eyes almost lost in lidless almond slits. He was not as large as he had seemed the night before. Most of his height was in his torso. Beneath his soft leather overcoat his legs were like short stumps.

"So. How's the head this morning, Vanya? A good time we had, eh?"

He threw an arm around Duvakin in a gesture that was more proprietary than hospitable. The length of his arms more than compensated for the length of his legs.

"It's nice to see you again, Ishan. My . . . superiors were . . . pleased to hear about my . . . new friends . . ."

"I'll bet, I'll bet they were! Everybody glad know Ishan!" His broken Russian boomed out over the street. The few passers-by stared with hate at this misshapen Asiatic with his fancy car. Possibly Ishan enjoyed their envy. If there was any other explanation for the manner in which Ishan slipped in and out of grammatical Russian, Duvakin would be damned if he could figure it out.

He hopped from foot to foot in the mashed-potato slush; his body desperately yearned toward the inviting warmth of the motor-car, which he feared with all his soul. He tried surreptitiously to peer inside, but the front windows were fogged and the back and sides curtained. He could see only a couple of black shapes.

"So . . . your car? Where are we going?"

"This isn't mine. I have a Zhiguli. Good car, little, but fast . . . so fast!" From Ishan's surprisingly genuine enthusiasm it would appear that he had only recently been elevated to the august rank of motor-car owner. He winked and squeezed Duvakin's elbow. "This one is a company car . . . Company business, you understand . . ." His grip made the elbow ache.

Duvakin slid into the middle of the back seat. As he had expected the seat was already occupied. On the far side sat Petka, the Russian from the Uzbekistan. He did not acknowledge Duvakin, but sat staring out his window through a crack in the curtain. In the front seat, beside the driver, was someone who had shoulders maybe a metre across and a neck the shape of an Easter cake. Ishan slid in next to Duvakin and, not without difficulty, slammed the door.

The car pulled out into traffic and turned right into Vernadsky Prospekt, heading toward the metro bridge and the centre of town. Ishan assumed the mirror image of Petka's pose. It was extremely difficult to tell where they were going and not only because of the angle at which Duvakin was sitting, crouching forward to look out of the low front window. He had very little idea of how the city conjoined, because he had rarely travelled through it in a motor-car. Often he recognised familar buildings, but he could not determine their location.

The car ran quietly, unlike the taxis Duvakin had taken. A special model, probably. The driver coped smoothly with the weaving, slithering traffic and inside all was silence and warmth, both from the men's bodies and from the automatic heater. Despite his tension, Duvakin found himself dozing off.

They drove for ages: lights, boulevards, streets, intersections, narrow lanes suited for droshkies and horses, large intersections again. Starting, stopping, turning, stopping. The sun set and the sky faded from grey to black, illumined by the violet glare of street lamps. Duvakin no longer had any idea of where he was, nor of how long he had been riding. He had not realised that Moscow was so large, although he had lived in the city for years now.

"Looks clear, Petr Ivanych," the driver said, so suddenly that Duvakin started.

Petr Ivanych. The Russian. He turned from the window and smiled at Duvakin. Not a reassuring smile.

He was about Duvakin's age, blond, balding. His face was scarred by smallpox or acne. His eyes were so light a blue that they seemed to glitter. He reminded Duvakin of a lynx, a resemblance that his fur collar and hat did nothing to dispel.

He reached into his overcoat and brought out a cigarette case made of some rare wood. "Well, Ivan Palych," he said, "it seems we can talk. Would you care for a cigarette?"

Duvakin accepted one in silence and had it lit for him.

"My name is Petr Ivanych, as you have heard. Petka to our friend Ishan here . . ." Ishan grinned. He seemed no longer like an overlord, but like a confident servant. Duvakin felt wiser. Nothing he saw going on around him, he thought, should be taken at face value.

The tyres clicked against the frozen concrete road-bed. They were going fast; probably they had left town. His heart began to pound. As he sat between the two men he saw with absolute certainty what was coming: a dead body, maybe with false papers, maybe with no papers, discovered next spring somewhere in the woods. If it was discovered at all. He fought down panic. If ever there was a time to keep his wits about him, this was it.

"Well, Pyotr Ivanych," he said, with a dry throat, "I enjoyed your party last night."

"I'm glad. But it wasn't mine. Was it, Ishan?"

"All friends Ishan. Ishan like throw big party . . ." He grinned again, playing the half-witted provincial. Then his grin disappeared and his voice became controlled and savage. "Besides, they hate Russians, most of them. Just as soon put a knife in your ribs as pass you the sardines. So Petka and me, we help each other out. Right, friend Petka?"

This reference to a knife did nothing to calm Duvakin's nerves. He could feel something gathering itself together around him. They seemed to draw closer to him on either side. He thought desperately. He had to find solid ground to stand on before they struck. Tanya's determination to find him a bargaining chip flashed through his head.

"Well," he said as calmly as he could, "it was a pleasant evening last night. Good company, good food, good lights . . ." He emphasised the last word.

"Lights," Petr Ivanych repeated.

Duvakin flicked his ashes into the metal pocket before him.

"Sure," he said. "It was nice and light . . . The photos turned out very clear. My friends thought they were good."

114

Both men turned their heads toward him. Even the humanoid in the front seat turned part way round, jaw agape. Ishan leaned forward to slap him irritably on the shoulder and he faced front again, but not before Duvakin saw his bushy eyebrows, small eyes and enormous jaw, like a shark or a tiger.

"Photos . . ." Petr Ivanych seemed genuinely puzzled, as though he had never heard the word before.

Duvakin assumed a nonchalant air, although his heart still pounded in his head. He felt the satisfaction of an angler who has just firmly hooked a big fish. Thank God for Tanya!

"Sure, photos," he said. "I always like to have pictures of my new friends, to show to my old friends . . ."

Petr Ivanych's voice had lost its silken touch. It was like a lash.

"Enough clowning, Duvakin, talk sense. What are you saying? What is your game?"

"I told you already. I'm a hotel security man, interested in dolls . . ."

Ishan's hand closed convulsively on Duvakin's arm, hard enough to make his eyes water. "You're lying," he said, spattering Duvakin with enraged saliva. "There's no way you could have taken pictures last night. We checked every god-damned millimetre—"

"Shut up, Ishan!"

The Uzbek closed his mouth abruptly, but his eyes still fumed through their almond slits. Duvakin freed himself from his crushing hand, with a dignity he was far from feeling.

"You had no camera last night, Duvakin," Petr Ivanych said.

"You mean you found no camera last night," Duvakin said sarcastically. "Any idiot could find a doll or a wad of money."

There was a pause.

"You lost the doll, and the money," Petr Ivanych said reflectively. "But you came with us tonight anyway . . ."

"As you see . . ." Duvakin said. He was pleasantly surprised by his own ability to improvise. He was even beginning to

115

believe himself, to feel the security of having left in an accomplice's possession photographs of last night's company. Instead of a description of the room scratched out by Tanya's leaky pen.

"You can't tell us that you switched the powder, or the money isn't real, you know," Ishan snapped. "We checked it already."

"Ishan, in the future keep your mouth shut until you are told to open it, understand?" Petr Ivanych looked closely at Duvakin, almost staring him down.

Duvakin leaned forward to stub out his cigarette. Through the front window he saw a sign pointing the way to Sheremetavo Airport. They passed the turn. Thank God for Ishan's big mouth. He might well have tried to tell them he had switched the powder.

"Of course they were real," he said, wearily. "My associates and I wanted . . . to find out . . ." What? "what sort of operation you have . . ."

"What do you mean, what sort?"

"Well, size, you know, what sorts of things you handle, how you do business. Because, you see, we had something of a problem with you people."

"What sort of problem?" Petr Ivanych's eyes were intense and unpleasant.

"Well, when we first got wind of you, we didn't know whether we hadn't heard about you because you were careful and pretty good, or because you're small . . ."

"We are extremely good. Very careful and clean." Pyotr Ivanych spoke rapidly and flatly. Duvakin wondered whether this might be the group's slogan. Petr Ivanych's face shone with pride, the first emotion Duvakin had discerned there. It was a pleasure to try to puncture that pride.

"Ummm, yes. Well, after that stunt last night we decided that you must be rather small. We decided to give you another chance anyway. That's why I'm here. Got any more cigarettes?"

Petka's cheeks flushed brightly. Ishan sat, mouth open, staring at Duvakin.

"No cigarettes? Well. I'll just have to smoke one of my own then," Duvakin said calmly. He dug about in his coat pocket.

He could understand why they would be startled by his words, for he was amazed at the dimensions of whatever it was he had poked his nose into. He knew already of several dozen people who were involved in this. There was the dead American, he himself had been slugged, had run across odd doings with KGB people, had found a crooked administrator in his hotel . . . Small was the last thing this bunch of lads might be called.

Petka gradually gained control of his rage.

"Listen, Duvakin, I don't know who the devil you represent, because we have never heard of you. But we are not little!" He said each word as though it were being chiselled into granite. "We have equipment, people, methods, organisation . . . Everything. And so far, no trouble of any sort. Good customers, good people, good business."

"Well, listen to me, good friend," Duvakin half turned toward him and poked his poorly-gloved index finger into Petka's crushed kid coat. "That may be . . . but from our end it looks a little messy. You can get yourself into a whole lot of trouble by playing these sorts of games . . ."

"What sort?"

"This sort . . ." A vague wave of the arm. "Taking a Lieutenant of the People's Control for a ride like this . . ."

"Ah. But you know what terrible accidents can happen around holiday time. People drink too much, freeze in the woods. Truck drivers don't watch where they are going . . . People get in fights. Anything can happen."

Duvakin once more fumbled for cigarettes. Ishan silently extended a pack. Duvakin inhaled deeply, avoiding the sight of Petka's God-awful light blue eyes and pockmarked cheeks. He made a special effort to keep his voice steady.

"Yes, people can get to drinking in a hotel room and do stupid things. They have to clean up their left-over bodies, don't they? But they might forget to pick up all their toys."

This hit home. It definitely registered.

"That again . . ." Ishan muttered. Petr Ivanych looked coldly at his colleague.

There was a moment of silence. The affair seemed somewhat clearer to Duvakin. Apparently Ishan was responsible for the sloppy Miller affair. Or at least responsible for trying to correct it. The murder itself appeared to have been unplanned. Had one of last night's faceless horde lost his temper with the American? Something like that . . . Duvakin moved restlessly, feeling insufferably cramped. They had been riding for an eternity. His legs felt wooden.

Petr Ivanych stared from Duvakin to Ishan, and then back again. He vibrated with hate, but at the same time he appeared frustrated. Suddenly he appeared to make a decision.

"Volodya. Turn around. Take us back to Bolshaya Vpadina."

Ishan protested. "Are you crazy, Petka? He—Volodya—said—"

"This isn't for us to handle any more," the Russian said. He sank back moodily into his seat.

So. Another layer was going to be peeled off this large and pungent onion. And how many Volodyas were involved? Did people name their children nothing but Vladimir? He did not know whether to be happy or sad that Petr Ivanych had changed his mind. In the meantime, his leg muscles were beginning to cramp: a cramp would be agonising in that crowded car and certainly he did not want to encourage a stop by the side of a dark, deserted road. His bladder was full too. He attempted to adjust his position, settled back and adjusted it again.

"Stop squirming, damn it," Petka said dispassionately. He appeared to have become calm again. "We'll be there soon enough."

The driver executed a neat slithering skid and turned the car in the other direction. Whatever Bolshaya Vpadina might be, that was where it lay. Death had probably waited in the direction they were originally going, but there was no guarantee that it did not also wait at Bolshaya Vpadina. Duvakin was not sure whether he should be relieved or upset. He could see nothing in the glare of their headlights except occasional trucks lumbering by.

They rode in dark silence, turning off of and onto main roads, rattling down lanes passable only because the deep ruts were frozen solid. Duvakin floated once more in a thick soup of drowsiness, now sinking, now rising with a start to the surface.

The car had stopped.

The Neanderthal got out to lift a crossbar on which was a 'No Entry' sign. The car glided past the bar, which was dropped into place behind them. They stopped again, the caveman got back in, and they were off, following a winding road. Duvakin tried to work some saliva into his mouth to rid it of the taste left by cigarettes and shallow sleep. He had a headache.

The headlights were dimmed. They appeared to pass through a grove of trees, and then to skirt an open place on a hill. Maybe a lake. More trees.

Duvakin's heart began to pound.

Dark green. That colour telegraphed a message. High party. A fence—steel. The giant in the front seat took a key from Ishan's extended hand and got out. With hands the size of cauliflowers he fumbled with a padlock. Finally he got the gate open.

All his life Duvakin had heard rumours of places like this. As a child he had crawled through bushes on the far side of Lake Ershino to catch glimpses of what lay beyond the steel fences, but he had been driven away by the baying of dogs and the rhythmic sounds of footsteps. The mysteries of the private dachas . . .

Lights could be seen through the enormous yellow trunks of the pines. They came to a clearing.

There were only one or two lights near the doorway; the few lighted windows were curtained, but Duvakin could see enough of the building to be astounded. It was far too large to be a peasant's house; too small for an apartment house. The design was unusual: a flat roof, and a tall wing on the left joining a lower wing on the right, at an obtuse angle.

The walls were made of stone, roughly cut and unevenly placed . . . tricky to build it, and have it come out straight. In front of the house a Volga stood on an asphalt patch, from which a concrete path curved between high snowdrifts to the door. The walls around the door were glass; the view into the entrance hall was screened by large green potted plants.

Petr Ivanych got out of the car, and motioned to Duvakin to follow his example. He obeyed with some difficulty; his legs had long since lost all feeling. He stamped his decrepit shoes against the frost-spangled asphalt. Petr Ivanych leaned into the open door and spoke inaudibly to the men in the front seat. The car backed up and disappeared down the road, apparently headed for some place beyond the house.

"Come on, Duvakin," Petr Ivanych said, taking his arm. Duvakin was much taller than his guide and almost certainly stronger. The thought of a struggle flashed through Duvakin's mind. But Petka seemed to be one of those creatures which relies on cunning for survival . . . or upon some sort of concealed weapon. In any case, the night, the season and Duvakin's total ignorance of their location made flight a pointless consideration.

One thought haunted him. As he kept pace with Petka on the path to the house, he kept thinking about some traps he had read about, used by fur trappers in the Far East to catch some animals—sable, maybe. He couldn't be sure of the animal, but it was a cone-shaped trap. The entrance to it was ringed with toothed flanges. The animal could push in toward the bait, but whenever it tried to back out, its head was trapped.

It had to move deeper. Inside.

Until the whole animal was inside. Trapped. Then the trapper came along and picked him up. They gassed him to death. That way the pelt was not harmed.

Duvakin shivered. The protection given him by fictitious photographs and Tanya's report was not very substantial. He tried to clear his brain and control rising panic. He had to resign himself to whatever lay before him. But he could not. That was the worst part.

Perhaps Petka sensed his feeling of desperation. As they stood on the stones before the carved wooden door in its glass wall, Petr Ivanych said, "How do you like the doors? Copied from the church at Rostov Veliky, you know. And you said it was a little enterprise! Ha!" He made a sound which was probably as close as he could come to laughter.

His derisive pride was repellent. This building probably had no right to exist on Russian soil; the means by which it had come into existence would seem to have been more foul than fair. Duvakin felt his zeal returning. He pulled himself together.

"It's showy," he said, contemptuously. "Little doesn't always refer just to volume, you know."

"Ummm hmmm. You'll see, you son of a bitch . . ."

Petka carefully scraped his feet clean of snow on the doormat. Duvakin stood aloof; he did not bother to wipe his feet. At length his guide—or captor—pushed the door lightly with his fingertips. To Duvakin's utter astonishment the massive doors swung open easily. All his life he had struggled with massive doors. He had never seen any open without expended effort. Some sort of counterweights? A motor?

They entered the glassed-in lobby, and once more Petr Ivanych spent long moments wiping his feet on the big mats which lay in indentations in the slate floor.

The entrance was like a bridge. On the left a small fountain splashed, bubbling over rocks, and past a number of large-leaved exotic plants, and falling into a pool which ran beneath the slab on which they stood. Bright fish could be seen darting through the clear water. Among the plants hung a cage in which small birds flashed and warbled.

On either side of the lobby were large doors. Those on the left were made of blond wood; those on the right were made of glass.

Through the glass Duvakin could see a room even more fantastic than the entry room. Although he could name the furniture—a chair, a bookshelf, a sofa, a lamp—the familiar names did not really suffice. How could a word like 'armchair' describe both the hopsack and pine device in Tanya's sitting room and the creation made of dark wood and leather which stood here before the stone fireplace? Even the wallpaper—faded and peeled blue plastic at Tanya's—and here, what looked like black and red velvet . . . He shook his head. Lord, what about the rest of the place!

He turned to Petr Ivanych, expecting to be ridiculed about his low opinion of the enterprise. But Petr Ivanych looked rather pale and meek. Timid. Heaven forbid, he looked scared. That was a contagious feeling.

"Well, Petka," Duvakin said with false jauntiness, "Where's the welcoming committee?"

"Shut up, Duvakin, they'll hear you!"

"Well, isn't that the idea?"

"Shut your mouth, for God's sake!"

There was unmistakeable, urgent alarm in his voice. He stood staring tensely at the blond doors. Duvakin did as he was told. They stood in silence for so long that Duvakin sneaked a look at his watch and was surprised to find that it was not yet seven o'clock.

Finally the door opened.

The man who came out was medium height, heavy set in a well-fed, average sort of way. He wore a black suit with a white shirt and gold-rimmed spectacles with black plastic temples. His black hair, plastered across his round head, matched his suit. His eyes stared rather dully. It was difficult to tell where his attention was focused, because he was wall-eyed.

"It's you, Tsyplyatin," he said, coolly. "What an . . . unexpected . . . surprise."

Somehow he did not look to Duvakin like the centre of the onion.

"I'm sorry, Leonid Nikolaevich, but it was un-un-unavoidable . . ." Petr Ivanych bleated, hat in hand. Duvakin looked at him, surprised. He had not stammered before. "But we didn't want to make a m-m- mistake . . . Ishan was afraid. He said to come back . . . I argued . . . You know, our directions, but Ishan insisted . . ."

Petr Ivanych, the steel-eyed killer, was truly earning the right to be called Petka. A babbling idiot.

"And now you want to see Vladimir Aleksandrovich, am I correct?" The irony was becoming acid.

Petka looked so miserable that Duvakin felt almost sorry for him.

"And you, I take it, are Ivan Petrovich?" The tone was more unctuous.

"Pavlovich."

"Beg pardon?"

"Pavlovich. Ivan Pavlovich."

"Oh, so sorry. Ivan Pavlovich," Leonid Nikolaevich said; his pronounced politeness was unpleasant. Duvakin, finding this little dance tiresome, decided to be brash. Lyonya here was obviously not top cone on the pine tree. Vladimir Aleksandrovich was. Digging into his breast pocket, Duvakin produced a cigarette.

"Got a light, Petka?" At first this request elicited no response at all. Finally, after a look of some surprise, Petka offered a lighter. Duvakin calmly lit up, and then turned his full attention to the cigarette, straightening its crumpled shape.

Leonid Nikolaevich smiled and said, in his oily voice, "Please make yourself comfortable, my dear fellow. I must apologise for the somewhat confused situation here. Your arrival was not . . . entirely expected . . ."

You might say, Duvakin thought, entirely unintended, even. He was supposed to be dead.

"You going to keep me standing here all night? My associates . . . value the old-time ways. Russian hospitality, you know . . ."

The 'confused situation', however, continued. His new 'friends' did not move. Although for some incomprehensible reason the windows were not fogged, the vestibule was as warm and moist as a bathhouse. Duvakin took off his overcoat and looked for some place to hang it or set it down. Then he decided to rely on the adage that, once you have the bear singing, you had better keep providing new tunes.

"Here, Petka, do something with these." He chucked his hat and coat at Petr Ivanych who reflexively caught them on his arm.

"Take the man's coat, Tsyplyatin," Leonid Nikolaevich said in his cream and vinegar voice. "Perhaps comrade Duvakin would care to sit down, to take some refreshment?"

In fact comrade Duvakin could hardly decide whether he were hungry or not. He did know that he had to use the bathroom—a luxurious vision of glass and coloured tiles.

When he came out Leonid Nikolaevich said, "Tsyplyatin, take the comrade into the next room and see that he is made comfortable. Then perhaps you would yourself join me in the library? . . . Comrade Duvakin, I apologise again that we are so poorly prepared for your visit . . . Do not judge our hospitality by our behaviour this evening. Please make yourself comfortable . . . We shall try not to keep you waiting long."

"Like they say, eh?" Duvakin said. "An uninvited guest is worse than a Tartar."

Leonid Nikolaevich's answering smile was like a pale winter sun.

Duvakin followed Petka up the slate steps into the big room beyond the glass. If anything, this room was even warmer than the vestibule. How could people wear clothes in here? Duvakin loosened his tie. Tsyplyatin bustled about, turning mysterious dials, vanishing into hidden rooms, reappearing suddenly. Lights came on here and there, brightening the room without illuminating it. It was enormous. Leather couches, stone walls, panelled at intervals in wood. An enormous fireplace with a copper . . . what? Chimney?

"Drink, Duvakin? Something to eat?" Tsyplyatin stood in an alcove at the end of the room, opposite the fireplace, behind a low counter at which stood long-legged stools. It looked like the tourist bar at the Red October, Duvakin thought, in much the same way that champagne resembles seltzer water.

Duvakin walked to the bar, through a dark purple rug as

thick as meadow grass. When he put his hand on the bar rail, a huge spark snapped at his hand. His heart leaped explosively into his throat, and turned over, almost strangling him. Fortunately Tsyplyatin's back was turned; he fussed with a kitchen-like device behind the bar. He looked up, surprised at Duvakin's silence.

"Have a cigarette," he said. "That box . . ."

Gingerly, with his heart still throbbing in his ears, Duvakin reached along the bar and opened a lacquered wooden box. He had seen this kind in tourist shops: black and gold, with a fairy tale scene painted on top. What would Tanya's reaction be if he could give her that box for a New Year's present?

"There's meat and piroshki," Tsyplyatin said. "Crayfish? I could get you something hot . . ." He seemed anxious to please; he was very nervous.

"No, that's all right, Petka. You run along and talk with your owners. I'll just wait." Duvakin's pleasure at baiting Petr Ivanych surprised him. He wanted someone to kick.

Petka left the room rapidly; the glass door shut behind him, apparently of its own volition.

Duvakin wandered over to a group of chairs and couches and sat down, carefully, avoiding another painful shock. It was very comfortable. But what in the name of the devil's grandmother was it for? The room was almost as large as the lobby of the Red October. It was too large to be a 'living room'—that ancient word—and the chairs were all in clusters and clumps. It was so warm, and smelled sweetly of birchwood.

A meeting place for diplomats or . . . some kind of official parties? What else could such a large room be for, furnished like that?

Of course people 'above' had to lead lush lives. The inside of the charmed circle must include this room. What the devil, it probably should be like this. A useful and important government bigwig ought to have the right to provide more room for his house-plants than Duvakin had for himself and all his wordly possessions.

But there seemed to be another side . . . a dirty side that did not mix with leather chairs, coffee tables of smoked glass . . . If a man had all this, the just rewards of service to the country, why would he need the other—the murder, the white powder in the child's toy . . .?

He rose and went to get another cigarette. The cracked sole of his shoe caught in the carpet, tripping him. He had to laugh: plastic shoes and enough leather in this furniture to make him a thousand pairs of shoes. The power behind this room was great. And yet here he stood. Duvakin. Alive. He took a handful of cigarettes and stacked them carefully in his pocket before he lit one.

He knew a great deal now, and he knew nothing about all this. It reminded him of the time in Krasnaya Sosna when he was a boy. A child's radio set was issued to the Young Pioneer club. Because of his father's rank Vanya Duvakin was among the few allowed to work on the project; he knew about radio, and he was anxious to learn about how it worked. They had followed the directions carefully, studying each part and its function. They assembled and disassembled the radio. Even now Duvakin could trace most of the pictures and remember some of the directions and explanations.

But the radio could never be made to work. There was a shortage of radio and electronic equipment. Most of the tubes and coils were blanks made of wood. Despite all their efforts all they had was a dead box of bits and pieces.

So too with this. Try as he would, he could not bring this situation to life. It would not run properly in his mind. Probably now he had enough information to give Polkovnikov; surely the KGB could find this enormous house. He might be now at the centre of the onion.

But he was interested in the puzzle for its own sake. And he had solved nothing. He did not know who had murdered Miller or why, or who had forged his log book, or broken into Tanya's apartment. He didn't know how the dolls travelled in and out of the country, or in fact anything about how the system functioned. Fancy furniture, houses, cars . . . proved nothing. He might as well go stand on Kutuzovsky Prospekt and scream to the four winds that each ZIL limousine that flashed past indicated a crime committed.

He paced across the room and peered out of the windows. They were as black as if they had been painted. Inside he could hear no sound. The wait began to seem interminable. Possibly his fortunes were rising; he thought he had thrown them badly off balance. He cracked his knuckles and took another cigarette. As he lit it, he laughed suddenly. He noticed that he had cigarettes burning in three ashtrays scattered about the room.

"Sorry to keep you waiting, comrade."

Leonid Nikolaevich had materialised without warning.

"As you should be," he said, continuing his policy of attack. "My associates certainly will not be impressed by this delay . . ."

"Vladimir Aleksandrovich would like to see you now, if you will be so kind as to follow me."

A door in one of the wooden panels opened, revealing a spiral staircase. That explained how Leonid Nikolaevich had entered so silently. They climbed up one dizzy flight and walked down a long thickly carpeted corridor. Closed doors faced it.

"Please, comrade." Leonid Nikolaevich stopped just beyond an open door, and indicated that Duvakin should enter ahead of him.

A man stood with his back to the door, looking out a large window.

"Come in, Vanya, sit down."

The voice was familiar, but he could not place it. He sank into a chair, under a bright lamp. The man at the window stood in twilight; the glass pane probably acted as a mirror for him.

The man at the window was rich, that was clear. He was about Duvakin's height, but fuller in build, and his clothes had not come from any rag and bone shop, as Duvakin's had. He was powerful, inconceivably powerful. And now he was dreadfully quiet. And devilishly familiar.

"Well, well, Vanya . . . It's a real surprise to see you again . . . We're both surprised, I'll bet."

127

His host turned, with a broad smile, and enlightenment came.

"You!" Duvakin cried.

"As you see . . ."

Anger unlike any emotion he had ever felt exploded within Duvakin. Before he had time even to think about it, he had leapt up, crossed the room and landed a round-house left on his host's right ear. Eyeglasses went flying; Duvakin's awkward right slammed into the middle of a look of myopic amazement.

"You son of a bitch, Volodya Ishakin, you son of a bitch," Duvakin muttered through clenched teeth. His victim slid to the floor.

11

Duvakin crouched in a deep velvet armchair, nursing his aching frame. All hell had broken loose after his attack upon Volodya. Presumably it was Leonid Nikolaevich who had wreaked vengeance upon him. Through his agony he had dimly perceived shouts, running feet, people on the move. And someone going through his pockets while he gasped for breath.

"How are we feeling now?"

A woman dressed in yellow stood at the far end of a tunnel of pain. She appeared to be smiling. Slowly the tunnel widened. She grew cleaner.

"Are you feeling better, Ivan Palych? Can I get you anything? Cognac? Cigarettes?" She seemed a pleasant sort, genuinely concerned about him.

And she was beautiful. Dark blonde hair in ropey curls, white teeth and white skin, with a tinge of golden olive . . . and tight pants and tighter sweater in fluorescent yellow.

"A little cognac, maybe. Cigarettes . . . What's your name?"

"My name? Margot." She pronounced the 't'.

"That's a strange name."

"It's exotic, don't you think so?"

She was the country girl, decked out to her delight in fancy clothes and a sophisticated hairdo. Slowly a light dawned.

A public house. Actually a very private house. That could very well be what Volodya was running here. Everyone had heard rumours: in addition to all their other perquisites, higher ups had private whore houses. Duvakin had always tended to discount these rumours; he thought they resulted from ignorance, jealousy and scurrilous imaginations. Now it would appear that he had been wrong.

Margot disappeared; he hoped on an errand of mercy. Carefully, he rose to his feet. He had his wind back; the pain lessened.

Volodya Ishakin, you spotted devil! You really got yourself into something, didn't you? The beautiful Finnish furniture, big black windows, fancy stone walls . . . Volodya, the brains behind an international smuggling ring . . . a cynical warlord who had had the American dispatched . . . Duvakin could not help feeling proud of his childhood friend. After the army Volodya had risen fast in the hotel game . . . An apartment in Moscow, a house in the country, a car. He was able to hire old friends, get them fixed up with places to live . . .

Little Volodya, helping his father take special rations out to the big houses beyond Lake Ershino . . . the houses that Duvakin could not even catch a glimpse of. And now big Volodya . . . doing what? Renting rooms by the hour to a select clientele . . . No small service. A hotel manager who could discreetly solve problems for influential people . . .

Margot returned with a big bulbous glass on a small tray, and a pack of cigarettes. Duvakin drank; a welcome warmth spread through his aching muscles, along with a feeling of wellbeing.

"Where's Volodya?" he said.

"Mr. Ishakin? He'll be here . . . You gave him a . . . headache . . ." She giggled, covering her mouth with her hand.

Duvakin flexed his fist. His knuckles hurt. He had not really punched anyone in years, and never in his life had he managed to land a good one on Volodya. Their childhood scuffles had always ended with Duvakin getting the worst of it. Never mind his present doubtful situation. He had settled an old score. He lit a cigarette and inhaled in a desperate ecstasy.

Volodya could do a lot with his hotel . . . Couldn't it be a funnel for scarce goods . . . What goods he was not sure . . . How much would people pay for them? He could not really imagine a vast number of needs pressing enough to generate the kind of money Volodya seemed to have . . .

And that, Duvakin thought bitterly, was why he wore cracked plastic shoes and a suit like a potato sack while Ishakin had leather furniture and this velvet armchair . . . and Margot. Who suddenly stiffened and left, without a goodbye.

Volodya had begun speaking while he was out in the hall; a light breezy speech.

"Well, Vanya, you really landed one on me that time, you old bastard you!" He nervously crossed the room and built himself a kind of barricade behind his desk. "And you—how are you? A little calmer now? Sorry about Lyonya, but you know, you took us by surprise. How do you feel?"

"Oh, don't worry about me, Volodya. I'm tough . . . I've had some practice lately, anyway. And relax. I won't hit you again."

"Vanya, come sit here. It seems we have a few things to discuss." Ishakin's voice lacked the bubbling cheerfulness of his entrance. It had the steely tone, overlaid with velvet, that was becoming familiar to Duvakin. Polkovnikov, Ishan, Tsyplyatin . . . Lord, even Tanya spoke that way sometimes.

He got up and moved, still feeling sore, to another deep comfortable armchair beside the desk.

Ishakin's face had changed over the years. The satiny cheeks and well-groomed hair did not really offset the red flare of his nose, and the puffiness around his eyes and jaw. Alcoholism? And his air of sleekness, of wellbeing, was disturbing. The rectangular eyeglasses were foreign. So was his suit.

"Well, Vanya, it seems we've caused each other a certain amount of trouble, doesn't it?"

"You might say that . . ."

"You might not believe me, Vanya, but I'm genuinely sorry that it happened to be you . . . Honestly, I didn't know . . ." His face and his tone were sincere.

After a silence that seemed to last for an age, Duvakin said, "Well, Volodya, I know how it can be . . ." He lit another cigarette, drawing out the ritual of stubbing out the old one, searching for matches, and so on. He was groping his way. "But then, we are both businessmen, aren't we? And these things will happen. The important thing . . ."

"Is the business! Right you are, Vanya, I'm glad to see you're being sensible about it . . ."

Volodya's face became more animated; his voice regained its bounce.

Now was the time to become more specific.

"The business, Volodya. Let's discuss dolls."

"Dolls?"

"Dolls, yes. Matryoshkas. With braids . . . Dolls."

"I'm afraid I don't follow."

Duvakin could feel his anger rising.

"You don't follow? Let's try it from another angle. How about dead Americans, lying around hotel rooms during duty shifts of childhood pals? Does that ring a bell?"

"Vanya, I'm trying. I have no idea what you're talking about."

Duvakin wanted to shriek at Volodya, to batter that white face gleaming moistly in the lamplight. But . . . could it be true? No, not possible. The chain of contacts he had followed had led to this room, this desk. But . . . how many layers of the onion had been peeled back? Four? Five? Could each layer protect the next, did the ones near the centre really not know . . . Possible. Or was he just playing dumb?

The glossy face told him nothing. But a wave of caution splashed over Duvakin's anger. He had a bull by the tail . . . powerful, dangerous . . .

"Very well, Volodya, we'll put it this way then. I represent a . . . large circle of associates. Until last Friday evening we were unaware of your existence. But then a certain . . . housekeeping problem, shall we say? . . . came up. Since I happened to run across it, I was delegated to find out more about your . . . enterprise . . ."

He sipped again from the brandy glass he held in his hand.

"Not easy to do, of course. You're not listed at the telephone information kiosks . . ."

Volodya laughed loud and hard. It wasn't that funny.

Duvakin waited. Finally Volodya wound down, wiped his eyes, and looked serious. Was he nervous?

But his face was once again a dangerous blank.

"And what have you discovered, Vanya? What is your interest? And—by the way—who is 'we'?"

"You will understand, I cannot answer that last question at the moment. I had a roll of money . . . We don't need it back. Does that tell you something? We are concerned with problems of supply . We want to . . . redress certain—no doubt temporary—inadequacies of . . . economic distribution."

Volodya thought that over for a moment. A slow, appreciative grin spread across his shiny face.

"I find it difficult to say what we have discovered about you," Duvakin said, fortified by the cognac. "Frankly, we're impressed . . . But there's still a lot to be desired . . ."

Ishakin shook his head, smiling broadly. "Vanya, Vanya, you astound me, old man! But then you always did. Remember Krasnoya Sosna, the apples? Same damn thing all over again!"

"I remember, sure . . ."

Volodya had wanted to steal apples; Vanya had refused. Stalin had just at that time extended the age of criminal culpability downwards to twelve years old. Apple-stealing was included in the category of 'destruction of State property'. School books were filled with stories about evil little boys who stole apples and whose fathers spied for England. Vanya had therefore left Volodya and returned home where, by some miracle, his mother had half a dozen apples, which she had acquired through Lord knows what stroke of luck. She had proudly presented two of them to Vanya and he, in turn, had trotted off to give one to Volodya and save him from a life of crime. Volodya refused to believe Vanya's story, and was convinced that the apples resulted from Vanya's secret prowess, from a clever and admirable piece of thievery.

"Yes, Vanya, you're a deep one, that's what you are. Deep. Eight years in that stinking hotel, and not one peep from you. No money, a lousy apartment . . . Not even girl friends to speak of. And now it turns out that the whole time you're in an *association*." He smiled benignly and rolled the word lovingly on his tongue. He seemed proud of Vanya: he, the benevolent older boy with his young, devoted playmate.

"Volodya, my . . . colleagues and I are interested in doing business. But certain things disturb us. We have to know more about . . . the operation . . ."

"But what bothers you, Vanya? Tell me what it is."

"Well, the outfit seems sloppy. Too many thugs . . . Loose ends left lying about. And petty things. My money . . ." He remembered Tanya's books. "Petty, stupid crooks . . ."

Ishakin nodded, toying with a pencil on the desk. He frowned. "You mean the American, don't you?" he said.

So!

Ishakin threw down the pencil and swore vividly, stunningly. Ishakin not only knew about Miller . . . but it seemed that murder annoyed him, even tormented him.

"Vanya, I'm going to tell you something, and only because you're an old friend . . . and a colleague. You're right, you're absolutely right. An organisation that takes eleven years to put together, it expands, it strengthens . . . And then a lousy street thug risks everything, and for no reason, no reason . . ." He shook his head.

Duvakin's militia instincts rushed forward before he

thought. "So you know who did it?" he asked. He bit his tongue and grasped the chair arms. Fortunately Volodya appeared to be too caught up in his own anger and disgust to notice the question's oddity.

"Yes, the devil take his mother! Scum, a pervert. One of those perverted bastards. And why didn't they check out Miller better? At any rate, we won't have that particular problem again . . ."

He brooded. Duvakin cleared his throat.

"Well, all right, Volodya. So you got rid of the . . . pervert . . . But you left a trail. I mean, I found it, and I could have been someone else, you know. And Miller's gone now, he seems to have been vital to the organisation. And the way it was handled afterward. It was so sloppy. And that worries us."

Ishakin drummed fingers the size of milk sausages on the desk top. Although his mouth already felt like the inside of a trash chute, Duvakin lit another cigarette. Tobacco seemed to be replacing food and sleep.

Faint noises filtered through the walls. Voices, the slamming of car doors, laughter . . . He looked at his watch. Almost eleven now. Ishakin's clients arriving . . .

The silence stretched on. The armchair in which he slumped cradled his outraged body like a mother. The hell with all of them, he thought. He was their problem; let them figure out what to do about him.

Volodya finally spoke, thoughtfully.

"Vanya, you've got me stumped, I admit it. To tell you the truth, I don't know what to make of you. I *know* Moscow . . . Name some names, give me some idea who you're working with . . ."

"Listen, the only name you can have is Ivan Pavlovich Duvakin. See? My own neck is on the line. I know a lot of your people already . . . You only know me. You're big, maybe too big, you're loose. Those two clowns that searched Miller's room . . . It was sloppy, Volodya; they just didn't give a damn."

Ishakin flushed. "Damn it, Duvakin!" he shouted. "What the hell are you after? I can't sit here all night . . ."

"Listen, Volodya, it's for your own good . . . Can't you give us some idea of the things we can expect from you, a demonstration of your methods . . . ?"

How could he be more specific than that? He didn't even know what he meant himself.

Volodya stood up. It wouldn't be a bad thing to have a suit like that. It would probably wear like iron.

"Vanya, can I trust you? That's my problem, you understand. Can I trust you? I want to . . ." Volodya's face was worried, mournful. A little boy's face. Duvakin felt a surge of guilt. Here stood Volodya Ishakin, who had begun with the same nothing as Duvakin, and now he had a house like something out of a fairy tale. He made people happy, after all, he gave them what they wanted. Pleasant sounds drifted from downstairs. Important people came here to relax, people the country needed. Ishakin was his boyhood friend, his only boyhood friend.

"Yes, of course you can trust me," Duvakin said. He felt dirty, disgusted. His eyes ached, and so did his ribs. He wanted nothing more than to be sitting in Tanya's kitchen drinking tea.

"Vanya, it's late and I have some things to attend to. Why don't I drive home with you, and we can talk on the way, all right?"

Numbly Duvakin nodded. Ishakin picked up an object on his desk. It resembled a strange fruit. It fell in half and Ishakin poked at something on its underside. Then he put it to his ear.

"Cute, eh? An American telephone. The great lovers of democracy call it a Princess . . . Hello? Ishakin. Send the Chaika round, out front." He hung up. "Got everything, Vanya? Let's go."

Wearily, Duvakin pushed himself out of the armchair.

"I don't remember where I left my coat . . ." His mind felt like buckwheat kasha left out overnight in the rain.

Ishakin coughed. "Vanya, I owe you an apology. Tsyplyatin was a little . . . over-enthusiastic . . . It did not survive . . ."

His martyred coat, twice a victim. And his funds would allow him to buy two-thirds of a new scarf. Freezing fogs, icy winds lay ahead . . .

"But don't worry, old friend! That overcoat was hardly worthy of your . . . lofty station, anyway. You must allow me to replace it. No arguments! I owe you something, after all . . ."

Ishakin ushered him toward a closet door. Opening it, he pulled out a heavy coat of dark leather and fur, which he hastily threw over his own shoulders. Then he lifted out a long overcoat of heavy white leather. He held it open enticingly. It was lined with loose, curly wool. Duvakin did not think he should take it. Knowing that he would die of cold before he got into the car, he looked at it longingly.

"What the hell," he mumbled. "Thanks, Volodya." Its fluffy warmth embraced him.

"Isn't it great? It looks marvellous on you, absolutely grand. It's French, you know."

Walking awkwardly because of the stiff leather and the unaccustomed weight and length of the coat, Duvakin followed Volodya out the door and down the hall. He could not turn his head because of the high collar.

They turned, descended a new set of stairs, passed through more halls. Duvakin, having lost his bearings, followed Ishakin meekly. They emerged into the night from a side door and followed a walkway of flat stones carved in the chest-high snow. The cold hit only Duvakin's face and feet. The vast coat was impenetrable.

A black and chrome Chaika gleamed in the parking area, its engine inaudible. Clouds of steam rose from its rear. Duvakin looked back at the house. Its lights were warm and inviting against the white snow, the dark blue evergreens and the black night. Two men were struggling to fit an enormous fir tree through the open front door.

"Later tonight we're going to put it up," Volodya said. "It's always quite a party. We were lucky this year. There was a very nice tree over in the cranberry bogs, that's on the grounds. Three metres tall, almost . . ."

Duvakin thought fleetingly of plump, Ishakin-like men and slender Margot-like women decorating the bright holiday tree. He found the thought repellent.

"Let's get going, Vanya. Got to get you home."

Duvakin had difficulty folding his new coat under him comfortably; it took him a moment to appreciate the luxury in which he sat. The car was twice normal size. Its cloth seats were trimmed with leather; the dashboard knobs were shiny wood, and there were Oriental rugs on the floor. As they pulled out of the driveway, Volodya asked, "Seleznovskaya still, Vanya?"

Duvakin nodded. It was unfortunately not in keeping with the image he wished to project. Vanya knew his place; he had arranged that room for him. For a moment he thought of Tanya's warm apartment, and her lovely hands. Better not to go there, though. Better not to drag her into this any further.

Ishakin spoke the address into a sort of telephone. The driver was separated from them by a glass partition.

12

The ride home was a blur of light and dark, underscored by the warmth of the Chaika and the new coat, the hypnotic hum of the engine, and of Volodya's voice.

The car glided from Butyrsky Val onto Seleznovskaya, passing from the twentieth century of brick buildings, asphalt boulevards and harsh blue street lights into the nineteenth of log buildings, basement shops and old tram rails. Duvakin loved this little neighbourhood; it had a village air. There was even a functioning church nestled between the Sadovoye and Butyrsky Val, hidden in a copse of birch. It had always been a working class neighbourhood, and Duvakin thought that for years and years knots of sturdy men in coarse cloth coats and caps had gathered laughing and swearing at the beer stand, while meek women in head scarves had scurried past them, intent on errands, or on their way to church, where a tiny bell softly tolled . . .

"Pretty run down, isn't it? How can you stand it, Vanya?"

"Oh, you know . . . You get used to it . . ."

They stopped before his house, a dark red-brick building with a silver-painted tin roof that looked snow-covered even in summer. Duvakin half-hoped that someone was awake to see him. His stock would certainly go up in the neighbourhood: there had probably never been a Chaika on the crumbling asphalt of Seleznovskaya.

"All right, old man," Volodya said. "Everything clear, then? We'll meet on Friday . . . You still hoofing it? All right, then we'll make it outside the Aeroport metro stop. At three . . ."

Duvakin watched the car glide out of sight. The stairs were as dark and slippery as ever. Thank heaven he lived only one flight up.

There were two doors on the landing, both heavily padded and surrounded by a thicket of door-bells. He dug out his spoon-sized key and rattled it around in the lock for a moment, before he realised that the door was not locked.

He looked at his watch. Astoundingly, it was not yet midnight. He felt as though it were infinitely late at night before a day that would never dawn. He pushed through outer and inner doors.

The apartment hallways smelled, as always, of cabbage, wet coats and children. Pots could be heard rattling even at this hour in the kitchen; someone was humming in the bathroom. The coat-rack had fallen over again, so the tenants had hung their coats wherever there was space. From long habit Duvakin chucked his coat onto the pile, and then rescued it, when he realised that if he left this new coat there, it would grace a new back in the morning and he would be stranded in the house until spring. He looked closely at his prize. Already the fine white French leather was speckled a bit with the black and grey of Moscow.

Attempting to rub it clean, he trudged down the hall into his corridor. Once this apartment had had large rooms, but these had been divided up so often that the house had turned into a labyrinth of corridors and cubby holes. He thought of something, as he passed the telephone on the wall, and fished in his pocket for a two-kopek coin. His limbs flamed with exhaustion, his brain was numb. The coat felt as though it weighed fifty kilos.

Tanya. It was not too late to call Tanya. The phone was the old-fashioned kind, which accepted only two kopek pieces. But the coin in his hand was a ten kopek, not a two. It was useless to ask anyone still awake for change or for a two kopek piece. Those coins were the poor man's wealth; even a matter of life and death would not coax one from his neighbours. Oh, what the hell, the ten kopek piece would work. It was really funny. Thousands of rubles had slipped through his hands in the past few days, and here he was worrying about eight kopeks.

He dropped the coin into the box, and waited. The earpiece made coughing noises, and then the buzz which meant he could dial through.

One ring. Two. Three.

"Vanya? Is that you, Vanya? . . . Are you all right? Oh, thank God . . ."

He was taken aback by her fervour. "Where are you now, Vanya? Can you come here?"

"I'm home, Tanya . . . I'm fine . . ." A lie, really. "But I'm pretty tired, it's been one hell of an evening. I'm going to bed. Thanks for waiting up. I'll call you tomorrow . . ."

"Poor Vanya . . . But can you talk now? What happened . . .?"

"Tomorrow. I'll tell you tomorrow. Now I've got to sleep."

"I understand. Tomorrow then, I understand. Sleep well, my little Vanya . . ."

Duvakin grinned involuntarily. Little Vanya! Even his mother had never called him that.

"Good night, dear Tanya." He hated to hang up, but his legs and arms felt as though they belonged to someone else.

He fumbled the lock open, found the switch behind the wardrobe and turned on the overhead light.

Oh, damn it! He had forgotten. Volodya's playmates.

His clothes were piled in the middle of the floor, along with his bed, and his few books and magazines. The boxes and cardboard suitcases in which he kept his belongings had been torn open and tossed on the heap. Even the door to his little refrigerator stood ajar. Probably now whatever was left in there had spoiled.

He waded through his possessions to the bed. But the effort of reassembling it was too much for him. He pulled off the blankets and dragged them to the divan. Everything that lay there he threw on the floor, and he lay down, still in his clothes, and wrapped the blankets around him. The arm-rest was scratchy and smelled of dust; his head lay at an odd angle. He sighed and almost immediately fell asleep.

13

Duvakin opened his eyes, and shut them again; there was a red curtain behind his lids. The sun must be shining in his eyes. Which meant that it was late. He rolled onto his side and squinted cautiously.

The hideous pile was gone from the centre of the floor.

"Morning, Vanya."

"Tanya!" He looked quickly at himself to make sure that he was decent. Of course. He still wore street clothes.

She was sitting in his armchair with her back to the window. A dove-blue aura of cigarette smoke circled about her head. She was smiling. The room looked better than it had before it was sacked. There was no dust on the table, the refrigerator was as white as when it had first emerged from its carton.

"You're no housekeeper, Vanya," she said.

"True enough . . ." He looked at her with pleasure. "Pass me the cigarettes, huh . . ."

She threw him the pack and the box of matches.

"Want some coffee? I brought some."

"Coffee! Please . . ." He lay back, his arms behind his head. Even cramped on the sofa, the luxury of lying down and smoking, awaiting coffee to be served, was overwhelming. He was grateful.

In a short time Tanya returned from the kitchen with a tray of steaming thick Turkish coffee and two cups. He sat up. He could not remember when he had welcomed a liquid more. The coffee was gritty and bittersweet; he was awakened and warmed. He wondered how she had gotten in without awaking him.

"Don't be a goose, Vanya. You forgot to close the door last night. When I got here it was half open, and you were snoring like a troll . . . And you were so fast asleep I could have painted and papered the whole place, you wouldn't have noticed!"

She came and sat on the edge of the couch. Stroking his head, her long fingers were cool. He felt younger than he had in years. Almost a child again, in fact. He snuggled deeper into his blankets; his shirt and pants were twisted about his body.

"Poor darling, you must have been so tired . . ."

Suddenly she said, "Akh!" and slapped him lightly on the head.

"There now, you see? You've spilled your coffee."

Duvakin lazily twisted his neck to look. Sure enough, the cup was gone from the sofa arm where he had set it down. Tanya went to the kitchen again to get a wet cloth. Duvakin sat up and straightened his clothing. The warmth of the sun had brought out the moisture trapped between the double windows; the panes were frosted into a golden rectangle of light. Duvakin remembered winter mornings in Krasnoya Sosna, lying in his warm bed while he waited for the stove to heat the house. When the house was warm, his mother would

141

come into the room where he slept, sit by his bed, and gently coax him awake.

He sighed softly. These pleasant memories were gradually displaced by the events of the previous evening, by anticipation of what yet lay before him.

Tanya reappeared with a rag. She bent down to mop up the small amount of coffee. Duvakin was touched by her serious desire to protect his entirely worthless but irreplaceable furniture.

"Vanya, who's the woman in the kitchen with grey hair?"

"She yell at you for stealing her soup bones?"

"That's the one."

"That's Firsovna. She lost those bones sometime during the Crimean War. She accuses everyone who goes into that stinking kitchen of taking them."

"Well, I'll take her the rag. She can squeeze the coffee into her broth."

"Do that, she'd like it!" Duvakin yelled after her. He hopped up and began hurriedly to change his clothes.

He was standing in the middle of the room with one leg in his pants, when Tanya returned.

"There, she loved it. Vanya! Where are you off to? You ought to rest, eat something. I'll make you whatever you'd like . . ."

"No, no. I'm not hungry . . . I've got a lot to do . . ."

"But . . . what need is there to get up so early?"

Duvakin looked at her, puzzled. She sat smiling on the edge of his sagging bed, her knees primly together, one hand toying with her hair. "You know . . ." The familiar pronoun in her husky voice flooded Duvakin with an emotion he could not name.

"Tanya . . . Tanenka . . ." To lie down with her, to immerse himself in that world, in that woman, to forget everything . . .

He could not do it.

"Tanya . . . Not now, not today . . . I can't. Lord . . ." His voice was strangled.

Tanya turned her head away for a second, and then looked back at him. To his surprise, she was still smiling.

"Easy for you to say, citizen, but then why are you standing at half-mast, open to the scrutiny of the collective?"

Blood flamed in his ears. He leaped quickly into the other leg of his trousers and, off balance, toppled back onto the couch.

Tanya collapsed in laughter on the bed.

Finally Duvakin righted himself and his clothing. His face still burned. He lit a cigarette from Tanya's pack, and coughed.

"Not used to ours any more?" Her question had a cutting edge.

"I just smoke too much, that's all," Duvakin said vaguely. He fumbled into his socks. "Anyway, maybe Polkovnikov will take the thing over now. Maybe I can get out. I learned a few things last night, you know; I have something to tell him . . .

As he tied his shoes he could feel Tanya's eyes on him.

"What's the matter?" he asked. "Do I have my shirt buttoned wrong? . . . Why are you looking at me like that?"

"I was just wondering, Vanya . . . Are you beginning to enjoy this?" She spoke very softly.

"*Enjoy?* Which part? Getting hit on the head? Punched in the stomach? Playing slap and tickle with a bunch of murderers?" He stared at her in amazement.

"No, playing God . . ." She shrugged. Getting to her feet she began to pace the room, her arms wrapped tightly about her body. Duvakin stood and watched.

After a moment she smiled at him.

"It's the future, Vanya. That's why I worry . . . I want a future . . ." Her eyes were liquid; her lower lip trembled. She said softly, "Take care, Vanya. Don't get caught."

Duvakin was puzzled.

"Caught?"

Visibly, she banished her tension; driving it somewhere within herself. She came over to the divan and sat down next to him, encircling his arm with hers. For a blissful moment Duvakin relaxed against her.

"Tanya, my darling. I have to go. This has to be done, you know. And I guess it's fallen to me to do it. But soon it will all be over, I swear to you. Maybe today even. Tomorrow for sure . . . And then . . ." And then what? Duvakin was afraid to try and imagine an answer to that question.

Half in jest, he spat at the Devil over his left shoulder. And so did Tanya, at that precise moment.

That broke the dam of tension between them.

He spoke huskily. "If my mama were alive, she'd say you're too thin . . ."

After a while he stood up.

"I've really got to go now, Tanochka. I'll come to your place as soon as I get through. Shall I? Or do you want to stay here?"

"I've got to work today. Then I'll go home. This place is too gloomy."

"It is, isn't it?" Duvakin looked around his room as if he were seeing it for the first time. "All right, I'll see you at your place, but I don't know when I'll be finished . . . Maybe if it's early we can go visit Lena?"

"Just immediate family, you know that. And you're not that, you know! . . . Besides, it's Thursday. Visiting is every other day. She's fine now, Vanya, don't worry. I'll try to find something special for us tonight, all right? Try to come . . . say, at four."

"All right, good. Come on, you can walk to the metro with me."

"It's a date . . . Just a moment . . ."

Tanya fussed around the room gathering her coat and hat, purse and carry bag. Duvakin shrugged on his overcoat.

"What do you think of it?" He did a clumsy model's turn.

"Nice . . . You got it last night?" Tanya did not seem delighted with the coat.

"Yes, a gift . . . or a replacement, rather. My other one . . . uh . . . expired during the execution of its duties. Or was executed . . ."

"You got it from the people you called a pack of murderers? The one with the heroin?"

"Yes, but I didn't buy it from them! It was a gift . . . I mean . . . It's all right . . ."

"And now you're going to wear it?"

"Damn it," Duvakin said angrily, "Yes! I don't have anything else. Am I supposed to freeze to death? And I didn't do anything dishonest to get it!"

But he had extracted the coat under false pretences. He had no need to be made to feel guilty about it. His pretence was for a good end. But probably she was right . . .

Tanya laughed at the expression on his face.

"I'm not worried about that, little Vanya. Lord! But . . . did you happen to examine the merchandise?"

He was dumbfounded. Her point suddenly sank home.

He pulled the coat off.

"Vanya, I can save you the effort. I looked already. But it was sort of dumb of you, my darling. I would be happier if in the future you managed to be a little more suspicious."

She took the coat from him and sat on the couch with it laid, lining out, on her knees.

"I was just looking at it. I wanted to see how it was made. It's French, you know; I wanted to see the seams . . ." Her fingers rummaged through the fleece, as though she were looking for lice.

"There. See?"

She held back the fleece and pinched it upwards. Duvakin saw a metal flash.

"Copper?"

Tanya nodded.

Duvakin was fascinated as well as embarrassed by his own credulity. Tanya helped him trace the copper wire down the back of the coat to a seam at the bottom hem, where it separated into two wires, following their own seams upward. Sewn into the leather of the enormous collar, just where it was stiffest, was a miniscule power unit, as big as a matchbox and quite flat. It would snuggle comfortably into the back of

145

his neck. If Tanya had not pointed it out, he would never have suspected it was there.

"What is it? A radio? A microphone?"

"A transmitter, I think. It would make it easy to follow you . . ."

To follow him to Polkovnikov.

His fingers trembled as he helped Tanya carefully pick the wire from the seams of his beautiful coat.

14

From the phone booth Duvakin looked across at the Berlin Hotel and Children's World. No enemy eyes seemed to be peering at him from the turbulent crowds. He could not be certain, of course. Fumbling with coins, gloves, the receiver, and distracted by the constant need to look about him, he finally managed to dial Polkovnikov's number.

It was Tanya who had said that destroying the bug would be almost as risky as wearing it. Duvakin, the clever detective, had simply stared numbly at the curling wires. If they were lucky the bug was still functioning, reporting that Duvakin remained inside his apartment. It was more likely that the bug had stopped functioning. In either case Duvakin could not simply waltz out the front door, for at the very least he would be followed. The very least. The words were chilling.

They had slipped out the rear of the building and had gone down the street to Sadovoye, not up to Novoslobodskaya as might have been expected. There they separated. Then Duvakin had gone around to Mayakovsky on the bus, out to the Ring Line, which he had ridden almost completely around the city, switching trains a couple of times, cutting back toward the centre on some of the lines. Twice he had entered a car and then jumped out just as the doors shut, earning bitter glares from old women passengers.

It took ages, but ultimately he had ended up at Sverdlov Square, where he had cut through TSUM, and come to rest, exhausted, worried and frightened, in the phone booth.

He dialled. The phone went dead, as it had before, and then rang.

"Yes?"

Lord, that tone of voice. It sounded the way old fish looked.

"Sasha?"

"Wrong number, chum . . ."

"Wait!" Duvakin yelled, just as the line went completely dead. Cursing himself, the phone and everything else he could think of, including the stiff leather of his coat, he fished out a coin and repeated the process.

"Yes?"

"Listen, damn it, get me Polkovnikov. This is Duvakin. And it's urgent!"

Sounds of a muffled consultation.

"Duvakin?"

At last! "Yes!"

"You've got something important?"

"What the hell do you think? I called to pass the time of day? Get me Polkovnikov. Do it *right now!*" He was shocked at his own impertinence. But he was sick of it all. Every person he came in contact with seemed to aim a kick at him; he was kicking back!

"Comrade Polkovnikov isn't in right now."

"Oh . . ." His anger slid away. He had not expected this. "Will he be in soon?"

"Well, that's hard to say. He doesn't normally come here at all, Duvakin."

"Doesn't normally come there." Duvakin repeated the words in disbelief. How could Polkovnikov not normally come there?

Again a muffled conversation. Duvakin waited, looking out into the street. Where were Volodya's men—in that mob of shuffling women with sacks, of men balancing New Year's trees and briefcases—in those lines of cars and trucks bumping through clouds of exhaust fumes—where were they, watching him? He wondered if he might be going crazy, imagining unseen eyes upon him. Struggling with the folds of his new coat, he dug out a cigarette, and noted with regret that he had picked up a black smear on his elbow from the phone booth shelf.

"Duvakin? Where are you now?"

"Berlin Hotel, across from Children's World."

"Ah, good. You're not far from Polkovnikov, from his office . . ."

So. That spanking new, unworn office. All for show.

"You go over there, why don't you? We'll call ahead and let him know."

"All right. And just where the devil . . .?"

"Twenty-Fifth October Street. Number Eight."

"Where's that?"

"Used to be Nikolskaya Street."

"What in God's name does that mean? I'm only in Moscow since Khrushchev!"

"North side of GUM. That narrow street. You know it? All right then, Number Eight."

"Eight."

"There's a sign on the door. Says it's *Yidische Folkszeitung* . . ."

"What's that? German?"

"A newspaper office. I don't know. The sign's in Russian and yid letters. Means Yid Worker or something. Anyway, you can't miss it."

"All right. And Polkovnikov's there . . ."

"Second floor. He's there."

He pushed his way out of the phone booth. Lord God in Heaven! This reminded him of one of those fairy tales, filled with stuff like 'It was a flock of swans landing in the lake, no it was not a flock of swans, it was Elena the Lovely with her white hand upon her bosom . . .'

It's Polkovnikov's office, it's not Polkovnikov's office, it's

148

a security office, it's a newspaper office . . . And why in hell a Jewish newspaper? Forty-eight years he had lived in this country and never before had he heard of such a thing as a Jewish newspaper.

He smoked nervously as he walked, regretting that his foreign cigarettes were gone. The Tu-144's he had picked up at the corner kiosk were stale and acrid. If you sucked on them too hard, the filter popped into your mouth. He crossed the street to the underground pedestrian walkway. As usual, it was a madhouse of jostling, shoving people. But for some reason he was able to pass through the crowd more easily than usual. People seemed to move out of his way. One young man went so far as to apologise for bumping into him.

He grinned to himself. The coat! It must be the coat. They thought he was Someone . . .

It was a heartening discovery.

He passed through the gate of the Kitai-gorod wall and paused to get his bearings. Twenty-Fifth October was a street from old Moscow, one of the maze-like streets east of the Kremlin, narrow, dark and lined with ornate, oppressive buildings. Lights burned late at night behind heavy curtains; black limousines slid in and out of inner courtyards . . .

He found the house after passing it once and retracing his steps. The sign said *The Jewish Solidarity* in Russian, and probably the same things in two other Latin alphabets. The Jewish letters looked like candle flames.

Pushing open the curtained door and stepping down into a dark hall, he found an ancient guard seated at a desk, the inevitable decanter of yellowish water at his elbow.

"What do you want, citizen?" The old man's voice was the rude, half-drunken one in which all guards speak to the intruding world.

Duvakin answered him in kind. "What business is it of yours, old man?" Before all this, he had hardly ever spoken to anyone that way. Now, he thought, I'm becoming a bastard in my own right.

This question provoked a long, heated largely incomprehensible diatribe about why this was the precise business of the guard and no one else, accompanied by imaginative slurs on Duvakin's person, source of income and ancestry.

At last the aged drunk subsided into muttering.

"Now get me Colonel Polkovnikov, old man. And don't tell me that there is no one of that name here. Tell him Duvakin wants to see him. Got it?" Duvakin threw his cigarette on the floor and ground it viciously beneath his toe.

He might as well have spat in the guard's face. The gesture was crude, unforgiveable, uncultured.

It had the intended effect.

The guard stared at him, one eye purblind and one rheumy blue. In his face malevolence fought with fear. Finally he said, "Room 231, second floor."

Duvakin stumped furiously up the stairs. He was tired of being the butt of every desk-squatter in town, of getting thumped on the neck and punched in the ribs by every damn thug who felt like it, of chasing all over Moscow after Asiatics and phantoms . . . And now some half-witted old sot in a phony Jewish newspaper office thought he could bully him . . . By the time he reached the second floor he was breathless with rage.

The search for room 231 did nothing to improve his temper. The corridor was lined with unnumbered doors. Opening some at random, he was greeted with sullen stares and even rude shouts. Finally he found the right place, an office similar to the one further up the street: a boxy room with a desk and a wall cupboard for papers. A young woman sat behind the desk. She wore a sky-blue uniform, and a mohair olive-green cap. Duvakin wondered, as he often had, why women wore winter hats indoors.

"Yes?" she said. She had not yet decided whether to be polite or abusive.

"Duvakin to see Polkovnikov. And tell him to hurry." Duvakin, nursing his anger, lit another terrible cigarette.

He was gratified to see her greyish eyes widen in disbelief at his audacity. They narrowed again almost immediately.

"Of course, at once. Just have a seat."

There was no chair. He stood, smoking. His anger began

to dissolve in the intimidating atmosphere of this kind of office.

He smoked the cigarette slowly, tapping the ashes into his hand. Then he lit another, and finished that. He lit a third from the butt. His feet hurt, he was broiling inside his coat, and, worst of all, he felt cowed.

At long last the inner door opened.

The secretary smiled, bowed slightly, and gestured for him to enter.

Polkovnikov sat at a large desk; a number of files were piled on its green felt top. All sorts of files: grey cardboard folders, boxes, notebooks, loose papers, all covered with ash, some with dust. This was a working office, unlike the one in Dzerzhinsky Street.

It was not as grand as Dzerzhinsky Street either, of course. No Oriental carpets, no fancy padding.

Polkovnikov leaned back in his chair and looked closely at him. "So, Duvakin, you've actually found something out?"

Duvakin hesitated. Now that he was here he was not really sure what he intended to say. After all, in the last three days all sorts of things had happened. He had lost, for instance, Lord only knew how much State money.

"I sincerely hope you have, comrade, because I can tell you quite frankly that our work here has gotten us here's what." The Colonel made a flatulent sound with his mouth. Then he smiled amiably. He was markedly friendly, or not even friendly . . . He was treating Duvakin like a colleague.

"You know, Duvakin . . ." He settled comfortably back, and rocked slightly in his seat. "It's funny about this case . . . I've seen a lot of bad types pass through these offices. But this is the first case in a long time that really had us puzzled. Usually there's nothing much to this business. You get wind of something, you haul somebody in . . . You have a nice private little talk . . . Add a little private encouragement if you have to . . ."

The Colonel looked him dead in the eye. An unpleasant sensation.

"And then my dear fellow, it all comes out. This isn't your

151

political side, where you have to stand around for hours in the freezing rain or try to unwind kilometres of magnetic tape. CID is pretty cut and dried. This one, though . . . Very confusing. My friend, you would be doing us a great favour if you can give us any help . . ."

As he spoke Polkovnikov held out a box of cigarettes. Duvakin was surprised by his own eagerness as he took one. Splendid, he thought. Now I'm hooked on foreign cigarettes.

But how to proceed? He himself did not come out of the story with flying colours, and there was the problem of Volodya. True, Volodya had not shown much consideration for Duvakin in the last four days . . . It was obvious—although almost incredible—that he had in fact ordered his execution. But still . . . A childhood friend is a childhood friend. And he had done him a good turn once . . .

"Well, Colonel, I have some things to report. But I don't know whether the time is right yet. I mean, there's a lot I don't know yet . . . all the facts, names of everyone who is involved . . ."

"That's not your business to decide, is it, comrade?" Polkovnikov's tone was suddenly dry. His face had changed.

"Oh, no, no . . . I know that . . . I know that—"

"It's just that your girl friend is mixed up in it, eh? That Tanya Kaplan of yours . . ."

Duvakin stared at him in horror. How the devil had Tanya's name got into this?

"Wonder how I know she's mixed up in it?" Polkovnikov swivelled to and fro in his chair, a cigarette in his fingers. He chuckled to himself.

"No . . . I mean, yes!" Duvakin took a deep breath. "Good Lord, Colonel, believe me, she has nothing to do with it. I swear to you!" His voice broke.

"Smuggling, money, and a girl named Kaplan? And there's no connection? Come now, what do you take me for?"

"No, no! It's not that at all. No, the head of the whole thing is Volodya, he's a childhood friend of mine, he—"

Duvakin stopped abruptly. Oh, damn! His self-confidence

crumbled like the cigarette which Polkovnikov stubbed out in his ashtray.

"Volodya. And I presume Volodya has a full name?"

Damn it, Volodya had had someone killed. He was a profiteer, he had people followed, he wired French coats, he broke into flats . . .

"All right, Colonel. Vladimir Aleksandrovich Ishakin."

"Address?" A mechanical question, pencil poised.

"I haven't the faintest idea . . . Well, his address . . . No . . ." Well, even if he lived in that big house . . . Where was it?

"Look Duvakin, get hold of yourself. Try to calm down. Just tell me what you've been doing since Monday, when we spoke." Polkovnikov was apparently friendly again. "Would you like some coffee? Or cognac perhaps?"

"Thank you, no. It's hard . . . it's hard to start, to put it together."

"Start at the beginning," Polkovnikov said. "Take your time. I can help you put it together." He leaned expansively back in his leather chair, fingertips together.

Duvakin began slowly, trying to give as much detail as possible, describing interiors, atmosphere, his own reactions. He had no affection for the girls at the hard currency store, for Liudmila Grigorievna, even for Ishakin. But he could not overcome his lifelong aversion to naming names.

Polkovnikov listened, at ease, as though this were a simple friendly chat; as though Duvakin were an underling who had come to him for advice. Duvakin ran through the story: the shop, the Uzbekistan, the ride in the Volga, the house in the country. Occasionally Polkovnikov smiled.

". . . so that's where it sits now, comrade Colonel. As you see, Tanya Kaplan has nothing to do with it. I'm not sure myself what it all means, which is why I hesitated when I first came in . . . But I thought I had better come to you for direction before tomorrow night. I'm supposed to meet Ishakin tomorrow at three, outside the Aeroport metro station. He agreed to a demonstration of some sort to me; I convinced him I represent this important, wealthy group of black marketeers . . . He was reluctant to trust me, but I convinced him. I don't know where they'll be taking me . . ." Duvakin's heart rose toward his throat as he spoke the last words.

"And what are we supposed to do?" Polkovnikov sounded disinterested, sleepy. His tone alarmed Duvakin as much as his question.

"What do you mean? Don't you know? I thought you would close in on them . . . You told me . . . I thought you could—"

"That we could pull your ass out of the fire?" Polkovnikov was smiling. His face was cold.

"Well . . . I can't bluff them any more. They're suspicious, naturally they're suspicous. If I don't show up . . . They're following me."

"What, here?"

"No. I hope not, anyway. I was careful, I was very careful. We took the wires out of the coat . . ."

"What wires?"

"Oh, they chopped up my old coat. I mean, it fell apart. So Volodya gave me a new one . . . this one . . . It's French. I found some copper wires and a transmitter . . . I thought it might be a transmitter . . . sewed inside the collar."

Polkovnikov stood up abruptly, and began to pace the room. He looked more than two metres tall today. Even though he was very thin, his hands and shoulders were muscular. Duvakin closed his eyes. He would be very happy to say a pleasant goodbye to Polkovnikov forever.

"So. They gave you a new coat, did they? You've done all right, haven't you?"

"But, my God, what do you mean? How could I go outside without a coat?"

"No, no, you couldn't, of course not, my dear fellow. Of course not." He stood still a moment in the centre of the room, apparently lost in thought. Then he turned suddenly and left the room.

What was going on? There could be no reason to worry, he was Polkovnikov's aide, his ally. He had said himself they had no leads except for Duvakin. He had acted in good faith. So why worry? The talk about Tanya . . . He became conscious of the heavy silence in the room. Due no doubt to the thickness of the walls. And why were there no windows? The location of the office, undoubtedly.

He got up, feeling stiff, and walked to the door. Should he try the door-knob? Would someone see . . .? There was no earthly reason why Polkovnikov would lock him in . . .

His heart thudded and skipped a beat. He cupped his breast with his hand, to aid and protect that fragile organ.

He was still standing at the door when Polkovnikov briskly returned. The two collided, and Duvakin almost fell. He staggered back, noting that Polkovnikov made no move to catch him, a thing one usually did by instinct. He caught himself against the chair.

"Restless, eh, friend Vanya? Please do sit down again. We won't keep you much longer, but there are a few matters we need to discuss." Polkovnikov took his arm and guided him to sit down. Polkovnikov was strong.

Duvakin felt belittled. The entire matter had gotten thoroughly on his nerves; he did not wish to talk about it any more. He kept his eyes down, on his worn, shiny trousers. How had all this happened to him? Less than a week ago he had been a simple, happy man, wandering vaguely toward old age.

Polkovnikov fussed with the papers on his desk, making notes. After a moment silence fell. Then he spoke, softly.

"Comrade Duvakin, it appears that you have rendered us an invaluable service."

Duvakin looked up in surprise.

"Yes, that's right, an invaluable service. For the Motherland. We're proud of you."

"I'm afraid, comrade Colonel . . ."

"You don't know what I'm talking about? Come, comrade, there is no need for such modesty. You have done your job well, you have endangered your life, performing valiant services for the socialist Homeland."

In a flash Duvakin understood. He smiled, but not with

pride. Polkovnikov had gone out to check with somebody. Now they had decided they needed him to do something more, so they hauled out this newspaper language to try and butter him up.

Polkovnikov continued.

". . . medal, but unfortunately in this line of work that is not possible. However there are other rewards; a communist in any case has no need of material recognition . . ."

"But you know I am not a Party member, comrade Colonel."

Polkovnikov was thrown off his stride.

"Oh yes . . . But still . . ."

"So I may go, knowing my country is well pleased with me?" Duvakin asked sarcastically.

Polkovnikov looked at him expressionlessly for a moment. Then he laughed.

"All right, Vanya. You get the point, though?"

Stupid though he knew it was, Duvakin could not help warming toward the man. Deliberately he looked away from him, trying to concentrate his gaze on the corner where walls and ceiling met.

"Vanya, let's get down to business. It looks as though you've managed to provide the missing pieces, or at least most of them. We knew a lot of this, but we never put it together; it never formed a picture for us, if you know what I mean. The hard currency place, the Uzbekistan, that blackass Ishan . . . Yes, but we didn't know what we had . . ."

"Do you know now?"

"Since you ask, yes. And no. It's something large. Devilishly large. And it's clear, the house, the killings . . . There's no place for that in Russia! But should we just pinch off the buds or go for the roots? What do you think, Vanya?" Polkovnikov had switched unobtrusively to the familiar. Duvakin felt himself being sucked into this inviting comradely warmth.

"I suppose," he said lamely, "the roots." He knew he had no other choice. "The roots," he repeated.

156

Polkovnikov had chosen the antiquated image of the tree of evil. An air of artifice, of falseness, hung over his speech. But perhaps it was simply natural to him.

"Excellent, comrade! I hoped you would say that. It is a great responsibility we are giving you, but I think I can say that it is also a great opportunity. A grateful Party and country will not forget."

Again Duvakin was forced to lower his eyes, to conceal his distaste for the Colonel's rhetoric. Normally Duvakin was oblivious to the verbiage of political idealism; it was so commonplace as to be almost unnoticeable. But in this context these fine words seemed almost blasphemous. That Polkovnikov's appraisals of men and the State were not idealistic had been apparent to Duvakin from their first encounter. And for the Colonel now to act the noble patriot . . .

A great wave of fatigue and disgust washed over Duvakin. He felt indifferent to this task, anxious only to be free of it all. Let Polkovnikov play the commissar if he wished. But it made Duvakin feel silly, like an actor in a crude war propaganda film.

A sharp pain in his fingers. His cigarette. He leaped forward to crush it out. The sudden movement startled Polkovnikov. The look of exaltation froze on his face; the liquid in his eyes turned to ice. Then slowly, visibly, the muscles of his cheeks and neck unknotted.

"Clumsy idiot," he said calmly.

"Sorry, it was the cigarette," Duvakin mumbled. "I was so caught up listening to you . . ."

"Garbage, you didn't hear a word I said," Polkovnikov continued in the same mild voice. "To business then. We've got to figure out the best way to handle this thing."

"What handle? I've told you everything I know."

"Fool, I know what you told me. I mean, motivations! Reasons! These guys are clever, I think; they're not in it just for the money. Something's going on. I want to know what it is."

"Why don't you round them all up? Bring them in and ask

them? A little talk . . ." He tried to keep bitterness out of his voice.

"Mmm . . . we could." Polkovnikov appeared to be thinking out loud. "But we'd have to have them all, and they'd have to be in one piece. Did they search you? I mean, did they search you close?"

"What do you mean, close?"

"They look down your throat? Up your ass?"

"Good Lord, no! Of course not!" Duvakin was indignant and embarrassed. But he remembered his drinking bout with Ishan and its ignominious end. Could they possibly have . . . ?

"Good," the Colonel said briskly. "Careless of them. But it helps us."

"You can't mean . . ." Duvakin was horrified.

"Oh, don't worry. Don't be such a baby. It's quite small. Besides, you want us to be able to find you again, don't you?" His grin was wolfish.

Duvakin sighed heavily, resigned. Anything. Just finish this comedy.

"All right then. Now. Assuming they still want to keep you among the living . . ."

Duvakin shuddered. The Colonel's tone reminded him of someone saying, 'Assuming it's sunny tomorrow,' or 'If the train is on time . . .'

" . . . then we can find the place. We'll need something to back up your story, something convincing. What do you want to buy? What do you think you could want to buy, Vanya?"

Stupid question. A new suit. Two books for Tanya. How the devil could he answer that? Maybe oranges for Grisha's New Year's party.

"Well . . . that can be worked out as you go along."

Not too comforting.

"You still have the money, of course . . ."

Damn. There it was. Bracing himself, Duvakin said, "Well . . . They . . . The alcohol . . ."

"Lost it?" Polkovnikov spoke drily. "Well, I suppose we'll

158

have to get you some more, then." He scribbled something on a sheet of paper.

Duvakin was startled, and wary. Was it going to be that easy?

Polkovnikov thought a while longer. He leaned forward.

"All right, Vanya, here's the way we'll do it. You meet your friends tomorrow, according to their arrangement. Go with them and we'll be following, a discreet kilometre or so behind you. Flash money around again, talk big. Make them think you're interested in something huge. Really huge."

"Such as?"

"Oh, I don't know off-hand. Short-wave radio, maybe. Pocket calculators . . ."

"What's that?"

"A new American toy. You hold it in your hand, it does arithmetic for you."

"Like an abacus."

"You might say so, I suppose. Anyway, use your imagination. All we really want is information. Get them talking. We need to know as much as we can before we start. We find it helps in the questioning, you know."

"But . . . what information? What sort? I ought to know . . ."

"Anything, everything. Who thought of it, who set it up, where the heroin goes, what comes back here . . . How does Ishakin hold the damn thing together? Anything you can get. Understand?"

"Yes, I understand. But—how will you know when to come?"

"Just a second," Polkovnikov said, "and I'll show you." He pressed a button under his desk.

The woman with the hat entered the room, attractive, plumpish.

"Larechka, bring me that box, will you? The one they sent over from Derzhinsky yesterday afternoon."

"Yes, of course, comrade Colonel." She departed in an unmilitary perfumed rustle of silk.

Duvakin looked after her; she was well worth watching. Polkovnikov seemed gratified by Duvakin's interest.

"We have the best here . . . Good resources, you know." He winked.

Duvakin grunted.

While they waited for her to return, Duvakin asked, "How come they put you in an old newspaper office? Temporary or what?"

Polkovnikov was amused. "The yid sign out front, you mean? That's left over from Khrushchev. They used to use the ground floor when foreigners came looking for their long-nosed brethren. We'd trot out our tame Jews; everything was tea and cakes. We leave it there because a lot of tourists come down this street since they finished the Rossia."

The woman bustled back with a small wooden box.

"Will there be anything else, comrade Colonel?"

"No, Larechka, that's all . . . for now," he added significantly, no doubt for Duvakin's benefit. She left. "Ahh, the life here certainly has its compensations . . ." Polkovnikov fiddled with the box as he spoke. Then he looked up, speaking thoughtfully. "It is ironic, you know," he said. "You wouldn't believe how many of them pass through here."

"Tourists?"

"No. Jews."

Duvakin had no idea of what this meant. He smoked and waited.

"You know," Polkovnikov said, "it's the way they are. Good with money, slick with figures. They look out for each other. Anytime we run across a big case—like this one here—we always look for a Jew involved in it. When we find him, we know we've got our ringleader, the brains behind the whole thing. Bring him in, bend him around a little bit, and wham! Case shut!" He smiled broadly. "That's why I wonder about your Tanya."

"Kaplan is her married name," Duvakin said. "There isn't any Jew involved here . . . I haven't found one anyway . . ."

"We'll find him," Polkovnikov said pleasantly. "Don't you worry. They're clever devils, but not clever enough by half." He was trying to pry the top off the box with his letter opener. "God damn fucking box! Spend a fortune on scientists and then hire a drunk to make crates!" The lid came off at last. He rummaged through the contents. "New toys," he said.

KGB 'toys' were legendary. As long as he could remember, people had been fearful of simple everyday objects: they covered the telephone with a pillow, they refrained from conversation near a radiator or a wall socket; they regarded even their own toilets with suspicion. Since the Japanese and the Americans had begun to sell equipment to the government, this fear had escalated; faith in foreign technology was blind and boundless. People now feared their walls, their ceilings, and many of their possessions as much as they had once feared only their friends.

Now here was a wooden box filled with these legendary products. It was fascinating.

"Here we go, the little devils," Polkovnikov said. He removed two objects and put the box into his desk drawer. "They told me about these, but I didn't believe it at first." He beamed with pride.

On the green felt desk top lay a Hungarian fountain pen, a Balaton, and a capsule about forty millimetres long, rounded at both ends. Duvakin eyed the capsule with suspicion. "What are they?" he asked. His excitement was mixed with loathing.

Polkovnikov held up the pen.

"This," he said, "is your whistle." He pulled off the cap. It looked like a pen. He wrote on a scrap of paper. The Balaton baulked, then blotted, then scratched a few curlicues.

Polkovnikov held it up. "Inside is a tiny transmitter, battery-powered. It doesn't have much range, half a kilometre or so. But when you open the lever to fill it with ink, it starts to send a signal. We'll be listening for it. When we hear it, we move in."

That was comforting. But the capsule. It closely resembled a suppository.

"And the other?"

"This? This is your leash." Polkovnikov picked it up and juggled it gently in his hand. "A transmitter too. Slightly different frequency. More range, maybe three times greater than the pen, depending on conditions . . . You don't turn it on, it's on all the time. Maybe a little like the toy you found in your coat: you put it somewhere where nobody will look . . ." he gave Duvakin an evil grin, "and it continues on its merry way, beeping at us the whole time. We follow in our car, picking up the signals. Neat little devil, eh?"

"Do I really have to . . ." Duvakin shuddered.

"Oh, there's lots of ways. If it's a woman, then . . ." He made an obscene gesture. "And sometimes, my dear Vanya, it's simply swallowed. A little butter and gulp! All gone!"

"Wonderful choice."

"Oh, my dear friend, don't worry. We won't give you a choice. This one is to be swallowed." Polkovnikov was clearly enjoying himself.

So now he, simple Vanya Duvakin, was about to be transformed. You think it is a man you see before you? It looks like a man, but it is a subtle device whose function is solely to carry a transmitter about the Russian countryside.

"Well, that's it, Vanya. Take the pill like a good boy before you go to meet your friends tomorrow. And then just play along." He fished in another drawer and took out a roll of foreign money, no smaller and no cleaner than the first one. "Here's more oil for your machine. And this time, try to be a little less generous, eh?"

Duvakin sighed and picked it up. There was no longer the excitement he had felt with the first roll of money. God knows that had brought him no pleasure. "I don't know what I should try to buy with it," he said.

"Oh, use your imagination. You've proven yourself a pretty fair liar so far, Vanya." Polkovnikov's voice was not entirely pleasant. There was no point in worrying about it; Duvakin

162

wanted only to take his leave. The walls and furniture pressed in upon him; the room seemed airless.

"Just pull the lever on the pen when the time is right, and we'll come." Polkovnikov's voice was curt, dismissive.

And then I am through with this forever, Duvakin thought. He found Polkovnikov exhausting. It was almost easier to deal with Ishakin, whose motives seemed clear. With Polkovnikov he felt sometimes like a colleague, sometimes like prey.

"That's all? I can go?" He rose.

"Yes, that's all. Be sure to sign for the money and the gear on your way out."

The Colonel went back to the papers on his desk.

The outside office was empty. Slowly he put on his heavy overcoat, which now looked quite grey, and waited for the girl Larisa to return. This room too was windowless. His temples throbbed in time to the flicker of the buzzing tubes overhead.

Finally he shrugged his shoulders, conscious of miming. He meant to say, Well, there is no one here, I have waited long enough, I am a busy man. I must go. He half-expected that the gesture would have an effect. Perhaps the wardrobe was really a television set, or the walls were made of one-way glass.

But no Larisa appeared. He walked out.

He emerged on Twenty-Fifth October Street. The sky was leaden and the first few snowflakes were drifting down over the crowds of people with their sacks, bundles, briefcases, string bags, sleds, cribs, holiday trees, chickens . . . It looked like an evacuation. But it was not war that was approaching; it was the New Year's holiday. A week from tomorrow.

Duvakin entered the sea of people and was buffeted by degrees into the metro, through the slush, past the change machines in the marble lobby, to the escalators moving downward. He ought really to do something for the New Year, get presents or something. Lenochka might be home from the hospital already; Tanya might not have her tree . . .

Determinedly he shook off the sense of compromise and compulsion that had resulted from his conversation with Polkovnikov, and lost himself in the warmth of his meditations.

15

At Matveevo the snow was coming down fast and dense. The trees were feathery white.

"Pretty, isn't it?" Duvakin said to the man next to him, a heavy-set, important-looking type with a Bulgarian raincoat and a leather briefcase.

"Damn right it's pretty, a pretty fucking god-damn mess, that's what it is," the man said. "Fucking nothing works, slush everywhere, and everything to get for New Year's. Yes, fucking beautiful it is, friend." He flicked his cigarette butt off the platform, where it was swallowed by the storm.

Most of the people disgorged by the trains did not venture at once beyond the shelter of the concrete wings above the platform. They peered anxiously into the rustling white sheet. With each new train the platform grew more crowded.

Up until two days ago Duvakin had hated heavy snow; he had a nightmare vision of falling and tearing his poor overcoat. Now he gathered the leather folds of the sheepskin about himself and stepped fearlessly into the wind.

It was like walking through a cotton world. He remained in a clear circle, while before and behind him the air was thick and impenetrable. The falling snow was private and quiet; it built up in gentle piles on his lapels, cuffs, hat, eyebrows, and then fell in miniature avalanches to the silent street.

He was smiling when he knocked on Tanya's door.

"Vanya?" The muffled question.

"Yes, Vanya!" he bellowed. Down the corridor a door opened at once; a stooped old woman with a wrinkled hairy face scowled at him.

"Shoo, Granny! It's not you I'm after!" Duvakin felt as if he had been drinking. Lord above! It was intoxicating just to be away from Polkovnikov.

"Tfoo!" The old woman spat. "Young people . . ." She retreated inside, slamming her door.

He turned to find Tanya standing before him in the open doorway, smiling.

"Roving eye already, eh? Sniffing around Granny Antonovna's door? Men are all alike . . ." Playfully she pushed at his chest with flour-covered hands.

"But she has me bewitched! And she's fascinated by my youth . . ."

"Youth? You?"

"Well, I must be. She said so."

"Well, all right . . ." She stood aside and he slipped past her, a most pleasant sensation. "Perhaps you are almost a baby. You're almost bald and you don't have many teeth . . ."

"Baby! I'll show you baby . . ."

"No, later . . . Come on, I want to show you something." Gracefully she eluded him and went into the kitchen.

It was bright in there against the stark grey windows. And it smelled delicious.

"Blintzes!" He looked over her shoulder.

"Well, not really, just pancakes. But that's not the surprise. Look at the bag, Vanya, hanging out on the hook." She pointed a smudged white finger at the window.

He opened the double windows and leaned out into the blowing snow.

"A goose! Tanya, you found a goose!"

It was odd that life could change so rapidly almost from moment to moment; that in the same day he could feel desolated and drained, and then light-headed with joy. Odd, and wonderful.

"Isn't it marvellous? The goose is for New Year's, next Friday, for you and me and Lenochka . . ."

"And have you got a tree too?"

"Oh, God, no, Vanya. I tried . . . but you wouldn't believe the mess. I went to this mudlot way out past Sokolniki . . . Truck after truck, and they dump out these pitiful twigs. Everybody's trying to find the best ones. It was kind of funny, but it was sad too . . ." Speaking with her back to him, she worked rapidly at the stove. A pleasant odour of frying butter and cooking flour floating through the room. Duvakin sank onto his usual stool and leaned his head against the wall.

"Tanya . . . Thank you. So pleasant here . . ." He spoke softly, almost to himself. Then he sat up briskly.

"Tell you what. I'll get the tree. That'll be my part. You got the goose . . ."

She turned half-way toward him, laughing. "Oh, good! But where are you going to find one? Two days ago I was there, and there wasn't much left."

"Almost gone already?"

"Vanya! Why do you think I bought a goose a week ahead of time? I only had to stand in line an hour and a half, two hours to get it. Because there it was, on sale, and heaven only knows whether they'll toss any more out to us before the holiday. Almost everything is sold already, Vanya. It's the same every year."

"The goose won't spoil?"

"Not if it stays cold out there. Let's pray the wind won't come up and blow it away! Maybe I'll come on something else . . . some kind of fruit, maybe. Two years ago I found some caviar, did I tell you? That was really a fluke . . ." She turned around, her hands on her hips, a broad smile of satisfaction on her face. "Now I don't have to worry about the goose, I can look all around, and who knows what I might find?"

Duvakin felt vastly incompetent before this slender creature. It had been ages, he realised, since he had paid much attention to what went into his mouth, or on his back, for that matter. This buying and selling, the market . . . He seemed to have been dumped into a new world. Or perhaps what he had thought was the real world was something else entirely.

Why was all of this necessary? If bananas or tangerines or Finnish eggs or Polish chickens were for sale today, for the New Year, why couldn't they be for sale every day? Why did the powers above 'toss out' food just before the holidays? And why toss them out in such small quantities, so that people had to stand in line for hours and hours? For some reason he thought of an American comedy he had seen years ago, probably just after the war. Two men were laying a carpet, and each time they got one corner down, another popped up. Two grown men, hilariously spending untold time, attention and skill—such as it was—on a simple inanimate object . . . And here were two grown people spending a full week or more gathering food for one single meal. It wasn't funny.

But at the same time it did represent a goal, something to work for, something in the future . . . beyond the unknown tomorrow. New Year's Eve, a goose, maybe a tree, Lenochka opening presents from Father Frost, a bottle of champagne, Tanya smiling . . .

It was relaxing, Tanya's air of assurance that when the holiday came, he would be present . . .

Tanya set the table, bringing blackberry and lingonberry preserves, and a platter of steaming, fragrant pancakes to set before him.

"Here, eat. You must be starved . . ." She slipped into her place at the table. "Poor Vanya . . . How did it go?"

He shrugged, stuffing forkfuls of pancake into his mouth. He was starved. He could not remember the last time he had eaten freshly cooked pancakes. All that came to mind were the blintzes he occasionally forced down at a cafe near the Red October. Prepared, it seemed, for the first Five Year Plan, and kept on a steam table ever since. The colour of an undershirt, and the texture of the last snowbank in May . . .

"Damn good, Tanya! I haven't had pancakes in ages . . . Sometimes I have them at the Russian Kvas place, but they haven't been fresh since Lenin was a boy."

Tanya laughed. " 'Russian Kvas'? What kind of name is that?"

He looked at her, puzzled, although still eating. Why wonder about names? Names were there; everything had a name.

" 'Russian Kvas'," Tanya said. "It's like that bit from Gogol: 'Two Russian muzhiks were standing . . .' "

"But what on earth do you mean, Tanya?"

"Vanya, you simpleton. There are no muzhiks except Russian ones, you see? And no other kind of kvas . . ." She went off in laughter again.

He shook his head and grinned. The lines that wreathed her smile, the softly jiggling mass of curls above her blue eyes—that was sufficient reason to smile, whatever she was talking about.

"Seriously, though, Vanya. What comes next?"

"Oh, I don't know. That damned Polkovnikov, I can't make him out. One moment I'm comrade, the next I'm 'hey, you!' Sometimes I think I'm the one being investigated . . ."

Her face was grave. Her voice dropped low. "How will it end? And us. What of that?"

He finished the last pancake and leaned back against the wall. Snowflakes spun dizzily against the window, beneath which the radiator sent up a shimmer of dancing air. This is home, he thought, and six months ago, I didn't even know it existed. Incredible and terrible that he should ever have to give up this place again.

"Tanya, tomorrow night it will be all over. Polkovnikov wants me to meet them tomorrow afternoon, as arranged. He'll follow me. He'll move in and finish off the lot of them. And that's that. I'll be home free."

"Will you, Vanya . . .?"

Duvakin rubbed his bald patch. She referred perhaps to his job.

"It's early to speak of that . . . I'm old, I don't know any other job. My family has always done it, someone has to do it . . . We can talk about it later."

She shook her head sadly, without looking at him. When she looked up, her face was brighter.

"Give me a cigarette, will you?"

He held out his crumpled pack of Tu-144's. She cupped her hand about his as she inhaled.

"I was at the hospital today. That place you got Lena into is beautiful. But their visiting hours. Two hours a week! Tphoo! . . . Lenochka looks her old self though. She's hopping all over the bed, laughing, singing. She's hell on nurses. 'Such an uncultured child!' Oh—and she asked for you."

"She did?" He was pleased.

He sat, well-fed, relaxing in the warmth, happy to smoke and contemplate future pleasures. Life, he always felt, came in three basic styles: better, worse, and the same. The last he had lived for most of his adult life, with flashes of the other two. Always in turns, though. Now things had improved magically. Like a fairy tale: the tablecloth that is always crowded with full plates, Vasilisa and the magic doll that grants all wishes. . . .

Of course his magic doll had made his life worse, at the same time that it seemed to have improved it. It was too much to understand. It was as though there were two Duvakins. One was setting out on a new and marvellous life filled with home-made pancakes and a holiday goose. And the other was about to be transformed into a radio set in order to catch a bunch of thieves and murderers for an unpredictable police-man.

He looked at his watch. Going on five o'clock. He had less than a day of this life left before he had to plunge into that life . . .

Reaching across the table he took Tanya's thin hand, and rubbed the back of it with his thumb.

"It is pleasant, isn't it?" she murmured. She touched his face gently with her free hand.

"Oh, yes . . ." He squeezed her hand softly, as though it were a delicate bird, a creature he wished neither to harm nor to release. He was overwhelmed by happiness, by gratitude.

The radiator hummed gently, doors slammed in the courtyard, someone walked over the crackling, broken tiles in the hallway. Suddenly Tanya pulled her hand away.

"Vanya, you dope! You've put my elbow in your plate!"

And suddenly she was hugging Duvakin so tightly that it hurt, and weeping.

16

The day had dawned clear. The thirty centimetres of new snow sparkled under the frosty red sun. The trains were solid with the crush of skiers leaving town and shoppers entering it. Even the grim determination of those shoppers melted somewhat in the unexpected sunshine. At Kiev station people stood about in groups, enjoying the warmth and chatting. Their breath danced in the sunlight like little flames.

The streets were alive with colour, a week before the holiday. Women's string bags bulged with oranges; the necks of wine and vodka bottles peeked from the men's coat pockets. Even the drunks and beggars surreptitiously haunting the station seemed cheerful.

Duvakin felt like a teenager. He smiled continuously to himself. In the gloom of the metro tunnel he received a sharp poke below the ribs.

"Hooligan! Where's your culture? Drunk on public transport!" A stern-looking woman with steel glasses and gold teeth was snapping at him.

He laughed in her face. "Whassa matter, Granny?" he asked, imitating a drunken slur. "Don't you know it's Karl Liebnicht's birthday?"

Shocked and offended, the woman left the metro at the next stop, and Duvakin returned to his blissful thoughts.

The Aeroport station seemed to be endless kilometres from the Kiev station. Station after station passed . . . Pink granite stained glass, crystal chandeliers, well-padded passengers, all streamed past the windows.

As the Aeroport neared, he tried to sober down. But his mind returned insistently to the night before.

An engaged man, that's what I am, he kept thinking in surprise! A groom! My God, Duvakin a groom!

During the night Duvakin's soul had unfurled in a way he had forgotten was possible, if indeed he had ever known it. Tanya was shy and withdrawn at some moments, aggressive and demanding at others. No promises were made. None were necessary. Both knew now that they would be married.

Come to think of it, he hadn't proposed. They had begun to discuss the best day to go to the civil registry; how Duvakin would go about adopting Lena and whether it would be difficult to get him registered to the apartment in Matveevo . . .

Finally the Aeroport stop was announced. Duvakin was squeezed through the double doors of the metro car in a crush of people jostling to board the single escalator.

He stepped off the creaking wooden slats. The momentum of the crowd carried him past the druggist's stand and the cripple who sold out-of-date chemistry texts.

It was just after three o'clock.

He went through the huge wooden doors into the street, and turned the corner onto Leningrad Chausee. He felt disoriented as he always did after riding the metro.

Moscow, as every schoolboy knows, had grown like a tree, in rings. The rings that Stalin had added after the war were indentical, thick and imposing. If one emerged from the metro on Prospekt Mira, Leningrad Chausee, Enthusiasts' Prospekt, or anywhere between the Sadovoye and the micro-regions, it all looked the same: grandiose buildings with ornate façades, gleaming spires and wide streets. The crowded sidewalks were dwarfed by the hectares of asphalt highways. There was no real relation between this kind of design and the human scale. It was architecture for giants.

He walked the long block to the corner and stopped next to the window of the shoe store. The double windows were fogged; the people inside looked like fish in an aquarium. Rows and rows of black shoes were ignored by shoppers anxiously snatching at some bins of stylish boots. He lit a cigarette, and spat. Lord, if foreign shoes felt as good as foreign cigarettes tasted, he could understand the eagerness of the people in the shop.

Leaning against the wall, he watched the sun sink behind the buildings opposite him. Briefly the statues of Agriculture Triumphant and Might Ever Vigilant on top of the colonnade glowed with light. Then they plunged into greyish gloom. Soon it would be time for the street lights to come on.

Cold seeped through his ancient shoes, while sweat trickled down his back. Already his new overcoat was streaked and spotted. At least it was still warm.

The Chausee was jammed with cars and buses. Twice Chaikas dashed past, in the inner lanes reserved for them. They were heading out of town, bigwigs going to their country houses for the weekend.

Several times he spotted a red Volga and mentally drew himself up for this, his last task. Through the overcoat he patted his jacket pocket, to reassure himself that his fountain pen was still there.

Each time the Volga passed, honking and squealing, and he sagged back against the building.

In the euphoria of the previous night he had decided not to make himself into a bipedal transmitter. He had not swallowed the radio, but had hidden it in his matchbox, burying the shiny metal beneath the wood.

He stomped his feet to get the blood going. These interminable waits.

172

Suddenly he had the sensation that someone was watching him, and had been for some time. Carefully he glanced about. His attention centred on the woman who sold meat pies at the metro exit. She was pretty in a slatternly way; a group of men stood about her, joking and flirting. A familiar face . . . Stumpy! the guide to the Uzbekistan. He appeared to take no part in the coarse banter. His eyes met Duvakin's. How long had he been there?

Two days earlier Duvakin would have hurried over to him. Now he did not move. If they wanted him, let them damned well come and get him. He shrugged and looked away.

"Ivan Palych?" Someone slapped an enormous hand on his shoulder. Duvakin, startled, dropped his cigarette.

It was the gorilla who had sat in the front seat during his last ride in the maroon Volga.

The creature was perhaps a hundred seventy centimetres tall, and at least that wide, bundled into an overcoat. His lantern jaw and beetle brow were prehistoric.

"The car," he said, pointing over his shoulder. It was surprising that he could talk.

Duvakin nodded curtly, steeling himself. They walked around the corner, Duvakin clinging to his composure with grim determination. Lord, he was lucky to have returned at all from that first car ride! The lad there could have torn him into little bits and deposited him in various waste baskets.

Sure enough, the maroon Volga was parked across the street from long rows of buses that carried peasants out to the countryside. Its motor was running. As they approached, the door was pushed open from within. Duvakin's heart speeded up a notch. He put his hand in his pocket, checking once more on his matchbox.

The gorilla indicated the back seat. Obediently Duvakin slid in. The Neanderthal shut the door behind him and climbed into what was apparently his accustomed seat in front, next to the driver.

Duvakin was alone in the back. Grey curtains covered all

the glass, even the partition behind the front seat. Dimly he could perceive the backs of the driver and his companion. The sensation was unpleasant. He fought back an impulse to open a side curtain as they pulled away from the curb. Soon he lost track of turns, direction—everything but the fact of motion. Street lights and headlights flashed through the curtains. The car ran so quietly that only the tyres hummed. After a while they appeared to leave congested traffic areas, and picked up speed.

Probably they were leaving town. The driver relaxed and began to talk about the Dinamo-Red Army hockey game. It was either just coming up or it had just ended, Duvakin was not sure which. The gorilla was indifferent; he grunted at intervals. At length the driver's monologue dried up. Kilometres rolled past in silence.

Some light came from the stars in the clear sky, and from the fingernail sliver of the moon. It would be extremely cold before morning.

He began to drowse. Because of last night the events to come seemed not a climax but an annoying task which had to be completed before he could get on with his new, interesting life. For instance, the question of his work . . . What could he take up at the age of forty-eight? Maybe Polkovnikov could pull some strings and get him transferred to station duty at a militia post. Or perhaps the passport office. That was simple work, and not political. Maybe a traffic post, sitting in a glass box and watching the cars go by. A bit dull, that. Tanya did all right at the bookstore. He could scratch together a couple hundred rubles a month. Maybe he should take one of those training courses that were advertised on buses and on the fences around construction sites. 'Interesting Profession! Become a Bus Driver! Become a Linotypist!'

Dreamily, he thought of summer picnics: he and Tanya on the grass while Lena galloped around chasing butterflies, or whatever little girls did. Tanya and he sitting at home, drinking tea at the kitchen table. Who knows, even a baby of their own. He was only forty-eight, she was young enough . . .

The car slowed and turned sharply. He jerked wide awake and tried unsuccessfully to read his watch. Abruptly they stopped.

The driver blew his horn. Could they be stuck in traffic? It didn't seem likely.

"Spotted devils," the driver muttered.

He blew the horn again. This time Duvakin noted a rhythm. A signal.

"Stop it, once is plenty."

There was a metallic scrape, and they rolled forward again. Maybe they were back at Ishakin's stone palace . . . It didn't feel like it, though. They drove a bit further, and then stopped again.

The driver turned off the ignition and the gorilla got out, and opened the back door. "Let's go," he said. "They're waiting."

Duvakin sat frozen, gripping the seat. The thought shot through his head of overpowering the driver . . . Ridiculous. Apart from anything else, he had not driven a car since he was in the army, and not much then.

He got out.

It was not the stone house. There were the outlines of a big squat structure, a warehouse? . . . with a sheltered dock of some sort. High up in the distance, above the dark slash of the forest, red lights twinkled. An airport?

The gorilla walked up a short flight of stairs and along the dock. Duvakin pulled his coat tightly about himself and shivered, only partly from the cold.

The gorilla looked back at him.

"They're waiting."

Duvakin followed him. A bull by the tail, and I can't let go now.

Part way down an enormous concrete pier, the gorilla halted, indicating a door. There were no lights. Duvakin could make out only varying shades of black. When he stepped through the doorway into the building, it was even worse. He could see nothing at all. He took four or five tentative steps and ran into rough wood. Crates? Instinctively he reached out his hand to push himself away; large splinters shot into his palm. In pain, he leapt back and something jagged poked him.

He froze. His heart boomed like the carillon in Spassky Tower.

"This way," the gorilla said softly. Judging by the sound of his voice he had walked past Duvakin. If they were trying to unnerve him, they were doing an excellent job.

"What way?" he asked, in a voice that was intended to be irritable. He prayed that it did not sound as reedy to his guide as it did to him.

"Oh, all right. Put your hand on my shoulder." The huge creature sounded disgusted. Was he able to see in the dark?

The man backed up to him. Duvakin ran his hand over the guide's coat, searching for his shoulder. When he found it, some sense of place returned to him.

"Why so dark?" he asked. They were threading their way through a maze of some kind.

"Vladimir Aleksandrovich likes it that way," the gorilla grunted, after a pause. "Watch it, there's a step." The warning was timed perfectly. Duvakin stumbled and barked his shin. Damn them anyway! But he knew now that Volodya was somewhere about. That was something.

A voice spoke from the dark.

"You got him?"

He had no sense of the dimensions of the place. How many men stood around him in the darkness? Perhaps he was about to be delivered up to his ancestors as neatly trussed as the goose that hung from Tanya's window.

"Yes. The office?"

"Yes."

A door opened, squeaking on its hinges. No light. Could they be sitting in the dark? Or had he suddenly gone blind? He pressed hard on his eyeballs, setting off a series of spots and flashes. At least he saw those.

He was propelled rapidly through a doorway, which was then shut behind him. He stood still.

176

Once he had read a novel about the horrors of life in the middle ages. He suddenly thought now of the oubliette. The prisoner was led up a flight of stairs. A dark door opened. Told he was free to go, the prisoner rushed gratefully forward. Into nothing.

Nonsense, of course. A twentieth-century warehouse near a Moscow airport would not have an oubliette. But he stood rooted to the spot, trembling like a new-born kitten.

Gradually he realised that the dancing red spot he had assumed to be the product of his own eyes was in fact a cigarette.

"Volodya? Turn on the lights, damn it."

"Turn them on, Tsyplyatin."

Of course the effect was devastating. Duvakin's eyes slammed shut. Coloured lights whirled behind his lids. He was still helpless. He had not been prepared for this light.

"Welcome, Vanya!" Volodya's voice. Cautiously he opened his eyes.

An office, yes. Directly opposite him sat Volodya, at a long table with a green felt top.

Other men there as well. Ishan, who gave him a cheery wave and a broad, gold-studded grin. Tsyplyatin—Petka— stood against the wall, every centimetre a ferret.

"Kind of melodramatic, isn't it, Volodya?" Duvakin spoke as coolly as he could. "A devil of a way to treat a customer."

Volodya rose, grinning, and extended his fleshy hand.

"Well," he said, jocularly, "you know that the science of customer service is regrettably underdeveloped in our great land. Only one of the insufficiencies we seek to correct."

He was pink and soft as an April rain cloud, and almost as fragrant. Shaking his hand was like squeezing fresh bread.

Two or three strange men leaned against the walls, and there were two strangers seated at the table. They were all as plump as Ishakin. Of the two men at the table, one was almost entirely bald; steel-rimmed glasses covered his eyes, the ice-blue eyes Duvakin had always hated. Snakes have eyes that colour, he thought. So do mad dogs.

The other man had a pleasant, wrinkled face and a nose like a boiled potato. He wore a military greatcoat. Insignia had changed since Duvakin's army days, but the man's broad epaulets seemed to signify that his rank was a good bit higher than sergeant.

"Vanya, my associates," Volodya said in a grand, ceremonial voice. "Gentlemen, my childhood friend, Ivan Pavlovich Duvakin."

The soldier rose and extended his hand.

"Sasha," he said simply.

"Vanya," Duvakin said.

Ice Eyes nodded behind his spectacles. He did not rise. Apparently he did not indulge in such social amenities as introductions and hand-shaking.

"Have a seat, Vanya. Can we get you something? Tea, cognac? A cigarette," Volodya hovered solicitously about Duvakin who sat down at the table folding the bulky leather overcoat so that it would fit in the chair. "I must apologise for the inconvenience of these accommodations. This is a temporary location, a business necessity. You understand."

The long table was set for a conference. Bottles of mineral water, ashtrays, paper, pencils.

Volodya whispered to Tsyplyatin, who disappeared through the door. No one spoke while they waited for him to return. Sasha looked at him with frank curiosity. There was something naive about him, or there seemed to be. The other man—the third man—stared as a blind man would, icy eyes unmoving, a dead gaze.

Duvakin busied himself, toying with the pencils and paper before him. He might have expected a warehouse, if he had thought about it. It made some sense. Tonight was to be a purchasing session. He felt his coat pocket, where the bankroll bulged next to the matchbox which, he hoped, was bleeping away.

178

There was a muffled, distant roar. Yes, an airport. Whether Domodedovo, Sheremetevo, Vnukovo or some other of which he had never heard . . . An airport. Goods come in, are whisked away in trucks . . . Taken—where? One of Volodya's hotels? An airport meant customs, officials, people . . . That was good, too. Confusion, laziness, inefficiency. And greed. He thought of Dima, his colleague at the Red October. Give him a pineapple and the man would let Nicholas the Second and Admiral Kolchak check into the hotel.

Tsyplyatin reappeared soundlessly. Ishakin conferred with him, and then returned to the table, where he began to speak, loudly, as though he were addressing a meeting.

"Well, Vanya, it seems all is in order. We might begin now. I hope you are comfortable?"

"Quite," Duvakin said. He poured some mineral water into his tall green glass and drank. The bitter metallic taste was not pleasant, but it was calming.

"Forgive me for my curiosity, Vanya," Volodya said, benignly. "But I can't help wondering . . . Little Vanya Duvakin, my childhood friend. The policeman's son. And grandson. And so on, to the nth generation. Militiaman in a pigsty of a village—you will forgive me—then security man in a fire trap of a hotel—"

"Fire trap?" That was surprising. But he realised that it was true. He had never thought of it that way. The interior framework of the hotel was raw logs; the bark was not even peeled from it. Well, if he hadn't noticed it, he hadn't worried about it either.

Ishakin looked at Duvakin with amusement.

"Education, Vanya? Tenth form and the Army . . . Is that right? You're damn lucky you know how to sign your own name!"

Sasha laughed loudly. The man with the dead eyes turned his head toward him. Sasha's guffaw died quickly away.

Duvakin thought he was beginning to see where power lay at this table.

Ishakin went on, a little more quickly. He did not seem to be relishing his words quite so much.

179

"A tiny little room in a rotting section of Moscow, clothes you couldn't give away, no friends to speak of, no car . . . Nothing."

He paused, apparently for effect.

"Yet here you sit! A week ago, you were a nonentity . . . Now you have landed on my friends and me like snow from a roof." His voice rose irritably. "Why, damn it? What is it you want?"

Duvakin did not reply. He could not. This was fortunate, because Volodya calmed down and began to answer his own question.

"The same things as anyone else, presumably. Money, nice things, a little excitement . . . Or who knows? Maybe you want something else, something new . . . Anyway, here you are. And something has to be done about you, eh?"

"Vladimir Aleksandrovich, with your permission . . ."

It was the dead-eyed man. His voice was rather hollow, but filled with self-assurance.

Nonchalantly Volodya waved him on.

As he turned his head once more toward Duvakin, it became clear that the strangeness of his gaze was produced by the thick lenses of his spectacles. Without his glasses, he would probably look like a mole.

"Ivan Pavlovich, comrade Ishakin is telling you that our gathering here tonight is most unusual." He made a tiny movement of his lips, as though he were spitting out spoiled milk. A smile. "But we believe there is good reason for it. Moscow, my dear fellow, is like a small village in many ways . . . Oh, many people, but very few . . . men of spirit . . . who have kept in contact with each other for several years now. Our business is sensitive; we really need to know about our competitors . . ."

Good Lord, Duvakin thought. Could that mean that just as he was getting to the core of the onion, he was being told that there was actually a whole bag of onions? Could Polkovnikov force him to spend his lifetime crawling through this muck?

"And we know of no group such as that you claim to represent . . ."

Duvakin disliked the idea that men stood behind him. Men like Tsyplyatin. Like Ishan. He ought to say something, he knew, but his mind refused to function. He was afraid. Afraid of another attack from behind . . . something hard and this time final, crashing into his bald head from behind . . . With trembling fingers he dug for his cigarettes. He remembered this feeling from his childhood, on the road back from Gzhel. An empty church stood on a rise above Chernaya Rechka. At night winged creatures flew in and out of its plundered dome. The wise child whom cruel fate drew there after dark always whistled as loud as he could, and ran past it toward home as fast his short legs would carry him.

"So, my dear Ivan Pavlovich," the Mole said. "We find ourselves at something of a loss."

Sasha the soldier suddenly leapt into the conversation.

"Yes, by God, what the devil is your game?" His face was red and his eyes popped. Oho, Duvakin thought. The nervous conspirator. He sees the shadow of the noose.

"If you don't mind, Aleksandr Matveevich, I have a few more words . . ."

Despite all his stripes and gold stars, Sasha slammed his jaw shut so fast it was a wonder he did not bite his tongue.

The Mole continued calmly.

"My friend's question is a good one, Ivan Pavlovich. You have been hounding us for a week; our venture has taken a good many years to perfect . . . A large enterprise, an effective enterprise. Until a few weeks ago, it was sealed tight."

"How could you do business if it was sealed shut?" Duvakin instantly regretted his tendency to ask impulsive questions. But still, it was puzzling. A black market operation without customers?

"Ah ha, a good question. A businessman's question . . ." Again the spoiled milk smile. "Business is not enough. Our method was time-tested. Cell structures. Most simple: those involved in certain aspects of the business need not be aware of the business as a whole. It is a system which Vladimir Ilich was quick to appreciate."

All his life Duvakin had heard Lenin's name invoked in everything from patriotic exhortations to coarse, pointless jokes. This was the first time he had heard the name in connection with the work of gangsters.

He remained impassive as the Mole, who obviously loved the sound of his own voice, continued.

"And . . . if I must cross the t's and dot the i's . . . I will tell you that any and all contacts with competitors were initiated by us. In eleven years we have not once, not *once*, had an experience like this one with you . . ."

Eleven years! You can get sloppy in eleven years, you smooth bastard. There'll be no twelfth.

"With you." The Mole regarded him a moment. "You have worked your way here in only one week . . . Perhaps you are exceptionally clever, you have hidden talents . . ." It was obvious that he didn't really think so. Eerily he echoed Duvakin's thoughts. "After eleven years any organisation can show signs of age . . . Too much success . . ." He looked briefly at Sasha. "You forget you have to be careful."

"Like with Miller?" Duvakin asked mildly.

The Mole moved slightly in his chair. His eyes returned to Duvakin's face. "Yes," he said. "That was . . . a bad situation. I was assured that we had made every effort to remedy that . . . but . . ." he smiled. "The wolf apparently was already among the flock."

The 'every effort' must have included those really inept searches as well as the attempt to make Duvakin look like a drunken incompetent, if not to kill him outright . . . And speaking of killing, they had presumably murdered the unfortunate psychopath who had dispatched Miller.

"But I do you an injustice, calling you the wolf," the Mole said. "After all, I find your story convincing . . ."

"Why?" Duvakin bit his lip. That was unquestionably the

182

stupidest question he had ever asked. *Why* could he never learn to think before he spoke?

"I like that question, Ivan Palovich, I like the way you think." A silence. Then, "For one thing, your money was certainly genuine . . ."

"I have more," Duvakin said, leaning forward eagerly.

"Oh, I'm sure you do . . . And what, after all, is money, my friend? You can get it, you can lose it . . . With a pocketful of Red Army belt buckles and a little determination, any pimply brat could accumulate the kind of wad you left with Ishan . . ."

It struck Duvakin that this was probably true. He had always taken it for granted that foreign money was as unattainable as the moon. No wonder Volodya had contempt for him.

"But you have something, dear Ivan Pavlovich, you have spirit. I admire your tenacity. We tried hard to discourage you . . . We did try hard, didn't we, Petka?"

So. That was the little weasel who had hit him from behind.

". . . and you have a certain cunning. The coat trick . . . Our final test. We don't use it often . . . It never fails . . ."

Perhaps they should hire Tanya. But the Mole had stopped talking. Really it was time Duvakin made some sort of response. "But that's so obvious," he said, expansively. "It was to be expected, even. That's what concerns us, you see . . . Predictable . . . Lax . . ."

The old soldier spoke up. "He's right, you know, Slava. You get soft, you relax . . . Risks have gone up . . ."

The Mole's name was Slava. Duvakin's confidence grew a tiny notch.

The dead eyes turned on the soldier, whose voice trailed off once more.

"You're right, Sashenka," the Mole said. "A dog knows his own prick when he licks it."

Sasha turned bright scarlet. His eyes darted about the room. Duvakin thought that Sasha was the weak link in this

183

chain of three. And that made sense, really. A soldier was in a bind: he answered not only to civil authorities and to the Party, but to the military as well. Say what you will, the Army looked out for itself. It served the nation but, as Duvakin knew only too well from his own Army days, it served itself at the same time.

"My dear Ivan Pavlovich . . ."

Slava's attention was back on him.

" . . . you worry me."

The hairs rose on the back of Duvakin's neck. The meat of their conversation was about to be served. "How so?" he asked.

"You tell me. Why have you come to us?"

The answer that rose to Duvakin's mind was, "Because I want to see you felling trees in Mordovia!" But instead he took the rhetorical tack that seemed to have worked fairly well for him so far. He answered with questions.

"Why does anyone come to you? Why does the peasant from Borisoglebsk try to go to GUM? Why does the football fan go to watch Dynamo?" He prayed that his questions would land right side up.

They appeared to.

"Well, we won't deny that we have had our successes. True, Volodya?" As Slava turned his unpleasant smile to Ishakin, Duvakin noted rolls of fat bulging over the back of his collar. Absently he rubbed the back of his own neck, where the bones protruded, knobby and unprotected.

Volodya smiled broadly in return. "Without question, Mstislav Abramovich," he said, "we cannot complain."

It was not just luck that had brought Volodya his comfortable paunch and his well-fitting suits. He balanced perfectly the manner of the admiring underling and the sympathetic equal. We are great, you and I, his smile seemed to say, and I particularly admire you.

Sasha the soldier was out in the cold.

"So far," he muttered gloomily. The other two did not bother to respond to him.

Duvakin cleared his throat. It was a good moment to take advantage of the self-congratulation in the air.

"Perhaps the time has come for me to tell you that . . . my associates find aspects of your operation most attractive . . . We would like you to help us with certain problems . . . We might be of use to you in return."

"There are problems in your organisation?" Volodya asked. His attitude was friendly.

"Who does not have problems?" Duvakin shrugged, the old campaigner philosophising on a bench in the autumn sun. "That's life, man's fate . . ."

"That's as may be," Slava said drily. "We deal here with material problems, specific problems. We leave the spiritual ones to others."

Volodya laughed approvingly. "Well put," he said. Mstislav Abramovich, smiling, drank mineral water. Clearly he prided himself on his wit. Who the devil was he, anyway? His name was odd: the given name pagan, the patronymic from the Old Testament. Was he the son of an ambitious peasant? A Jew whose parents wanted to pass? . . . Polkovnikov's Jew . . . He had the air of a man who was used to bending circumstance to fit his will.

And Duvakin in his whole life had been intent only on landing on his feet.

"My organisation is small compared to yours," he said. "That can be an advantage, you know. Remember the story of the oak and the reed . . ." Lord, Slava's rhetorical style was contagious. "In any case, we feel we can increase our scope now, the opportunities are there . . ."

Slava nodded. "It's true. Recently the possibilities have expanded . . ."

"Precisely, Mstislav Abramovich, precisely. My colleagues are cautious men, but they know what they want . . ."

"God damn right they're cautious!" The old soldier again. "We've been scouring the town for them, and all we've found is one lousy broad . . ."

With an effort Duvakin maintained his poise. He affected a weary sigh.

"That's a perfect example of the sort of thing that bothers us, friend. You want to make a surreptitious search? Go ahead . . . But don't leave markers. Don't steal things . . . I mean, stealing books!"

He looked into Slava's eyes, and shrugged.

Sasha turned nervously to Mstislav Abramovich.

"I warned them," he said. "Those bastards! I told them—"

Volodya's face had turned beet red. "Who was it?" he snapped. "Who did you send?"

Slava interrupted. "I knew nothing about this," he said.

Duvakin held up his hands, palms out, in appeal.

"Gentlemen, gentlemen, please . . . Don't excite yourselves. The books are a small matter, just an example . . . Other aspects of your enterprise are dazzling. Yes, they're really dazzling . . . I'm not here to make trouble." He looked at his watch. "And you will want to discuss all this when you are alone, when you have all the time you need . . ."

I'm a busy man, he thought. Let them digest that.

"We were impressed with the way you . . . contained the damage. Only an efficient organisation could have co-ordinated a thing like that . . ."

He was nervous about specifics. His success so far seemed easy. The bottom could drop out at any time. The other players in this game held the cards; he did not know their value.

"Like what?" Volodya asked grumpily.

"Well . . . after the murder, for instance . . ."

"You see! You see!" Sasha shouted, and jabbed the air with an index finger shaped like a sausage. "Those are good men, those two! They take big risks, all the risks; they do the dirty work, and you begrudge them a couple of stinking books! I've told you before, we're too stingy with them! The temptation is there. Give them more money, that's what's wrong, the devil take it!"

Volodya cut across the soldier's words, speaking smoothly.

"Ah, Vanya, my old friend . . . You see the troubles you bring on us? Those men who . . . contained . . . the original

186

mishap. Good men, believe me, trustworthy in the past. They always handled the most sensitive work. But now . . . Well, it appears that our two lads have begun to develop appetites of their own. Greed, it causes ingratitude . . ." He made an elegant gesture of resignation. Then his voice changed.

"Troepolsky and Vorobeikin," he said.

"Get rid of them," Mstislav Abramovich said curtly.

Duvakin was appalled. He did not want two lives on his conscience.

"But we can't, Mstislav Abramovich," Sasha said, in a tired voice. "That will kick up more trouble than we've got now."

Mstislav Abramovich lost his temper.

"I don't care!" he shouted. "Transfer them to Kolyma! Let them guard factories at Bash Sarai! Put them on the Chinese frontier, just get them the hell out of here!" Almost as an after-thought he said, more calmly, "Send them wherever you sent the last one."

Sasha laughed. "What, Kaplan? That courier? He's in his people's homeland. I stationed him in Birdzhan, on the Chinese border."

Duvakin stared at Sasha. Polkovnikov had said that people from the organs could be involved. Sasha, those greenish grey tabs were a disguise, he had replaced sky-blue epaulets with them. It would probably have taken the Minister of Defence himself to know whether the military insignia fit together . . . Yes, the weakness of State secrecy. There were unknown ranks all over the place. The uniform brought automatic respect and deference. Sasha the old soldier played on both sides of the fence . . .

The whole enterprise was marvellous, no wonder they were so proud of it. Sasha was high in the organs some-where . . . Maybe in charge of foreigners, maybe the militia, who knew? He could send anyone he wished to investigate a murder, to handle it conveniently, to search an apartment, to brain someone . . . And he could dispose of his pawns . . .

And Volodya. No less a big cheese . . . He could handle

187

goods from abroad, lubricate the wheels with doses of foreign cigarettes and liquor . . . Hotel construction, too. Or something close to hotel construction, that would give him the opportunity to siphon off necessary materials, labour, furnishings . . . He could build a fairy tale castle in the woods. He could get sympathy, he could buy averted eyes with a supply of fresh, beautiful girls . . . And his record keeping would be cleverly done . . .

The three men before him were caught up in recrimination and self-justification. Half-listening, Duvakin suddenly thought of something else. Volodya had the power to staff his hotels. The idea was not flattering. Vanya the Post, Grisha Zavalshin, Liudmila Grigorievna . . . and himself. People Volodya could trust. There were those he could trust to handle the proper business in the proper way. And there were those he could trust to be so enfeebled or so stupid that they would see nothing, think nothing, do nothing. Question nothing. Duvakin's ears burned with embarrassment and anger. Eight years! For eight years he had played the fool . . . Pink and beaming Volodya, his benefactor.

There was no reason now why he should feel guilty about anything that happened to his childhood friend. No, why should he? He would show him!

Watching the conversation, he received the impression that Mstislav Abramovich was not really a friend to Sasha and Volodya. He did not seem to know them all that well. He was too superior in his bearing; he gave orders too quickly. It was not a triumvirate. So where did Slava fit in? Sasha the soldier, Volodya the hotel keeper . . . A link was missing. Polkovnikov had stressed the foreign connections of this group . . . And certainly one unhappy American had been inveigled into the game. Someone had to make arrangements, someone had to see that payments got outside the country . . . Someone who could travel.

A man who could travel outside the country was a man specially graced. If any man considered himself specially graced, that man was Mstislav Abramovich. So then who the devil was he? A scientist? The head of a factory? Chairman of something or other?

Well, it didn't matter. He had made it through the swamp. He had only to call Polkovnikov now and let him worry about the rest of it. Let him find out how friend Mstislav had arranged Miller's comings and goings. Let him learn about what they brought into Russia, and the details of how they transferred it here and there. Duvakin's part was done.

He reached into his breast pocket for the fountain pen.

As if on cue all three men stopped talking; all three heads turned toward him at once. From the corner of his eye Duvakin saw Ishan push himself away from the wall. Rustling and tension behind him from Tsyplyatin and the other gorillas. He froze, his hand inside his coat. A fine thing, to solve the puzzle, and die. He cursed his stupidity. He ought to have realised how delicate were the threads of their confidence. Luck alone had kept him alive so far.

"Cigarette," he said lamely.

"You have one burning," Mstislav Abramovich said politely. He indicated the ashtray.

"It tastes bad. Opals, you know." He tried to sound brisk. His voice quavered.

"Here," Mstislav said, in the same silky voice, "take one of mine." He reached across the table, extending a silver cigarette case. Flipped open, it revealed cigarettes in papers of different pastel colours. There was a gold band around each one. Duvakin chose a yellow one.

"What are these? I've never seen this sort," he said. He puffed at the little flame from Mstislav's heavy gold lighter.

"Sobranie."

"*Sobranie?* Russian?" Mstislav smoked Russian cigarettes?

"No, English. I don't know why they call them that . . . I have them made for me." The pride in his voice was unmistakeable.

Duvakin shook his head. A man who had cigarettes made for him. What wonders would come next?

"Not bad," he said, scrutinising the paper. He was trembling with fear and rage.

God damn Polkovnikov anyway! What was this silly game of making objects look like something they were not? The Colonel was no brighter than this bunch of elegant thugs. Couldn't anyone do anything right? The pen was monstrously inappropriate to this discussion. Polkovnikov might just as well have handed him a walkie-talkie and told him to call on it if he needed a hand. Was someone going to ask for his autograph? How—and why?—could he pull out a fountain pen and pretend to fill it? Oh, he could. But he wouldn't survive thirty seconds.

The business with the two transmitters had seemed smooth and clever in the office on Twenty-Fifth October Street. Now the whole thing was murderously silly. KGB toys!

There he sat, smoking a cigarette, one step away from the end, and there was nothing he could do. Except wait for fate to present him with an opportunity to remove the pen in a natural way, discover that it was empty, and—God in heaven!—find some ink to fill it with.

It wasn't likely. What could black marketeers possibly ask him to sign? The guest register? A complaint book? My God, there were pencils all over the table.

Another horrible thought occurred to him. What if Polkovnikov's suppliers were so stupid that they had actually filled the pen with ink? No, no, impossible. But what difference did it make if it was empty, anyway? Nobody would go and get him a bottle of ink. They would just lend him a pen.

Lord in heaven.

Through his terror he had to think of something he wanted to buy. What would his fictitious colleagues wish to purchase? Everything he could think of as desirable was too petty for this operation. Cigarettes? Liquor? Books? It was like swimming the length of the Ob in order to get your feet wet.

". . . so the initiative is yours, comrade Duvakin. Let's move on. We're here together . . . you've upset us considerably, you've spent your money and taken up our time. Now. What can we do for you?"

For a wild moment Duvakin considered leaping up, knocking over water pitchers as a diversion, setting off the pen, and praying that Polkovnikov would come bursting in before he himself was dispatched to a better world. He took a deep breath and flung himself into the arms of his luck, such as it was.

"Frankly, Mstislav Abramóvich, I have to confess that a large part of what brought me here was curiosity, simple curiosity . . ."

Mstislav Abramovich stared at him. The tension in the room increased.

"Curiosity," Duvakin repeated firmly. "When I discovered that dead American, I started wondering . . . An American, that means power. And heroin. That means power and money."

Slava appeared to relax somewhat.

"Our own operation is so small, you see. Quiet . . . Little dealings here and there. Oh, lucrative, I promise you. We've had trouble finding appropriate . . . outlets for . . . profits . . ."

Slava's face was a mask. Not encouraging.

"I can't reveal too much about my colleagues. So . . . I came here to explore the possibility of a relationship. We want to make a first purchase. A test, you might say . . ."

"Purchase of what?" Slava sounded like a bored shop girl.

"Of course we have no real idea of your . . . inventory . . ."

"It doesn't matter. Whatever it is, we can get it. For a price, of course."

Duvakin wished Dima were with him. He would know what was hot on the market right now. Maybe even Tanya would know . . .

"Jeans, maybe. Overcoats . . . A set of tyres for a Zhiguli?"

Sasha exploded.

"The devil, man! Why come to us for that? Any half-witted brat on the street can get that stuff for you!"

"Our impetuous friend here has a point," Mstislav Abramovich said, in a purring voice.

"Well, that's true," Duvakin said slowly. "In a way . . . We have channels already for getting the things we've been interested in so far . . . Jewels . . . Money . . ."

It was not that Duvakin was not greedy. He could gorge himself sick on delicacies when he could get them, which was rarely, and on many sleety days when slush dripped down his threadbare collar and soaked his broken shoes he would have traded his own grandmother for a ride in a taxi cab. He took all the privileges he could get; he would have accepted more. It was like a line from a story he had read somewhere: 'Everyone wants to eat first and die last.'

It was pleasant to eat first, when the pot was still full, and he certainly was in no hurry to die.

Now he was being offered a chance to dip into a full pot, to rub a magic lamp. A new overcoat and a goose for New Year's, these had represented the outer limits of desirable possession. Oranges, maybe. Now he could ask for anything.

And he could think of nothing.

"We don't really need more than we have now," he babbled. "But there are items we've never seen. Things we've only heard about . . . They're bulky . . . And expensive, we can prove to you we can pay for them. Two items . . . The first is calculators," He enunciated the foreign word carefully.

Slava's face did not change. "What sort of calculators?"

"Hand-held ones. Good ones, that will do a lot of different things . . ." He really was not sure what he was talking about.

"Well, there is a possibility. Volodya, what do you think, would you say that was a possibility?" A curious drawl, an arch teasing tone, unsettled Duvakin. He pushed on.

"Now the other thing . . . We're really interested . . . That trick you pulled with the duty register at the Red October. We want a machine like that. Or maybe a couple, maybe three. It depends on the price . . ."

Slava frowned and looked at Volodya.

"A photocopier, Mstislav Abramovich. To replace the page in the register reporting Miller's death. Vorobeikin and Troepolsky used one of our photocopiers."

"Ah," Slava said. "Not terribly efficient, was it?"

Sasha's face again turned the colour of beet borscht. Volodya smiled and shrugged. Mstislav Abramovich turned back to Duvakin.

"You do know a great deal about us, don't you, my friend? It's impressive. Our relationship should really be a lasting one . . ." He smiled his curdled smile. "We should be bound together for all time, so to speak."

And what in hell did that mean?

"I certainly hope so, Mstislav Abramovich, I certainly hope so . . ."

What now? Prices, arrangements for delivery? Too crude, right now? Or should he mention something . . .?

He caught Volodya's eye. There was a remnant of the childhood relationship: Volodya was uneasy. But he smiled and shurgged.

The smile was enchanting. Duvakin found himself smiling back; some tension slipped from his neck and shoulders. Volodya's smile was boyish and cheerful, so different from Slava's dreadful grimace. It almost made this seem like a game, a childish round of Whites and Reds.

"Well, gentlemen," Volodya boomed. "It seems we have reached a satisfactory conclusion to our business this evening . . . And now we should follow that time-honoured Russian custom . . . A dry bargain is a bargain that soon wilts, eh?"

Duvakin looked at his watch. A drink. The general distraction. He could set off his pen radio. He forced a look of delight.

Sasha's delight was not forced. He rubbed his hands with relish. "Like the priest says in the joke, 'The Church has no objections!'"

The man was really too perfect, almost a caricature. A drunkard, savage and paranoid, a lover of pointless anecdotes. In earlier days he would have made a good member of the Black Hundred.

"Tsyplyatin, Ishan . . . Get cognac . . ." That was predictable, too. Mstislav Abramovich would not propose a toast, nor would he enjoy it, but if it were to happen, he must be the one who gave the orders.

If only they would adjourn to do their drinking at the stone house. Movement of that kind would give him the chance to set off that damn pen. Besides, the warehouse was chilly and draughty. He wanted dearly to wallow one last time in that beautiful luxury . . . soft chairs, lights, green plants, the woman Margot . . . He had an inner ache, an itch . . . 'Eat first, die last . . .' And smoke a cigarette with Latin letters on the packet . . .

The atmosphere lightened; it was a party atmosphere now . . . Experimentally he rummaged in his pocket again. No tense reaction this time. But why had they designed the damn pen so you needed two hands to set it off? He bit his lip.

"Cigarettes?" Volodya was solicitous. "Here, catch."

He snapped his fingers. One of the men from the shadows stepped forward and tossed Duvakin a packet. In a cardboard box. Foreign. He was annoyed at the eagerness with which he seized them.

There had to be a way to set off that damn pen!

It was in keeping with the events of that ludicrous week that Duvakin was saved by luck. Luck had for that entire week been chucking him into the mire and hauling him out again. Now he was plucked from this quandary by being thrown into another.

Concentrating frantically on the problem of the pen, he absent-mindedly bit off the filter of the cigarette. Inhaling in surprise, he drew the little fibres against the back of his throat; they floated to the top of his lungs.

Rising in panic, pulling off his coat, he began to cough. His whole body seemed to turn itself inside out; he choked, his ears flamed with pain; his jaw muscles tried to close.

After a frozen moment the three men at the table burst into chaotic activity. Volodya tried to hold Duvakin's arms up in the air; Sasha pounded him frenziedly on the back, causing fireworks to pop behind his eyes. Slava thrust a glass of Bormozhi water beneath his nose. Everyone had a recipe to stop choking.

He forced down the water, spilling a good deal of it onto the green felt. It began its journey downward, but suddenly returned, spraying everything around him and destroying all sensation in his nose. His outraged body was now desperate. He knew with absolute certainty that he was going to throw up.

They saw him attempt to cover his mouth and look wildly about the room. Without further ado, two of the men hustled him clumsily through a doorway on the right and down a short corridor. His feet barely touched the ground. They thrust him through a plywood door at the end of the hallway, and slammed it shut behind him.

Shoved violently into the tiny room, he banged his shin against the porcelain stool. If he had been wearing his overcoat he could not have fit into the room at all; as it was he could barely move. He hung over the toilet, as his stomach tried hard to bring back everything that it had accepted in the last three days. Since he had eaten so little, his retching was agonising.

Despite his pain, the burning heaves that rolled back and forth across his body, he was pleased. He dug a quivering hand into his pocket, pulled out the pen and fumbled with the lever.

Don't drop it, don't drop it, he thought desperately. How could he ever retrieve it in that constricted space? Or if it fell in the toilet . . .

His thumbnail forced itself over the top of the lever and he pulled hard. The lever resisted, for the cap was still on the pen and the air had no place to go. But at last, at last, while he suffered his last spasm and his frame quietened, he felt the lever open.

The weakness of relief caused him to slump against the wall. His knees were like aspic. Thank God, he thought. It's over.

17

Everyone looked at him solicitously as he re-entered the office, squinting against the bright light. Even his escort back from the toilet had given him a slap on the shoulder in the hallway and asked gruffly, "All right now?" He felt like an invalid. His legs shook and his pelvis ached. Carefully Volodya took one arm and Sasha the other. They helped him back into his chair.

"You're all right now?" Volodya asked. "What the hell happened?"

"I'm fine . . . Please." Instinctively he shooed them away. "Stupid thing . . . Sorry I . . . accidentally bit off the filter. Wasn't thinking . . ."

He indicated the ashtray where the amputated cigarette still smouldered. Someone had mopped up the Bormozhi water; the felt was still black with dampness.

"Sorry," he said. "Tired, I suppose. It's been a long week, gentlemen, a very long week."

There were nods of sympathy. He noted that the cognac bottle had appeared. It was disappointing that the label was Russian; he had expected something exotic, magical, from some unbelievable place like Andalusia, or Patagonia. But ordinary Georgian? His disappointment faded after a closer look. There were seven stars on the top label of the bottle. Only on one occasion had Duvakin drunk cognac with more than three stars; that was a Dagestani which could only have been given three stars in relation to other Dagestanis. In relation to petrol it would have received two stars.

"So," Mstislav Abramovich said drily, like a rather nasty nurse, "feeling better, are we?"

This tone put the wind under Duvakin's tail. He replied with beer-stand chumminess, even dipping into the familiar.

"Damn right, little friend, now that I've seen the bottle, waiting for us. What say, it's the Russian way after all! I buy your machines and you take my money? That's how a German does business! The Russian way . . . that's wetting the bargain with a friendly drink, another matter entirely!" Idly he waved the roll of money about. He was almost drunk with relief.

Volodya took the bottle in his elegant white-bread hand and began to pour the lovely amber fluid into the crystal glasses. These were received with murmurs and glances of anticipatory pleasure from nearly everyone—except Mstislav Abramovich.

Volodya raised his glass.

"Well, gentlemen, it seems that we have acquired at least one new associate, a friend. May he live long among us, may he be ever our friend, may we be his friends always!" He extended the glass to the centre of the table. Crystal clicked against crystal.

To the successful completion of my task, Duvakin thought. The liquor flowed easily down his throat, forming a pool in his empty stomach from which waves of pleasant heat lapped gently through his body. He felt the heat so vividly that he thought he should probably not have drunk so deeply since he had not eaten. But somehow he could not worry about it. All he had to do now was wait for Polkovnikov. And his life would flow once more in one channel only, as life was meant to do. He thought of Tanya . . .

Sasha tossed off his drink, belched, and wiped his lips with the back of his hand. The atmosphere in the room was relaxed, comradely. Sasha stood this time to pour and hand round the glasses.

"To the Red Army!" he said.

Everyone clicked glasses and drank automatically. Volodya winked at Duvakin; often in their youth these pompous irrelevant toasts had set them off into fits of half-suppressed laughter. It did so, now. The double fistful of cognac created a haze of good feeling. Sasha thumped Volodya good-naturedly on the back. Duvakin, chuckling, took a cigarette. He wiped his sweating forehead with his hand; his match would not light.

It was suddenly suffocating in the office.

"Phew," he mumbled. "Hot . . ." He began to shrug off his jacket.

Mstislav Abramovich's voice cut like a knife through the clouds of cognac.

"Your fountain pen appears to be leaking," he said.

Duvakin froze, his coat half off, his shirt exposed. A bright blue stain glistened on the white cloth, just above his heart. He looked quickly at the breast pocket of his jacket. The stain was there, but barely visible against the dark textured fabric.

"The devil take it!" He exclaimed. "That lousy, stinking . . ." In his alcoholic fog he had been about to utter the name of Polkovnikov. He stopped. ". . . Hungarian pen . . ." he finished lamely.

"A Balaton?" Mstislav Abramovich inquired politely.

"I'm . . . not sure . . ."

"Might I have a look at it? I'm surprised, those pens are usually very reliable." Slava leaned far across the table, very close to him.

Volodya and Sasha clucked at the spoiled clothing; drinking went on. Only between Duvakin and Mstislav, the tension grew.

Duvakin shrugged and pulled the pen from his pocket. It caught for a moment, and he realised that he had forgotten in his haste to shut the fill lever. And some idiot had given it to him filled with ink.

"Well, well," the Mole said, helpfully, "Here's your problem straightaway. The lever is open."

"Well, I'm damned," Duvakin said. He smiled gratefully and reached for the pen.

But Mstislav Abramovich made no attempt to return it. "But why," he said, "why on earth would the lever be open

198

like that?" He looked at Duvakin; his eyes were as bland as two boiled eggs.

"Caught on the fabric when I pulled it out, I suppose," Duvakin said casually. He reached his hand out again.

"But then it wouldn't have stained your shirt first, would it?" Mstislav Abramovich smiled at him. "Before I asked to see it, I mean."

The attention of the other men in the room had been attracted to this little scene.

"Well, damned if I know," Duvakin said. He shrugged.

"Just a leaky pen," Sasha said. He poured himself another cognac.

But Mstislav Abramovich continued to be absorbed by the problem. "No," he said. "You see? The lever is recessed a fraction; that makes it hard to snag on anything. That's why it's a good pen, because you need to get your fingernail down into the groove in order to open it. You have to want to open it. I know this pen."

He held it in both hands. "This brings up still another question, good friend Vanya," he said. "Why does a man who is throwing up in the toilet try at the same time to fill a pen that is filled with ink?"

As Mstislav Abramovich spoke his knuckles turned from pink to red to white. As he finished his question the pen snapped in half.

Ink flew across the room; it spattered the table. Sasha put down his glass. Volodya stood as if turned to stone.

"An interesting pen, dear Ivan Pavlovich. Most unusual," Mstislav Abramovich casually tipped something out of the broken pen and extended his open palm. On it lay a silvery ink-stained object. The fill lever was still attached to it.

Every eye in the room was fastened on Duvakin.

Sasha was upset and mystified. "What the hell is that thing?" he said. "Slava . . . Volodya . . . What is this?" Duvakin felt almost sorry for him.

Mstislav Abramovich rolled the silvery object around on his palm for a moment. Then he wiped the ink from it fastidiously with a white linen handkerchief. His eyes did not leave Duvakin, as he replied to Sasha.

"You are in charge of security, you work for the organs, and yet you have to ask me that? My dear Sasha. In your work you have never encountered a tracing transmitter before?"

"Vanya, is that true? Is that what it is? You were followed here?" Volodya's voice was soft; shock and hurt drifted through it.

Duvakin lowered his head. Childhood friendship, patronage, even the meeting with Tanya . . . all these things he owed to Volodya, whose face was an open accusation of betrayal. The game was finished, the cards were down.

"Yes, Volodya," he said quietly. "That's what it is."

Sasha was bug-eyed, his face turned from red to white. He was the weakest link, the first to break. His voice gargled in his throat.

"Shoot him . . . Fascist bastard . . . Kill the Fascist . . ."

The whole thing was a nightmare. He sat nailed to his chair while slowly his blurred enemies prepared for his murder. His head doddered feebly.

Mstislav Abramovich spoke softly, gently. Everyone looked at him. "One moment," he said. A man behind him dropped his pistol to his side as quickly as if his tendons had been cut.

Sasha was frantic. "But Slava . . . I'm security . . . This is my job . . ."

"Oh, yes, my friend. And a fine job you've made of it, Aleksandr." Mstislav Abramovich looked at the soldier with a sarcastic smile. It occurred to Duvakin that Sasha's life expectancy might not greatly exceed his own.

"Control yourself for just a moment," Slava said. He turned briskly to Volodya. "Bolshaya Vpadina?"

"Not a good night . . . Friday, the week before New Year's . . . A lot of people."

"The boat house maybe," Mstislav Abramovich responded, somewhere between a question and an order.

"We have to be careful about disposal, though," Volodya said. "The ground's still frozen out there. But you're right as usual, that boat house is just the thing . . ."

200

Duvakin longed desperately for Polkovnikov. At any moment the circle shrinking about him would be broken and he would be freed.

But nothing was happening. He was alone.

Slava purred at Sasha, "Please ride with me, Aleksandr Matveich. I do have several things I would like to discuss with you." Sasha nodded jerkily. Slowly he buttoned his overcoat on the wrong buttons. Curtly Slava nodded toward Duvakin. "Immobilise him," he said.

Duvakin was snatched to his feet; his arms, seized from behind, were jammed together behind his back. He heard his shoulder joints pop. His nerves signalled that this hurt like the devil, but a kind of blissful mental blackout had descended upon him, blocking reality.

Cold metal bands encircled his wrists, shutting with a rasping noise. Instinctively he tugged at the chain between the handcuffs and the bands clicked more tightly. American handcuffs, with the ratchet. The more you thrash, the tighter they grow.

A hot September afternoon in the dusty, stifling lecture room at the militia station. A pair of cuffs like this had been handed round . . . It was a source of some amusement . . . They locked one another up and pretended to swallow the key, or to throw it away . . .

They began to shove him toward the door. "Wait!" Duvakin called. "My coat!" The habit of a lifetime would not permit him to believe he could be sent outdoors without his overcoat.

Behind him, Petka gave him a rough jab below the ribs. "Don't worry, you bastard," he said viciously, "you won't have any time for catching cold." The jab propelled Duvakin into the sharp corner of a low cabinet. He doubled over with pain. Through his agony he saw his overcoat, still lying invitingly open on the chair where he had been sitting. The fleece still bore the odour of his sweat, of his tobacco, perhaps even a faint odour of Tanya. Suddenly the coat assumed more importance than the life he was about to lose. His eyes filled with tears.

"The cars are ready? Good . . . But be careful . . ."

Mstislav Abramovich was in command. At least half a dozen pistols were aimed at Duvakin, toy-sized, silly militia pistols.

The light in the office was put out; they moved forward through the darkness. Duvakin stumbled several times against treacherous invisible objects. Spots of light danced before his eyes. Deprived of hands for balance and eyes for guidance, he was utterly disoriented, almost paralysed. After taking a few steps he tripped and fell heavily, taking the full weight of the fall on one shoulder.

From somewhere in the dark Sasha said, "Pick the son of a bitch up." Perhaps it was Sasha who kicked him, unexpectedly, and hard. Fortunately the blow caught Duvakin in the back of his thigh. No real damage was inflicted, but he could feel the tight knot of a cramp as he was hauled to his feet and quick-marched forward.

The sensation was appalling. He was being flung through an impenetrable darkness, his feet barely able to keep up with the speed of his passage, his arms pinioned and bursting with pain.

"Clear?" someone asked. Duvakin could no longer identify voices.

"Clear. Let's go!"

He was flung through a door. Again he lost his balance and fell forward. He lay on his side on the frozen cement, a salty trickle of blood running into his mouth from his nostrils.

The world now had varying shades of darkness. The one eye which was free of the concrete told him that they were back on the loading dock. With immense effort he straightened his body, to try to struggle to his feet. Directly in front of him were three wide black shapes. Even without lights it was apparent that they were ZILs. ZILs, for God's sake. Where could they have gotten ZILs? He could hear their engines purring and smell the fumes from their exhaust.

Once again invisible hands hoisted him unkindly to his feet and pushed him to the edge of the dock. For a moment he stood on the edge, unable to keep his balance.

The doors of the limousines were open. A shadow moved to open the trunk of the first car. It was pretty obvious that that trunk was to have a passenger.

Duvakin's arms throbbed violently. He knew his cheek was already swelling from his last fall. At least his nose had stopped bleeding; it was filled with clotted blood. Someone spoke behind him.

"Down, motherfucker."

"I can't. I can't do it with my hands cuffed," Duvakin said reasonably. As he said it he realised how distorted his thinking had become. He had seriously expected that this objection would cause them to free his arms.

He was shoved hard from behind, and sent hurtling off the dock. If he had not landed in a pile of crusty, frozen slush, the fall would surely have broken his shoulder, if nothing else. As it was, the wind was knocked out of him. Galaxies of light exploded behind his eyes. He snorted and gasped, trying to force his paralysed diaphragm to help bring air into his lungs. His efforts drew gritty vile snow into his nose and mouth. He choked and rolled over onto his back. Cold snow soaked through his thin suit. In a few minutes he would begin to shiver uncontrollably. I'll never be warm again, he thought. He began to sob; tears ran down his face.

Suddenly floodlights illuminated the yard. There was a shout.

"Stand! The Cheka!"

Men scattered in all directions. From where he lay, Duvakin could see little, but he heard the sound of running feet, more shouts, and heavy breathing. Gun shots rang out, ludicrous popping noises, like bursting soap bubbles. Someone pitched forward from the dock to lie still, face down on the asphalt.

One of the ZILs accelerated and drove rapidly forward. The driver wove his way in a zig-zag intricate motion; rapid flashes puffed from the car window. That someone could drive like that, and still shoot! The car careened up against the corner of a loading ramp, and flipped over onto its side. It slid along on the driver's side before toppling majestically onto its roof, where it lay, its wheels spinning.

In the sudden silence someone was bellowing, "Stop it! Stop! Stop shooting!"

Duvakin struggled to sit up, leaning his aching shoulders and insensate hands against the concrete dock. The voice which had shouted the order belonged to Mstislav Abramovich. His rotund little figure emerged cautiously from the protection of a packing crate. Then, incredibly, he walked down the stairs of the freight-dock and crossed the floodlit asphalt. He stood apparently waiting in the centre of the parking lot.

"All right, who are you?" he said imperiously. "Please show yourselves, so that we can straighten this thing out." His voice was a little shrill.

After a black and frostly silence a tall, angular figure detached itself from the shadows. Polkovnikov! Duvakin's relief was so great that he smiled through his tears. He shook all over with sobs and with the cold.

The two men spoke in steamy puffs which dissipated in the air. No sound carried across the frozen blacktop. Duvakin huddled in upon himself, shrinking from the cold. In one shovel-like hand Polkovnikov held a pistol; he gestured with it to Mstislav Abramovich, who at first continued to talk, and then shrugged. He turned his back to the Colonel and raised his hands. Insolence was in every line of his body. Duvakin thought that if he had had a pistol he would have shot the little man where he stood.

From the absolute blackness men emerged bundled in sheepskin coats and felt boots. They advanced slowly, crouching. Some even carried Kalashnikov automatic weapons. It was like a newsreel of the Great War.

One of these men from the shadows came over to Duvakin and pointed a rifle at him. His inner structure seemed to give way entirely. He was so cold, he was in such pain. He could not begin to explain why it was wrong, it was unfair, that he should once again be under a gun. He burst into sobs, which he tried to muffle against his shivering shoulders.

"Take him inside, corporal, and see that he gets a coat."

It was Polkovnikov, who loomed nearby.

"Go on inside and get warm, Vanya, while we try to straighten this out. On the face of it, you've done a good piece of work. These look to be decent-sized fish. Oh, decent-sized indeed!"

18

For the third time that day Duvakin stumbled through the total blackness of the warehouse. In a way this time it was worse, because now not even his guides knew a safe path through the wilderness of crates, and he had no hands to put protectively before himself. He banged his bruised body several times. Finally he smashed into what seemed to be a wall made of rough pine, stopping so suddenly that the soldier behind him slammed into him.

"Polkovnikov!" he yelled in desperation. "Can't you find the lights?"

The question echoed through the dark warehouse.

There was no answer. But soon the lights came on. After a few moments of blinking and squinting, Duvakin saw huge islands of crates and boxes in the centre of the enormous room. Mysterious addresses and directions were daubed roughly on the splintering sides. Along the walls were shelves bending beneath the weight of more cartons. Above each shelf was a name . . . Those Duvakin read: 'Paris . . . Peking . . . Prague . . .'

Curious. Alphabetical, not geographical . . .

"Over here! Vanya, come on over here and we'll take off your jewellery for you!" Polkovnikov's voice came from somewhere on the far side of the islands. Duvakin managed to weave his tortured way through the maze, to the door of the office. Polkovnikov stood in the doorway. He filled it almost entirely.

"Vanya, good luck! It looks as though we've got the entire ring, and the contraband too, a lot of it . . ." Polkovnikov's professional calm appeared to have vanished. He was excited.

By God, Duvakin thought, the job is done. I made it.

He was still shivering. He was rather taken aback to see that the room remained unchanged. Circumstances were now so different that he had expected somehow that the room would have changed too. But the cognac still stood uncorked on the table, ashtrays overflowing with butts were on the green felt table top. And there was his overcoat! His eyes blurred over again.

He turned his back to Polkovnikov to remind him of the cuffs. "My hands . . ." he said.

Then he turned to look at his saviour once more.

Polkovnikov was leaning against the wall behind the table. His little pistol was placed casually on a window sill near him.

The others were there too. Ishan stood, silent, emotionless, his face wooden and without expression. Volodya sat in Sasha's chair. He looked steadily at Duvakin, his face enraged and hurt. "How *could* you?" it said. Mstislav Abramovich sat in his own chair, motionless.

Outside the door a scuffle could be heard, and muffled shouting. Sasha was more or less projected through the doorway, threatening the soldiers, and protesting his innocence. They had found him hiding in an empty crate.

"That's the lot, sir," the soldier said. "Three dead, one shot through the leg. No mishaps on our side."

Sasha stood before Polkovnikov. His head was bowed, his shoulders drooped. He was doomed. His eyes brushed dully over Duvakin's face. An inner explosion of some kind appeared to happen. The old soldier's friendly potato-nosed face, no longer drained, was once more suffused with blood. His fist shot out without warning.

"Fascist! Judas! Spy! Traitor! Enemy of the people!"

The blow was awkward and wildly thrown but it had the power of terror behind it. It caught Duvakin on the point of his sore shoulder, near his neck. He pitched back and to his left, falling on one of the pinewood chairs, which collapsed to pieces under him.

Two enormous soldiers had Sasha in a tight grip.

"Shut him up," Polkovnikov said softly. There was a muffled thud and Sasha's inert body landed near Duvakin, who instinctively rolled away from him and staggered with tremendous difficulty to his feet. The room whirled and danced; he could not use his arms for balance. He more or less fell into the centre of the chair which held his overcoat.

Sasha was picked up off the floor and dumped into another chair, in which he lolled limply. He did not appear to be conscious.

"Well, gentlemen," Polkovnikov said, "it seems we are all here. Shall we have a bit of talk?" His voice was ironic.

Mstislav Abramovich said pleasantly, "This is really most tiresome, Colonel, surely you see that. And it is a great waste of time."

"That's as may be," Polkovnikov answered coldly. "I think that soon you will have time enough on your hands."

A silence ensued. Polkovnikov stood near the windows. He appeared content, even exalted. He enjoyed his role. Duvakin wished he could share that pleasure. But he was in intense pain, he felt old, exhausted. He wanted a cigarette desperately, he wanted to run his hands together to restore feeling to them, he wanted to put on his new overcoat. In his excitement the Colonel had forgotten about the handcuffs.

"So . . ." Polkovnikov said. "A pretty bunch you are. Murder, heroin, smuggling, contraband, black marketeering, currency speculation . . . Just the high points, you understand. The little things I'm leaving out for now. Like bashing up our friend Vanya here, who just happens to be a government official. Oh—and impeding an investigation, burglary, impersonation of State officials, destruction of State property . . . All in all, we need to ask you a lot of questions.

207

But there will be time to discuss all this. Plenty of time, the rest of your lives, in fact. Depending on how you answer, that could be very long, or . . . not . . ."

Volodya was looking at Duvakin.

"Why, Vanya?" he asked.

Duvakin looked at Polkovnikov. But the Colonel went on leaning against the wall. He seemed lazily interested in Duvakin's answer.

"Well, you heard the Colonel . . . you broke the law, damn it!" He caught his breath and tried not to strain against the handcuffs. He wished the devil Polkovnikov would do something about those cuffs.

"You subverted the internal organs of State security," Duvakin said.

"Oh, for God's sake! You talk like some idiot from the Thirties! . . . That's for old drunks and pensioners. We're not in danger of anything, except dying of boredom!"

Why did Polkovnikov allow this to continue? Why didn't he bundle everyone into the marias and haul them off? This was no place for all this . . . But the Colonel appeared to be enjoying himself. He was playing cat and mice . . .

Volodya was still ranting.

". . . drooling idiots who will stand hours in line to buy a half-rotten cucumber! My God, Vanya, give any one of them the chance to get to the head of the line or pick up three kopeks on the side and he'd trample his own mother to death to do it! Listen, life gives back what you put into it! Everybody takes what he can. Don't start with me about the law."

"Eat first and die last, eh?" Duvakin said bitterly.

"Yes, that's right," Volodya said. He appealed to the room, to Polkovnikov, "Look at him! A fucking monk . . . Ask him about his new French overcoat, or how he managed a Moscow registration . . . Or take up the question of his lady friend and her apartment . . . Oh, that's different, isn't it? The slut lives in a place with square metres for five people and runs around while her husband is away on business, but that's all right. That doesn't count! God damn it, Vanya,

208

everyone on earth spends his whole life trying to get closer to the trough. Yes, even you! Don't tell me how to live . . .!"

Duvakin was furious. Volodya was not entirely wrong.

"I didn't want to do this . . . You tried to kill me . . . Volodya, you clubbed me, you drugged me . . . I didn't have any choice . . ."

No one said anything. Duvakin felt he had not acquitted himself well. "Besides," he said, "someone had to . . ."

His rage mounted again. Somehow the roles had switched. Why should he justify himself?

"Comrade Polkovnikov?," he said. "Please! These cuffs are killing me. Can't you get them off?" He was tense; why should he have to endure the frustration of trying to explain the sky to a fish?

Polkovnikov started.

"Lord, I'm sorry. I forgot. Hey, Misha! Get the key, would you?"

One of the soldiers bent to touch the cuffs, and then looked up questioningly at Polkovnikov

Polkovnikov addressed the captives.

"Which one of you assholes has the key?" he asked jovially.

Mstislav Abramovich dug into his vest pocket. He tossed the little key out onto the table. "A question, comrade Colonel," he said.

Polkovnikov turned his hawk nose and pale eyes to the pudgy little man.

"You know," he said. "you are a queer one. I've met a lot of bastards in my time . . . All right. Let's hear what you have to say for yourself?" He winked at Duvakin. The wink said, 'Listen to this, this will be good.'

The pain from the handcuffs was unendurable, his body throbbed everywhere, his lips were bleeding, he could not breathe through his clotted nose. He wanted desperately to go home, to be rid of this room and these people forever. Why did this have to go on like this?

And why was Mstislav Abramovich so calm? Why did he seem self-assured? Why was he not angry like Volodya, white-faced and doddering like Sasha?

Why did he speak as though he were sitting at his own kitchen table?

"Comrade Colonel, we are both professional men. I will not waste your time, nor mine. I won't ask you what evidence you have for this arrest . . . We both know that the right belongs to the man who has the power to use it. Evidence is a toy, to give work to lawyers. You've found nothing illegal here . . ."

Polkovnikov interrupted him cheerfully. "Oh, we will, when we start to look at it. But you're right. Even if those crates are stuffed with sauerkraut, we still have you. And that's what counts, isn't it?"

"You seem to think so," Slava said. "Do you think we are guilty? Oh, of course you do . . . I even agree with you. We are guilty of carelessness . . ."

"Carelessness!" Polkovnikov said. His laughter sounded forced.

"Yes, and our friend Sasha here has to bear the brunt of that guilt . . . And Comrade Ishakin, guilty of sentimentality . . ."

Volodya leaned forward sharply across the table. "Me?" he roared at Mstislav Abramovich. "What the devil are you talking about?" So much for the honour of thieves, Duvakin thought. Slava was trying to save his own neck. He wanted to throw his colleagues to the wolves.

". . . sentimentality which dulled his suspicions and blinded him. He forgot to think of possible explanations for the actions of his friend Duvakin . . ."

Now, Duvakin thought, he will try to stress his own innocence. He will try to make some kind of deal. He tried to catch Polkovnikov's eye, to return his wink. But the Colonel was giving Mstislav Abramovich his full attention.

"And I am guilty, even more guilty than the others. I was too sure of myself, I let things run by themselves . . ."

But what the devil? He had just confessed that he was the core of the onion.

"I have to pay for being over-confident, I have to pay for my pride."

"Damn right," Polkovnikov said, with coarse heartiness.

"You should profit from my mistakes, comrade Colonel. I was too sure of myself, as I told you. Let me ask you one question. Whom have you arrested?"

Silence. Polkovnikov looked troubled. And puzzled. Duvakin was puzzled too. It was a child's question: "Why is the sky blue? . . . Why is the water wet? . . . Why is the fire hot?" It was too simple.

Polkovnikov answered slowly, a cautious man who suspects a trick.

"I just told you. Black marketeers, murderers, speculators, blackmailers, conspirators. A nest of thieves, in short."

Mstislav Abramovich waved these troublesome words away like gnats. "Well, those aren't absolutes, Colonel. The true measure of any activity is its success, isn't that right? In 1913, how was Lenin described? How did he look in the eyes of the State? A bandit, an outlaw, a traitor. Five years later he is a hero. Success is what worked the transformation . . ."

"Ah ha!" Polkovnikov said. "So now we can add anti-Soviet propaganda to our list."

Mstislav Abramovich gestured impatiently.

"Try a little harder, Colonel. It's failure that pushes people over the brink, failure, the lack of success. It's important to avoid failure. You want to spare yourself that."

Polkovnikov moved restlessly. He brushed at his forehead beneath his hat.

"What do you mean?" he asked.

"All right, an example . . . An employee of mine. I knew that boy for years, I trusted him. He gave a little . . . twist . . . to a job I gave him. The twist brought him something he wanted, it gave him an advantage. He pursued the advantage. He forgot the larger picture. An important enterprise was damaged because of this. At the moment that boy has plenty of leisure to repent his forgetfulness, working on a sovkhoz outside Birdzhan, in his national homeland."

"So?" Polkovnikov said. "A yid gets up, a yid gets slapped down, he's packed off to the East. Who cares?"

"Well, that's it. No one cares. I don't . . . Our work, as you see . . ." he made an expansive gesture. "Even his personal

211

life goes on without him, his place has been taken. At work, by Ishan . . . At home by him . . ."

He jerked his thumb at Duvakin.

Mstislav Abramovich suddenly tossed an ink-stained object onto the table. The remains of Duvakin's pen.

"We should have found this," he said. "But we had searched him twice, he was clean . . . We should have found this, and the other little transmitter as well, wherever it is. A nice little device, a tracer with a signal. We've used it ourselves, you know. It is really inexcusable that Petr Ivanovich managed to fool us . . ."

"Ivan Pavlovich," Duvakin muttered automatically. Battered and distracted as he was, something was gnawing at the edge of his memory. Who was Mstislav Abramovich?

"Now," the little man said. "I have a question for you, comrade Colonel. Where do all these little toys come from? Eh?"

Polkovnikov's answer came slowly, warily.

"The labs make them up for us . . ."

"The labs make them up for you. And out of what? Bread crumbs and egg yolks?"

Really, the man was outrageous.

"Wire," Polkovnikov said. "Transistors . . . batteries." His temper flared suddenly. "How should I know? That's not my business."

"Oh, I know that," Mstislav Abramovich said. "It's mine."

19

In the silence that followed Mstislav Abramovich's confident assertion the pieces which danced through Duvakin's head suddenly fell into place.

"Krakmalov!" he gasped. "You're the one! And Tanya's . . . former . . . He's the one out . . ."

"Yes, in Birdzhan. Oh, very clever, Petr Ivanovich. But you've got my name wrong . . ."

"All right, damn it," Polkovnikov said. His voice was icy once more. "I'm getting a little tired of all these mysteries. Now just tell me who the hell you are. And remember. Lies make me unhappy."

"Korshunov, Mstislav Abramovich, at your service. I am rationaliser in Kaluga, at the Maurice Thorez Foundry and Metallurgical Kombinat."

"Never heard of it," Polkovnikov said calmly. "Or of you either, you shit-eating son of a bitch."

"Well, anonymity is my greatest asset," Korshunov said. "Unfortunately, I haven't been able to preserve it . . ."

Korshunov . . . Ishakin . . . Tanya's husband . . . the apartment. Duvakin sat back on his numbed hands, utterly bewildered. What about Tanya, in all this? Impossible that she could be involved.

"Do you know what a rationaliser is, Colonel? It's a curious kind of post, you know . . . I'm very good at it. I'm successful at it, a success. It's not good practice to tamper with success, did I mention that? A rationaliser has something of an open hand, as long as he's successful. He improves production, that's his job, output, effectiveness . . . Don't overlook the significance of the fact that you have never heard of the Foundry. A brilliant mind like yours can see the significance of that."

"You are a cocky bastard, aren't you?" Polkovnikov fingered his pistol idly. "A couple of years inside will take some of the starch out of your collar. Come on, it's time to go. Your friends will be upset to hear that you are now rationalising timber-felling on the Manchurian border. A reversal in your career, so to speak."

He gestured with the pistol to Korshunov to stand up.

"Listen, Colonel," the man said insistently. "I'm trying to spare you embarrassment . . . Any career can have a reversal . . ." He flicked his finger at the transmitter. "Do you know where these materials come from?

"All right." Polkovnikov pulled a chair up and plunked himself into it. His face wore a look of patient long-suffering. "Get it over with. We'll all have a laugh. I hope you've got lots of warm clothing. We have a long trip ahead of us."

"Yes, all right. You know, this transmitter has delicate microcircuits . . . Well, believe me, it has. These circuits . . . you don't use them just for pens that go beep-beep. You use them for missiles, for satellites. Our rockets are the most powerful, the best in the world, but you can't make their guidance equipment out of vacuum tubes and quartz crystals . . . Or take computers. Iosif Vissarionovich said cybernetics was a bourgeois science . . . That set us back, you know. Our computer technology, even now . . . Compare it with the Japanese, the Americans . . ."

Polkovnikov stifled a theatrical yawn. "Fascinating," he said. "I'll add one more count of anti-Soviet agitation to the list against you. Now let's be off." He rose to his feet.

"Hold it . . ." Mstislav Abramovich was a man fighting for his life. "Where does that stuff come from, the microcircuits . . .? In the sixties we made our own . . . Three straight probes to Venus turned into a couple hundred kilos of dead steel . . . We had to start buying it. But the problems . . . It's expensive, all that material. Your little toy over there, your pen . . ."

Polkovnikov sank slowly back into his chair.

"Do you know what that cost? Two hundred gold rubles, two-fifty, maybe. And that's without extra costs: negotiating, transport, assembly . . ."

"You're finishing up now, aren't you? Tell us where you fit into this . . ." Polkovnikov's face was impassive.

How long was this going to go on? The key lay on the centre of the green felt. Duvakin's hands were bound, but still he held the tail of the bull. Even now he ran where the bull took him. Ivan the Fool.

"I fit in the middle, Colonel. I saw the need; I filled it. I filled it successfully. I have a great reputation, I am a rationaliser of great resource. I can locate scarce material . . ."

"But you're not telling me," Polkovnikov said softly, "that you represent a policy of the State? Because, my slimy little friend, if that is what you are trying to say, I will kill you right here and now." He raised the pistol and pointed it at Korshunov's head. Duvakin crouched sideways in his chair, prepared for the shock of the blast.

"Please, Colonel," Korshunov said. His voice was fatigued. "Can't you understand that the needs of my Kombinat are very great? Tremendous sacrifice and effort are required to meet the complex demands of the State . . . These institutions . . ." he looked at the soldiers who stood about the room. "These institutions cannot be interested in the sources . . . The materials enable them to meet demands . . ."

Quotas, Duvakin thought, in some way he's talking about quotas. Every facet of life had a quota. You filled your quota, you were congratulated; you overfilled it, you got rewards, money. And a higher quota for the next year. You didn't meet your quota.

"Accidents happen, in the West," Korshunov said. "Ships sink, trains are wrecked, trucks disappear. Theft is part of the capitalist ethic. And the white powder . . ." He leaned forward, toward Polkovnikov. "I used my head. I found a way to get the white powder here, and to send there . . . And the necessary items they had there . . . We found the ones that were misplaced . . . It involved money, it involved men . . . But you know—it worked!"

Duvakin wanted a cigarette with all his soul. Pathetic to listen to Korshunov brag; his achievement, whatever it was, was pouring through his hands like sand. An involuntary movement of his wrists sent jagged shards of pain shooting up his arms and shoulders.

"The foreign end," Polkovnikov said. "You used Miller?"

"Later, after the organisation was set up. I had to have control at the far end . . . I thought he was perfect. A little sentimental . . . an ageing uncle here . . . Better pay even than in the West . . . Well, we didn't pay enough attention to his . . . sexual tastes . . . But it worked for a long time."

"The borders? Customs?"

Oh, why couldn't they find all this out later? Even the soldiers were bored, shifting their weight from foot to foot, brushing off their rifles.

"Sasha here . . . Marked crates, you understand . . ."

"And Volodya?" Duvakin said. Polkovnikov and Korshunov looked at him sharply. He felt embarrassed. It was as though he had interrupted a private conversation.

"Cultivation, nursing," Korshunov said, with some distaste. "Create a benevolent atmosphere, a little discreet surveillance. And hotels with plenty of rooms . . ."

Volodya was grinning. But why? He was a man whose vessel had foundered. The ship was sinking.

Duvakin could feel a violent nausea growing in his stomach. Panic was rising to his throat. The throbbing of his hands was filled with sound, with slow balloons of pain that swelled and burst in his hands, sending shock waves of agony up through his arms to his inner ears. He looked imploringly at Polkovnikov. His whole soul was in his eyes, he knew it.

The Colonel seemed deep in thought.

"In answer to your final question, Colonel," Slava said softly, "profits are very healthy indeed."

"I wasn't going to ask," Polkovnikov said.

"Somewhere in the vicinity of a million rubles last year. After expenses, of course."

"Buys a nice little whorehouse, a sum like that," Polkovnikov said lightly. "And it may buy capital punishment as well, my little friend."

"People who deprive the State of technological materials which it needs vitally deserve punishment," Korshunov said. "Short-sighed, narrow-minded men. Some of them will have a hard time choking down what they chose to bite off." He stood up and buttoned his coat. "Let's go," he said. "We'll see if guilt is an absolute entity."

Volodya stood up too and buttoned his overcoat. Sasha remained in his chair, limp and moaning slightly. After a moment Polkovnikov also stood up.

"It will be an interesting proposition, comrade," he said,

somewhat distractedly. He shook his head, as if chasing away a gnat. "All right, gentlemen, the comedy is ended. Lieutenant!"

One of the guards came out of his unfocused trance and stepped forward.

"Take these men to the holding cells at Nikitinsky Gates. We can sort everything out there in the morning. Oh—and undo our friend Vanya there, will you?"

While the soldiers forced their prisoners into convoy rank, two by two, the lieutenant took the key from the centre table and approached Duvakin, who twisted eagerly to one side to allow him access to his wrists.

The lieutenant fumbled with the little lock and then . . . incredibly, miraculously, unbelievably . . . a click. The cuff on his left hand swung open. Slowly, carefully, he brought his hands in front of him. They were a purplish parody of Korshunov's, swollen, puffy, the colour of spoiled meat. The second cuff opened. He was free.

20

Duvakin's relief was submerged in a wash of exhaustion, pain, and nausea. Of course he felt exaltation too, for the job he had done. He slowly chafed his hands. Quickly they became a cacophony of spiked, angry nerves.

As if in tacit recognition of his status, Korshunov was the last man to be prodded into line by the soldiers. He was not paired, but walked alone, behind Volodya and Sasha. Volodya. It was painful to see him in that line.

Almost as though he read his mind, Volodya looked at him with hate in his eyes.

"Judas," he said in a conversational tone.

Perhaps it was so. But he had ridden his bull. And he had made it. He was alive. And somewhere in the distance was Tanya, the New Year's goose, little Lena . . . And Sasha Kaplan? But that could be explained . . .

"With your permission, Colonel?"

"All right, lieutenant. Take them out to the wagons. But leave Korshunov for me."

The line moved out, jostling and bumping, forced through the door in awkward pairs. Korshunov stood to one side. Further bumping and cursing floated back from the warehouse. The sounds grew fainter. There was only silence in the room.

Duvakin, his hands less painful now, fumbled for a cigarette. All he could find in his pockets was a stale Tu-144, broken in half. He sighed. No more foreign cigarettes.

A small price to pay for the miracle of life. He lit the stub. The smoke entered his lungs like a gift from heaven, although somewhat acrid. He coughed, and then inhaled again. The matchbox.

He held it out.

"Oh, Colonel . . . The radio . . ."

Polkovnikov looked at him. His expression was ironic.

"Coward, eh? Couldn't swallow it? Oh, well, never mind. We can keep them clean this way."

Polkovnikov was friendly. A comrade, really. Duvakin smiled, worry falling away from him for the moment. "Well," he said, "that just about finishes it, doesn't it?" He wanted some words of approval.

"Pretty much, Vanya, pretty much. Just a few more words with your friend here, and then maybe we'll drive out to take a peek at the whorehouse, eh?" He leered and gave him a nudge in the ribs. It felt like a poke with a truncheon. Duvakin twisted slightly away and coughed.

Polkovnikov took a firm grip of Korshunov's arm.

"Well, Mstislav Abramovich, shall we go out to my car?"

They walked out the door; Duvakin laboriously put on his coat. He felt superfluous. Why in the devil's name did he

218

have to go back to Bolshaya Vpadina again? He had lost all interest in that luxurious retreat. But . . . really it didn't matter any more.

It was over.

His hands were clumsy and numb, and they still hurt, but they were free. He could move them. This was a blessing which he had never thought to count. He rounded a corner and found the open doors to the outside.

"Come on, Vanya, we're waiting!" He heard Polkovnikov's voice and saw the orange running lights of the car. The floodlights had been turned off. No bodies lying about. An efficient clean-up.

He shambled down the concrete stairs. The car was a Volga. Well, in a week he had scaled the heights of the automotive world, right up to a ZIL, although he hadn't actually ridden in a ZIL. It would have been the trunk for him, anyway. And now he was on the way down again.

Polkovnikov sat behind the wheel, Korshunov on his right. Duvakin snuggled luxuriously into the soft, welcoming seat.

Polkovnikov pulled smoothly out of the yard and drove some distance down the road before he put on the headlights. The car rocked soothingly, the warm air began to flow. Duvakin dozed off.

He woke with a jolt. "What?" he croaked. His throat hurt.

Polkovnikov laughed. "So. The conquering hero sleeps soundly after his victory."

Through the front windows Duvakin could see the lights of an enormous apartment complex, lights still shining even though it was now long after midnight. A comforting domestic picture. His journey was almost done. The building looked like Matveevo.

It was Saturday. It had all begun to happen only one week ago. The longest week of his life. Incredible. And most incredible of all, in hindsight—he had lived to tell about it.

Polkovnikov was drumming nervously on the steering wheel as he drove.

"But one thing more, Korshunov," he said. "I can understand the others. Money, a whorehouse in the country, a

Zhiguli, gold teeth . . . But you . . . All right, so you have a nice apartment . . ."

"You've been there . . ."

"Of course. You don't come as a complete surprise, you know. Jealousy breeds suspicion. It breeds denunciation . . ."

Korshunov laughed, a metalic, tinkling sound. "Oh, well. Perhaps my days were already numbered."

"The apartment, a car, a tiny dacha outside Kaluga. Nice, but ordinary. You could have had it anyway. Why take the risk? What for?"

"Does it matter?" Korshunov sounded bitter. Beaten. This was a source of enormous satisfaction to Duvakin. The little man's eloquence back in the warehouse had been his last line of defence. He was outflanked, overrun. Beaten.

"Money isn't everything, my dear Colonel. It can even be a curse. It can raise questions, you've just told me that. You use it to buy things with, they weigh on you . . . anchors, embarrassments . . ."

"And so?" Polkovnikov was clearly curious.

"But more useful than money . . . Position, influence. Power. You have scope, freedom. You are free from the herd." His voice dropped. "And power protects. You will discover that."

"Perhaps," Polkovnikov said.

"The factory chief gets his transistors in time to meet his quota . . . What does he care where they came from? But he knows who got them for him, and he will remember that. He'll need them again, or a calculator or a capacitor. The person who can get that . . . that person is his air, his water, his food . . ."

"So what went wrong then, Korshunov? If you are so clever . . ." Polkovnikov was serious; he did not taunt Korshunov.

"Ah, who knows? Too many people, too much success. Carelessness in little things, complacency, sentiment . . . or perhaps . . ." he jerked his thumb over his shoulder at the back seat. "Or perhaps there is simply no way to turn aside the blind luck of a fool. But still, you know, it's a shame . . ."

"Your career," Polkovnikov said.

"Oh, yes, of course. But remember it's a career built on real need, it's a function. Someone can step into my shoes, I suppose. But will he have the real needs of the country at heart? The damage while he is learning, and then . . . will he think of himself first?"

Was it really patriotism of a sort? He sounded genuine. Duvakin could not tell, but really he did not need to. He was going home. Tanya, the goose, the tree . . . He needed to get the tree. Of course he would have to talk to her about Sasha . . . Could he still get that tree? He could not help laughing a little. A pleasant worry, a New Year's tree.

The men in the front seat paid no attention to him. The tyres hummed, the street lights blinked in the misty night.

Suddenly Duvakin recognised where they were. Kutozovsky Prospekt! And Matveevo lay somewhere to the right.

"Colonel! Please. Drop me off at Matveevo, will you?"

"Duvakin, what about reports? Depositions? When will we wrap this up, eh?" Polkovnikov sounded displeased.

"Tomorrow!" Duvakin said entreatingly. "First thing tomorrow!"

"It is tomorrow, my little friend," he said. "My little Judas."

Duvakin exploded. "God damn it! I have been clubbed, drugged, cuffed, and almost killed! Twice! And if it wasn't for me you'd still be back in the office picking your nose! I demand to get out of this car!"

Polkovnikov laughed.

"So! My rabbit becomes a wolf! He makes demands. Your wish is my command, little hero . . ."

The car turned at the next intersection. Duvakin's heart leapt. The road wandered through fields and through what remained of the village of Solntsevo, and finally emerged in Matveevo. He settled back into his seat, pleased, excited, exhausted.

Polkovnikov negotiated the rutted, frozen mud road in silence.

Then he spoke again.

"Noon tomorrow then? At Dzerzhinsky?"

"Same office as the first time? Sure . . ."

"Good . . . and, ummm, do make certain to bring in all the equipment that you got from us. Details, you understand, but vital. Don't you agree that attention to detail is the first condition of a successful enterprise, Korshunov?"

Korshunov answered in an actor's voice. "Colonel, my agreement is both heartfelt and lamentably belated."

"I gave you the one radio and Korshunov the other," Duvakin said. He tried to remember what other equipment Polkovnikov might be thinking of.

"True, but the receipts will still have to be signed. We can do all that tomorrow though . . . Well, almost there, Vanya. It's that tall building over at the end, if I remember correctly." The car wound obediently around the frosty curve. "Oh, and the money, of course . . ."

Duvakin slapped his forehead. Of course. He had forgotten.

"Here, it's in my coat pocket . . . Just a second. I didn't have to use it . . ." He rummaged through the stiff leather of the overcoat; his only useful souvenir of the week's work. Finally he dug out the roll. "But I never signed for it. Your secretary was gone and I couldn't wait. Here you go . . ."

He held out the money.

"One more corner and here we are . . . Never signed for it? That is odd. I distinctly remember a receipt with your signature, for a large amount of foreign currency. It's right on my desk."

Duvakin rested his arm on the back of the front seat. He was confused.

"That was for the other money, the first bunch . . . Last Monday or Tuesday, I don't remember. Before I went to the Uzbekistan. They stole it from me, remember? When they took the doll . . ."

"The doll? Oh yes, I forgot . . . Well, here we are,

Vanya . . . Good night, see you tomorrow. Oh—remember to bring the doll with you too."

"But I told you. They stole the doll and the money, when I was at the Uzbekistan. Hell, ask Korshunov where it is!"

The car stopped at the curb by Tanya's building. Duvakin slid over and pulled on the door handle.

Nothing happened.

He turned to Polkovnikov, who still had his back to him. The Colonel was watching him in the mirror.

"You signed for a hundred grams of heroin, Duvakin, and a large quantity of gold-backed currency. And now you say you haven't got them? *And* you have an enormous wad of foreign money for which you have no receipt? My dear Ivan Pavlovich, I am appalled. You are an officer of the State militia, and yet you are telling me . . ." Polkovnikov turned in his seat. He looked directly into Duvakin's eyes as he spoke. ". . . that you are guilty of theft of State property, destruction of State property, and illegal possession of foreign currency?"

Duvakin would have understood the words no less had Polkovnikov spoken to him in Arabic. Again he pulled on the door handle. In vain.

Korshunov stared at Polkovnikov.

"But don't you agree, Mstislav Abramovich? State property is acquired at a cost too great to allow people to steal it or lose it or do as they wish with it. Why, that sort of behaviour threatens the security of the State! What the State requires, the State must have, and more than anything the State needs security. Power brings security and security power. Anyone who stands in the way of what the State requires is a dangerous man. Don't you agree, Mstislav Abramovich?"

Korshunov turned to look at Duvakin with raised eyebrows. For a moment he seemed speechless. Then, looking back at Polkovnikov, he said with conviction:

"Wholeheartedly! I agree with you wholeheartedly, Colonel!"

"We have a lot to discuss . . . I think I can make a contribution . . ."

"Most certainly! Most certainly!"

"But first . . . we had best do something with this danger-ous . . . fool."

Duvakin stared in frozen horror as the car slowly pulled away from the curb. His eyes stayed riveted to the building which disappeared slowly behind him and his hand pumped frantically at the handle of the unresponding door.